M000208908

FOREWORD

I first met Mike Hancock when he was a student in the MFA program where I taught. I remember the day Mike walked into my office, in his denim overalls, flip flops, and green T-shirt. He was quiet-spoken with a Texan drawl and thoughtful blue eyes—a gentle giant.

Mike was meeting with me to inquire into my teaching process and to see if I would be interested in working with him as his mentor over the course of the next semester. I was a tough writing instructor. My demands were high. Mike didn't flinch at that.

I asked him to tell me about himself. He mentioned a few things he'd done in the past—working as a hunting guide, spending time in Montana and Alaska. There were a lot of gaps, or rather there were a lot of words he wasn't saying. But there was also a breadth of living in his eyes, in his voice, in his gentle demeanor that conveyed the understanding of suffering and the humility of our humanness.

When I asked Mike about what he liked to read, his words became fluid and his voice carried an edge of excitement. Mike possessed an insatiable hunger and appreciation for literature, both the classics and the contemporary. He, like I, was inspired by landscape and language, and the power of the written word to make sense of the world. I had stereotyped this ex-college football linebacker, and I found myself eager to learn about his work in progress. What followed next was my introduction to two unforgettable men, Grey Wolf and Calvin, with deeply personal and powerful quests for redemption and salvation.

Mike and I continued to work together throughout his final semester in the program, and I have carried the lives of those two protagonists with me ever since, as well as those of Yellow Leaf, a young Piegan wife and mother, and Ivey, a beautiful teenage girl afraid to dream.

I must admit I was anxious when Mike turned in his first submission. I wanted it to be everything I hoped for from him. I didn't care if it was rough; I knew there would be work ahead of us. But I hoped it wouldn't disappoint in its depth of character and landscape. Mike surpassed all my expectations. Not only was I mesmerized by his descriptions of the natural world, Mike gripped me from page one with characters so real, their proximity felt tangible, and the kind of narrative tension that stole far too many hours of my sleep. Mike's storytelling is bold and transgressive and beautiful, and at times stretches the limits of the heart's capacity.

FALLEN is the powerful telling of two storylines. One takes place in the 1990s and follows the pains and foibles of a traumatized and abandoned child who grows up to become a wilderness hunting guide. The other storyline is a brutal survival tale from the point of view of a Piegan warrior and father in the aftermath of the Marias Massacre of 1870. Each story moves with great velocity and depth until, like the horizon and sky that can appear as one, the two storylines seamlessly blend into a climax of revelatory transformation. I don't want to say more about the plot, because in doing so I would be giving too much away. But I do want to discuss two themes of the novel that make it so relevant and timeless.

FALLEN is a story of tremendous sacrifice and forgiveness that defies cultural and racial boundaries. We are a divided people with deeply entrenched histories of inequality and exploitation. To bridge those divides we need compassion, empathy, and understanding of the histories that separate us, the wounds passed on from generation to generation, as well as the sins of our fathers. We need to listen to each other, and we need to be heard. It is the empathy from one broken man to another across cultural and generational divides that resonates with me the most in Mike's novel. Ultimately, we are one race—the human race—and we share much in common: grief, loss, trauma, love, shame, guilt, broken relationships, injuries to the body and soul, and the deep yearning for redemption and grace.

We also share something else in common. We stand on communal ground; we breathe communal air. We draw life from the same elements from which our ancestors drew life. When one injures our natural world, we all suffer. When one protects it, we share in the gifts of that protection.

The other day upon visiting with a friend, she spoke of a black bear that she saw, a beautiful sow, within twenty yards of her, who looked at her for almost a minute before moving on. I wondered what message the bear was bringing to my friend, but my musings were dismissed by others in the group. I thought of the spring over twelve years ago when at least five different bears made eye contact with me over the course of several weeks, including one in the middle of the college campus, whom no one else reported seeing.

I retreated that summer to a small cabin and reflected upon the messages the bears had brought me. Mike's book is filled with layers of the eternal lessons from the natural world, lessons that encourage each of us, if we will remove our blinders, to listen, feel, be witness to the wonders around us, including the wonders of each other.

— *Diane Les Becquets*
Award-winning and national bestselling author
of *Breaking Wild* and *The Last Woman in the Forest*

ACKNOWLEDGMENTS

Many people have helped substantially in the process of researching and developing *FALLEN*.

To that end, I would like to thank Cecil and Isabel Noble, formerly of Lion Creek Outfitters, Aaron Gesch, Jack and Rick Wemple, Bruce Maker, Conrad Vollertsen, Mark Lincoln, Roland Andrews, Jo Parker, Pat Brown, Ben and Virginia Hancock, George Hancock, my dear editor Susan Kennedy, Timothy Woodward, Todd Abernathy, Richard Adams Carey, Diane Les Becquets, Bob Begiebing, Merle Drown, Richard Rhodes, Alison Taylor-Brown, Laura Kuehlke, Tammy Ivey Cutts, Jason Garner, and Mindi Boston Horne. Included in this group is Daniel Charles Ross, a colleague and friend who believed in my work and talent.

Without the above, among others, *FALLEN* would never have been realized.

This is also dedicated to my many wonderful students. You've given me much inspiration and happiness.

— *Mike Hancock*
April 2020

FALLEN

"HANCOCK DISPLAYS SKILLFUL PROSE AND A HEART WISE IN THE INTRICACIES OF LOVE AND GRIEF. THIS IS GOOD STORYTELLING."
— RICHARD ADAMS CAREY
AUTHOR OF 'RAVEN'S CHILDREN: AN ALASKAN CULTURE AT TWILIGHT'

"IN FALLEN, HANCOCK EXPERTLY EXAMINES THE EMOTIONAL AND COMPLEX RELATIONSHIPS BETWEEN FATHERS AND SONS IN TWO RICHLY INTERWOVEN TALES. I WAS COMPLETELY SWEPT UP IN THIS POIGNANT STORY OF ADVENTURE AND SURVIVAL, SACRIFICE, AND REDEMPTION. IT'S A GREAT REMINDER TO HOLD ON TO WHAT WE LOVE."
— KELLY STONE GAMBLE
USATODAY BEST-SELLING AUTHOR OF 'CALL ME DADDY'

MIKE HANCOCK

FALLEN

A HISTORICAL THRILLER

SUMMIT & SEA

DETROIT

FORTES · FORTUNA · ADIUVAT

Summit & Sea is an imprint of Artisanal
artisanalpublishing.com

This book is a work of fiction. Except where noted, the characters, names, places, and any real people and places are fictitious or are used fictitiously. Any resemblance to people living or dead, or to places or activities is purely coincidental and the sole product of the author's imagination.

Copyright ©2020 by Mike Hancock

Cover copyright ©2020 by Summit & Sea
Library of Congress Cataloging-in-Publication Data has been applied for.

Summit & Sea eBook edition
September 2020 ISBN-13 978-1-7342007-3-7

Summit & Sea trade paperback
September 2020 ISBN-13 978-1-7342007-2-0

All rights reserved, including the right to reproduce this work or any portion thereof in any form whatsoever, now or in the future, without regard for form or method.

For more information on the use of material from this work (not including short excerpts for review purposes), please see artisanalpublishing.com or address inquiries to via email to reachout@artisanalpublishing.com.

Summit & Sea, by name and colophon, are trademarks of Artisanal.
This book was produced in Adobe InDesign CC 2020 using Crimson 11/16
for body copy and CF Klondike licensed from CloutierFontes for headings & dropcaps.

Piracy is theft. For information about special discount bulk purchases of paper or ebooks, please contact Direct Sales via email at reachout@ArtisanalPublishing.com
Manufactured in the United States of America.

For Mom.

FALLEN

CHAPTER ONE

GARLAND, TEXAS
1978

My mama had been bad again. I knew because he yelled at her. She was always bad on Fridays and Saturdays, almost always. He was gone those days, like every day. Didn't matter if he worked or not, Mama said, he just left. But when he came back on those nights, in the middle of the night when I woke to the breaking things, thumps against the walls and him yelling and my mama screaming, I knew she had been bad again.

My mama said he was my father and he sometimes, on good days, called me son. I didn't think he liked me too much most days.

He worked all day during the week for my granddad putting roofs on houses, came home to my mama and me when he got done. Red face from the sun, sweaty, his eyes almost shut like it was hard for him to see.

Supper was always ready when he walked in, his rule for Mama. The house smelled of fried pork chops or tomatoes and roast beef. I didn't talk. I just went to my room and shut the door when he walked in. That was my rule.

I always waited in my room, almost always sat in the chair Dad bought for me when he went to Mexico. Chair was little and made just for me. With my TV tray pulled up, I liked to look out the window at the squirrels playing in the big oak tree or watch Mr. Shepard next door working in his yard. Sometimes I heard him talking to himself and sometimes he didn't walk too good. He didn't much care for me but I still liked to watch him.

My mama always brought me my supper. She liked to pet the top of my head before she left.

I ate by myself. She said I couldn't eat with them because he was tired, wanted quiet. Mama looked like something was wrong when she told me that, like she had been stung by a fire ant. I was lonely at first because I didn't see her again until she took my plate away, then later when she kissed me goodnight and tucked me in.

Sometimes Mama watched me sleep. Well, she thought I was asleep but I was just pretending. She would open the door real quiet and watch. But one time I half-opened my eyes and it wasn't Mama but my father. Had a smile on his face and then he shut the door. I thought he wanted to be good to me sometimes but couldn't. Didn't know why.

But then one day Mama brought Ben the bear and I wasn't so lonely.

He was a big bear, almost as big as me. Chocolate brown fur all over. Friendly round face and little furry ears. I was eating one day in my room when my mama brought him in. Eating and humming a song that I heard watching cartoons.

That's what I liked to do in my room. Not just hum, but sing too. Songs Maw Maw sung to me when I was over there, or songs from Mama's records she played when she got home from work, which was way before he got home.

She brought him in, hiding him behind her back but it didn't work because I saw the brown fur sticking out. Ben was a big bear.

"Hey, baby, got a new friend for you."

She showed me the bear and I dropped my fork and ran up and hugged it.

"Thank you, Mama, thank you!"

"You're welcome, sugar. What you gonna name him?"

"Ben! I want to name him Ben! Like Grizzly Adams, Mama!"

"Okay, Calvin, okay. Finish your supper and I'll be back in a little bit." And she left, closing the door quiet.

Me and Ben went everywhere together. When Mama went to work she took me and Ben to Maw Maw and Dad's house. Maw Maw took me to preschool and picked me up, but Mama always got me when she was done working. To all the different places I went every day, Ben went, too.

I liked Maw Maw. She let me go outside and play with their dogs or with all the toys that Dad bought me. Me and Ben were never bored over there. They had a big backyard with a pecan tree. I set Ben up on a branch while I let Dusty, my favorite dog, out to play. He was a fox terrier and followed me wherever I went.

I didn't get to see Dad a whole lot because he was always working. He went around and told people what to do when they were putting roofs on houses. He drove a brown truck with ladders on it, but he also had a big red dump truck with six wheels at his work. He always let me sit in the cab when they weren't using it.

That's another thing I did at Maw Maw's. On days I didn't have school sometimes Maw Maw would take me to go see Dad. Me and Ben rode around with him all day. Dad said he really liked Ben because they had the same first name, and because brown was his favorite color.

Sometimes we rode to Dallas to visit a house bunched together with other houses and with people all over, and on other days we rode out to the country with woods and creeks, not like the creek by my house but way bigger. Dad said there were bears in the woods by those creeks but not to be scared because I was friends with a bear and the other bears would be my friends, too.

Dad was always smoking a cigar and telling me stories and talking. And we always, always went by and got ice cream after working. There was a shop close to his house that served all kinds of flavors, but he always got a chocolate malt and I always got a double dip vanilla cone. Then he would take me home.

Only there was a secret.

Mama said I should call Dad "Paw Paw" when I was at home, and especially around my father. She said he wouldn't like it if he knew I called my granddad "Dad." I told her that I wouldn't do it at home, but I thought it didn't matter much anyway. I didn't tell her that because she was worried about it and I didn't like it when she worried.

All of these things happened a long time ago but one night I woke up to the screams and I knew that she had been bad again. I felt around in the dark for Ben and I found the soft fur of his back. He was on the edge of the bed and had almost fallen down, but I pulled him back close to me.

I felt the cold button of his black nose on my face and his furry arm around my neck. Ben was warm and he protected me. My fan was set on high like I like it, moving back and forth, humming in my ears. A good sound.

Voices I barely heard through the walls.

Deep voice, then my mama.

Bad words, stinging words, tearing words.

"You remember when we played with Dusty yesterday, Ben?" I whispered to him.

Shiny black eyes looked back at me.

"It was fun, wasn't it? Dusty's silly. He wants to play with you but I think he would be too rough, so I don't let him."

Glass breaking. Scream. Deep voice talking.

"Don't mean to hurt you though, Ben. He's a good dog."

I held Ben closer to me, brown fur on my cheek. The fan humming in the dark, moving back and forth.

He called her the bad names again. Mama screamed for him to leave her alone and then she called him a bad name. I held Ben tighter, found a place underneath him and the humming fan where the bad words wouldn't go.

Loud smack. I heard her cry. Different cry this time, a new cry, a new scared.

"Hiding place, Ben. Let's go to the hiding place."

I felt underneath the bed for the big chalkboard that I liked to draw pictures on. I brought it out, dragging it behind me as I crawled with my elbows with Ben tucked under my arm. I got into the space under my desk and closed myself up with the chalkboard, and curled up in the corner.

Peeking through my hiding place at the door, I saw the shine on the handle in the dark. Mama still crying through the walls. I listened for him but didn't hear him. Back of Ben's head getting wet from my breath, wind from the fan coming in.

Then something happened on my insides. Never happened before on the Fridays and Saturdays, something different. A feeling. I felt scared before and I cried, but then I felt something more.

Mad.

Mad at him and his hurting words. Him hurting my mama. I was scared before but then I had Ben the bear, and Ben would protect me, keep me safe, because he was my friend. Maybe, I thought, maybe I'll give Ben to my mama, just on the Fridays and Saturdays to keep her safe from him.

That's what I'll do. I'll bring her Ben.

I pulled Ben close to me. Gotta get brave. Brave like Mighty Mouse. He was little like me but that didn't stop him from getting the bad guys. Tried to get up but scared, so scared but then I heard my mama crying through the walls and the sound made me mad so I pushed the chalkboard away and crawled to the door.

Bumped into things, toys, my chair. I was cold. I heard her cry, a long cry. Made me afraid and so I held Ben, held my breath. Had to keep going because Mama was hurt and she needed me this time.

I stood up in the dark, my hand on the door knob. Turned it slow and opened the door. Mama just around the corner, just past the kitchen. No more walls then. My bare feet touched the cold of the kitchen floor. I tried to be real quiet. No sound. Lamp in the living room was turned on so I could see even though it was still dark in the kitchen.

I saw the couch but nothing in front of it. Didn't know where he was. Brave like Mighty Mouse. Got Ben so it was okay. Mama needed him and he would make it better. Breathed too loud, had to breathe quiet.

Mama stopped crying. Just sobbed, not out in the open, but like her head was in a pillow. Saw something move on the end of the couch. Her foot. So she was resting. Maybe he was gone.

He's gone, and I'll just put Ben the bear in her arms while she's sleeping, and he'll protect her. She'll wake up and Ben will be there, and she'll be okay. That's what I'll do.

No more cold kitchen floor, my feet felt the gray carpet of the living room. Warm from the gas heater and I didn't want to move anymore. The last safe place. One more step and I could see if he was there.

I sat down, quiet as I could, watched my mama's foot, heard her breathing, sobbing. Funny smell, like cough syrup or the mouthwash Dad kept on his bathroom counter. But different. And then I remembered, because I smelled it before and my mama told me what it was. Whiskey, she said.

He wasn't there. Gone to bed. Just me and Mama and Ben. She wasn't crying anymore, just sleeping. Soft sounds of sleep. Good sounds. I stood up holding Ben, stepped forward, looked to see what was around the corner.

He leaned over. I sucked in my breath, held it. He was looking at me. Got up from his chair.

I kept my bear between him and me. Ben will protect me because he's my friend.

Blue jeans, white T-shirt that wasn't tucked in. Tear in his shirt at the collar. I looked up at him and he was staring at me. Eyes red, almost shut like it was hard for him to see. Hair messed up. I looked down at his hands, big hands, opening and closing.

"Why aren't you in your room?"

Whiskey smell came down at me, scary voice, nose hurting because of the smell. Tried to talk but nothing came out so I shook my head back and forth.

"Go to your room."

Couldn't look at his blue eyes gone red, not even with Ben. Then I heard myself talk, didn't sound like my talk, like somebody else said it.

"I want to talk to Mama."

"Yeah? Well I want to talk to you." He walked back to the coffee table. I saw the big bottle, the whiskey, almost empty, just a little bit of yellow at the bottom. Next to it was the regular stuff, papers and magazines and letters but also one of my things, my green tractor, one of my favorites. Mama was still sleeping on the couch next to him and he picked my tractor up and looked back at me.

"What's the rule about toys in the living room?"

He looked at me all quiet but then Mama woke up and she sat up real fast. She saw me and her face changed. Looked scared.

"Calvin, go to your room now," she said, her voice different like my voice was different, sounding like she was five like me. Her face was different, too. White, no color except around her eyes, red and puffy and one of them had purple around it. I wanted to run to her and put Ben in her arms because Ben would make it better, make her look like Mama again. But he was in between us and I was lost, didn't know what to do. Do what Mama said, I thought, so I took a step back and started to turn.

"No, no."

I stopped, looked back over Ben's shoulders at him.

"No. You didn't answer my question. What is the rule about your toys in the living room?"

Bad smell came down hurting my nose when he talked. Mama scared, looked at me quiet. My tummy didn't feel good, bad feelings, tears in my eyes. Hiding place. Needed to be in my hiding place.

"No toys?"

He took a step closer, slow, leaned down, stared at me with his red eyes, bad smelling whiskey in my face and hurting my stomach. I tried to hide behind Ben, my eyes just over his brown fur. So scared and I felt something warm and wet down there, went to the bathroom in my pants. Not supposed to do that. Couldn't breathe and I started to cry, tried to hold it in.

"That's right. No toys."

Hands came at me all blurry, fast like a snake. He had Ben, held him up, Ben the bear. Tore his head off, Ben's body fell to the table, bounced off to the floor. Soft white cotton came down slow like snowflakes everywhere.

I dropped to the floor and curled up, head between my arms and I cried, cried harder than I ever did. Something moved real fast and it was my mama jumping off the couch, eyes mad.

"You bastard! Oh, you sorry motherfucking bastard! He's only five years old!"

He turned with Ben's head still in his hand and he hit her face hard and my mama screamed, hit him back with her fists, again and again. He picked her up and threw her on the coffee table, magazines and papers everywhere, table legs breaking, Mama rolling off and onto the floor, then blood, blood all over her face and she crawled to the corner of the room and I cried louder.

He looked down at me and I curled up in a ball, tight as I could, so scared. I made a sound I hadn't heard before, high whining sound, didn't know why so scared. He kicked me in the ribs hard and I was going sideways, hurt so bad. Couldn't see real good, everything dizzy and spinning around, couldn't see no more cotton, no more magazines, no more Mama. Needed Ben.

Behind me, he picked up my favorite tractor, held it in his big hands, looked down at me, red eyes and bad whiskey smell.

"Take your fucking toys to your room!"

His arm came back fast and he threw my tractor and it hit me in the back and it hurt so bad I screamed, screamed *make it go away, make it all go away*. Had to get up then, had to go to my hiding place. Go to the hiding place.

Ran to my room, everything dizzy, slammed the door, crying, ran in the dark, crawled to my hiding place, chalkboard up and I was in my corner. Thought about good things then, Maw Maw's songs, thought about Dusty and Dad and ice cream, good things. But those good things weren't there, not there in my hiding place in the dark.

What am I going to do now? He's gone.

My best friend.

Ben the bear.

CHAPTER TWO

BEAR'S PAW MOUNTAINS, NORTH-CENTRAL MONTANA
JANUARY 1870

The arrow disappeared into the blackhorn just behind its shoulders, exploding both lungs. She rose and let out a thundering bellow. Grey Bear nocked another arrow; she turned a circle, kicking up dirt and snow. He released, the arrow disappearing into her paunch and she trampled downhill, hooves shaking the earth.

Grey Bear held a finger in front of his face and flattened his palm downward to the ground. Running Dog nodded once.

His young legs worked their way down smoothly, silent, and then he crouched down by his father's side. He gazed at the tracks before them, and his eyes followed the kicked up dirt and snow to the bottoms below. The boy returned his focus closer, inspecting every patch of dirt, every broken limb, every segment of the broken snow, for blood.

It was good, Grey Bear thought; he was learning.

They sat in silence, the bitter cold seeping through their bodies. Running Dog unconsciously edged closer to his father for warmth, his face dispelling the frost through flushed lips.

"We move," Grey Bear said. "She has had time to stiffen up. I want you to go ahead of me."

Running Dog followed the tracks, just off to the side. Already at ten winters, he moved gracefully, but with power and a strong body built low to the ground, like the wolverine.

The cow blackhorn, Grey Bear knew, had expired lungs, but she was strong and would go a distance before her strength left her. She followed the path he suspected, making her way to the bottom of the draw, and then walked parallel with the creek, always downhill, the easiest route. As they closed the distance, the blood sign grew heavier. Two drops turned into five, five into ten, ten into a pool here and there. Grey Bear signaled his son to slow, then to stop.

Through the alders and aspens, Grey Bear scanned, looking, smelling, hearing. Through an opening in the tangled brush, fifty paces away, he saw the clump of hair. Without moving his head, he glanced down to his son to see if he picked it out. He was still searching. Grey Bear bent down next to his face and pointed.

Arrow nocked, held against the soft rest of deer hide, he began to weave his way through the tangled willows, grasses, and trees, always keeping his line of sight on the patch of fur. He could not yet make out the cow's eyes, so he moved slowly, for if she had anything left she would immediately rise and attempt to run as far away as she could, her blood trail maybe drying up in the escape.

He saw her whole form now, but her head faced away from him and he could not yet tell if she slept. There was an exit wound from an arrow and a cake of blood behind her shoulders. Grey Bear drew back his bow, taking his point of aim below her wound, again in the lungs. The arrow disappeared into her, but there was no movement.

Grey Bear eased closer, ever wary. Animals do strange things.

Sometimes they come back to life.

He crept up to her. He was by her side then, moving around to see her eyes. They were open, but clouded over. With an arrow out, Grey Bear took a tentative stab at her head. Nothing.

He signaled to Running Dog, and the boy came bounding up to him, smiling. He squatted next to the dead cow, his hands running over her horns, her coarse hair. Grey Bear motioned for the boy to back away as he began to pray.

"I give thanks," Grey Bear whispered, "to the Creator and the four winds and the Above Ones and Below Ones. I give thanks to the Long Ago People, and I give you this shadow animal that you will have good meat."

Grey Bear took his skinning knife out of its sheath and cut a long incision from the base of the breast bone down to the intestines. He reached into her, the warmth spilling onto his hand as he gripped her heart and cut it out. Grey Bear held it out to his son. Running Dog smiled and bit into the hot flesh, salty blood smearing his lips. Grey Bear then, too, sampled the rubbery meat, the warmth making his body whole. The blood dripped from his chin.

"Go now and fetch the horses. We will make camp tonight on the river."

Running Dog sprinted back through the tangled forest, his short, wiry body weaving away and disappearing. Grey Bear watched, and the image of his own father came to him. He remembered what it was to be a boy.

Grey Bear skinned the carcass, first cutting a circular incision around the four hocks, then running his knife underneath the legs joining the cut in the abdomen. He cut and then pulled, cut and pulled, the hide gradually coming away from the cow's flesh. He placed the hide hair down on the forest floor and de-boned the meat, placing it on the hide as he went, the sweat pouring down his face.

She was a good fat cow, he saw, and will provide a great feast when they return from the winter hunt. There were forty-two hunters, all the able-bodied men of the tribe, the youngest being Running Dog. They left camp together but spread out looking for the scattered tracks of the blackhorn. The blackhorn were fewer in number than in years past, and then, in the winter, they sought refuge in the timber away from the open plains, often in isolation.

Grey Bear cut along the thick slab of a back strap and pulled it out, feeling its snakelike heft in his hands, and placed it on the hide with portions of hindquarter. He thought back to when he was Running Dog's age, maybe a little older, to the summers and the hunts before the Sun Gathering when blackhorns ran thick on the open prairie. He and the fathers and uncles and cousins had worked the jumps off the vertical bluffs.

Those days are over now, he thought; Running Dog will see these things only through his father's lips and memory.

Branches snapped, horses exhaled as they picked their way through the timber. Running Dog led them, with a horse hair rope tied to their rawhide halters, around the carcass and meat, both of them snorting and staring white-eyed at the blood. He tied his horse to a thick cottonwood, then rigged his father's bay up with the meat panniers, placing a blanket over its withers and then hanging the rawhide basket panniers on either side. He lifted the larger chunks of meat and filled them, careful to keep the weight on each side equal.

Grey Bear finished boning out the rest of the meat. Running Dog. Already he was showing promise: a fearless, hard-working young boy who he brags to his brothers and sisters of, who in a few winters will go alone on his vision quest into the Always Winter Land of the grass hills, to the top of the Alone Butte and hear his own animal guide. He will listen to the Long Ago People, and find what he needs to carry him through this life. He will honor himself in battle, own many horses, many buffalo runners, as strong and smart as the one he now loads with meat. Grey Bear smiled.

Taking the hide to a narrow sandy creek, Grey Bear washed the blood off, folded the hide and bound it with sinew. Running Dog was finished packing the meat, so Grey Bear placed the hide in the center of his pack and tied it down.

"We will head out of these foothills and try to make the banks of the river by nightfall. We will camp there," Grey Bear said. "Tomorrow we go home, and Yellow Leaf will make us a feast."

Running Dog stopped what he was doing when Grey Bear spoke, and looked up to his father with questioning eyes. Grey Bear nodded for him to speak.

"Father, are we not going to meet the others at the bluff where we separated?"

"No, we will go back to the lodge. Spotted Owl and Three Suns talked of heading north into the foothills of Woman Cry Creek, and the rest were venturing deeper still into the Bears Paw, so they will be longer in their hunts. We are doing them no good waiting, as our horses are loaded down."

Running Dog seemed to make sense of this, although Grey Bear knew he wanted to keep hunting. But he obediently gripped the lead rope, and began to follow the creek.

They worked their way out of the foothills of the Bears Paw, the cottonwood and aspen became more dispersed, and the clusters less frequent. The creek veered south into the Marias. A light snow began to fall as the sun edged off the western horizon. The lone man-child, dark eyes alert, moved through the forest, his feet quietly making their way through the tracks of his father.

Grey Bear looked around, to the north and the Always Winter Land, to the west at the great South Butte, rising out of the Sweet Grass Hills and looming over them.

His eyes moved across the nothingness of white around them, gently sloping hills and prairies that in the spring will harbor a green bounty of fescue that the blackhorn will feed on. The spring. Grey Bear longed for it, yearned for the end of the hard winter. The blackhorn escaped the deep snows and ranged into the mountains of the Bears Paw, but the tracks have been fewer, the hunting harder.

Grey Bear and Running Dog were out in the semi-open then, the pain and cold replaced with thoughts of Sun festivals and great feasts. And Yellow Leaf. Yellow Leaf with her bronze skin, black, glowing eyes that will dance when they come in from the hunt. Grey Bear thought about her warm lodge, about lying back on the thick blackhorn robes with a belly full of boiled tongue and Yellow Leaf next to him, soft braids across his chest. Fire crackling.

Grey Bear saw the glimmer from the moon's light casting off water. The Marias. The banks of the river were frozen, but the current still ran strong in its middle. Tall cottonwoods lined the river, giving cover for the many wags-his-tails that grazed along its edges. Grey Bear glanced back at Running Dog, just a hazy shape in the darkness.

"Running Dog," he said. "Drop the panniers next to those cottonwoods, and hobble the horses. We'll camp here and let the horses get a good feed."

Grey Bear constructed a quick lean-to out of down timber and started a fire with his flint and steel, and soon sat comfortably on his robes, quietly staring at the flames. Running Dog warmed his hands by the fire.

"Go cut up some more wood to last us the night," Grey Bear said, extending his hatchet out to him.

While watching his son cut up pieces of the timber, he pulled out his skinning knife. Running Dog finished piling the wood next to their camp, and admired the blade his father held up. Grey Bear inwardly laughed.

It was a fine knife. Handle of wapiti horn, brass fittings, blade of high-tempered steel. They were silent for a moment.

"Take my knife, son, and go cut us up some pieces of backstrap."

Running Dog's eyes widened. He, using a knife of that caliber, his father's knife. He took it and scampered off, new life in his young legs. He reached into the pannier and grabbed the thick backstrap. With his other hand he held up the knife, admired the glimmer of the blade against the moon's light, then began his cuts.

Grey Bear stretched his legs, feeling an angry tinge of pain shoot up his thighs. His body told him to lay down and rest, but he continued to sit up, watched Running Dog cut two sharp ends on a pair of sticks. Grey Bear gestured for his son to sit.

"It is a great knife, Father. One day I will have a knife like that."

Grey Bear smiled.

"And so you will, Running Dog."

Grey Bear picked up the two sharpened sticks, and jabbed them into big chunks of the tender meat before handing a stick to Running Dog. They held their steaks over the fire; the flames flared with the dripping juices. The wind filtered through the tall cottonwoods, bringing the sweet smell to their noses until they could wait no longer and began to feast.

They ate in silence, with only the winds and the slow moving water of the Marias and the occasional howls of far-off coyotes breaking the quiet. The cold wet of their clothing steamed, and with hot flesh in their bellies, they both lay down in the warmth of the thick robe, hands behind their heads, looking up to the tangled mass of branches and the cloudless sky beyond.

"Father?"

"Yes?"

"What happens when we die?"

Grey Bear's eyes shifted to Running Dog, who gazed up at the sky, his face expressionless. Grey Bear wondered why he picked this time to ask, but knew that a boy's mind always wandered.

"Son, that was a very important question. And the answer is … it depends. There is a barren land to the north, past the Sweet Grass Hills and into the Always Winter Land. This place is called the Sand Hills. It is a place, to our eyes, of a vast nothingness. But sometimes our eyes cannot see the things that are most real."

Running Dog lay on his back, his brow furrowed in concentration. He thought for a second, nodded.

"When I was a few winters older than you are now," Grey Bear said. "I ventured alone to a land not to the north, or to the east of our country like most do when seeking their guidance, but to the west. I knew that most who sought their guide failed, but I was young and determined and heard of this place from the others. It was a land of mountains, a land of wild rivers and thick timber, and my young heart knew that if I could make this journey, I would find my spirit animal."

Grey Bear paused, the fire's sparks shooting up into the blackness.

"So, I picked one of my father's best buffalo runners, and made this journey. I entered this vast land, and ventured on to the highest ridge where I constructed my sweatbox. It was through this vision quest that the animal came, a great he-grizzly that walked straight at me, and whispered the secrets of my medicine bag that will bring me health, luck in battle, and down meat in the hunts.

"I returned to my band and told of my success. It was then that your father became not Slender Bow, but Grey Bear. The elders spoke highly of my good fortune, and from then on, I was included in every raiding party, every hunt. I became strong medicine."

Running Dog kept his focus trained on the robe between them. His eyes briefly met his father's and, seeing approval, he asked, "Father, will this bear prevent you from dying?"

"No, he will not. But if I lead a virtuous life, and die an honorable death, he will guide me into the Sand Hills to be with my ancestors and the Long Ago people, where I will become a shadow. In death, I will do the things that I did in life. I will wage war on my enemies, hunt the blackhorn, have a lodge, have many horses. But myself, and all these things, the enemy, the animals, the others, will be as shadows, for they too were once alive."

Grey Bear sat up, crossed his legs, leaned forward, and peered at the darkness toward the river. He lit his tobacco pipe from a hot coal, and began to smoke. He glanced up at the looming timbers creaking in their hibernation.

"Father, what happens to those who do not find their way to the Sand Hills?"

Grey Bear took a pull on his pipe and exhaled the smoke, watched it funnel upwards, dissipating.

"Yes, many do not. Those who reject their spirit guides, who disgrace their people, who turn away from their ancestors. Many people. The Napikwans who wear their blue coats, the Crow, people from our own tribe, our own band. People who lose their way. Their fate is not a happy one, Running Dog. They are doomed to roam the earth near the place of their death, as ghosts. You see, ghosts do not live beneath or above the ground, but on it, and exist among the living. For them, there is no happiness, only sorrow.

"And know this: ghosts that are forever doomed to wander here, they can talk to us. They can talk to us through dreams, or even in our waking hours, whispering to us through the wind. Most of these voices come from vengeful souls who led a dishonorable life, so their intentions are spiteful. However, some intend to do good, to correct a past wrong, or help a loved one. So these voices are to be listened to with caution, and the living must always follow their own beating heart, and not those of the dead. Do you understand?"

Grey Bear inhaled the tobacco, content with its mellow taste, and looked down at Running Dog, who was considering these things, trying to decipher them.

"Yes, Father, I think so."

After dumping the ashes of his pipe into the coals, Grey Bear stoked the fire with three heavy branches. He settled back into the lean-to, and lay on his back, feeling the warmth of the flames. His tired bones relished the heat.

"Let us sleep now, Running Dog."

Running Dog nodded, lay down next to him. Grey Bear heard the steady sound of his son breathing, and knew that Running Dog was dreaming. Grey Bear wondered what his dreams were, and guessed them to be of future glories in battle, and of horses and a lodge to call his own. Maybe he dreamed of his own vision quest, his own spirit animal. Or maybe he just dreamed of his mother, Yellow Leaf, and her food and comfort.

These are the dreams I wish for him, anyway, Grey Bear thought.

His question made Grey Bear wonder if Running Dog also had the dreams that his father did, the bad dreams of Running Dog's little sisters, who were taken by the Napikwan disease, the smallpox. It was four winters ago, when Running Dog was still a young child, who would not likely understand the full measure of what had taken place, but Grey Bear knew that he remembered well.

Only I wish that his dreams would stay true and good, and that he would not be haunted by these ghosts as I am, Grey Bear thought.

Grey Bear turned his head and saw the black tufts of hair sticking out from the warmth of the robe. Heard his muted breathing, saw the robe moving up and down with each breath as the flames cast their contrasting lights and shadows. He closed his eyes and drifted off to sleep.

The dreams came, the good dreams of the warmth of Yellow Leaf and home, but then the old dreams returned, of his dead children now in the Sand Hills, and the dreams of the great bear, slowly walking up to him and starting to whisper.

CHAPTER THREE

WYLIE, TEXAS
1982

The old brown Chevy truck turned off the paved highway and onto the gravel road. The boat hitched behind us, the fishing rods tied together inside it vibrating. The road ahead was crowded with thick oaks and pecans on either side. Dad had the heater on, cab of the truck smelled faintly of dirt and cigar smoke. Dad, with an old blue plaid wool shirt on, brown slacks that had seen better days, an old baseball cap, one he always wore, that read "Retired: no job, no prospects, no money."

"Dad, do you think I could have a BB gun for Christmas?"

His brown weathered face crinkled in a grin.

"Nine years old, gettin' to be a big boy. I'll talk to Santa Claus and see what we can do."

I knew there wasn't a Santa Claus other than Dad but I didn't say anything. I saw through the thick trees the blue of the lake and was excited like I always got when we were almost there.

"Gonna run trotlines today?"

"Yeah, we can put one out if you want. Brought it along. Figured we'd string one out and do a little crappie fishing, then we'll run it when we get ready to leave, how's that?"

He talked to me like I'm big like him, and I liked that.

We passed by an old cemetery as he turned right on a "T" in the road. Real old, weeds growing up around the tombstones, some of them broke in two. He saw me looking at them.

"You know," he said. "Your mama named you after my brother. Me and Calvin used to fish together at the farm in Oklahoma all the time, like me and you do now. There was an old cemetery like that next to the river where me and him would fish, and we'd have to walk through it on the way back to the house. Always dark, 'cause we couldn't go until after we finished our chores and we'd always stay long as we could.

"Anyway, one night we was going through there, had our fishing poles and just walking, stepping over the stumps and weeds, couldn't hardly see nothing 'cause it was so dark.

"We was just getting out of that cemetery when a haint rose up from behind a tall gravestone and started hollering real loud and carrying on. Boy, old Calvin dropped his fishing pole and started tearing off towards the house, almost knocked me over."

My eyes got real wide.

"I started running too, but I was kind of curious 'cause something in that haint's holler sounded like I'd heard it before. I stopped, turned around, and saw my younger brother Randall taking off a white sheet and laughing. I liked to killed him that night."

I chuckled, started to say something, but Dad cleared his throat.

"Calvin ran all the way home, didn't stop once. I got in and never did tell him it was Randall. He would've been hotter than the old devil and whooped him good."

The sign to the boat ramp came up and Dad pulled in, circling the truck around with its whiny sounds and backed it down into the lake. He had his neck craned back, looking real hard so the boat went in straight. I stared at him, thinking.

"So you never seen a real ghost, Dad?"

The boat went in smooth, pushing back ripples of water, Dad easing the truck back some more and when it floated up off the trailer, he put on the brakes, hand on the door.

"Nope. Just my brother in a white sheet. Ain't no real ghosts, Calvin."

It was white-capping out on the open water, roar of the boat's eighty-five horse engine drowned out the cars that shot by on a bridge to the east. Hitting a wave head-on now and then, I was out on the bow like always, the cold spray against my wet cheeks. Stung a little.

Dad pulled back on the throttle as we headed into the trees, mostly underwater but there were lots that stuck up. I peered down into the lake at the stumps just under the surface. After killing the engine, Dad stood up and tied the trotline to a thick branch, unwound the line, the many hooks dangling in the water.

"Might as well bait up while I'm stringing her out," he said with his back to me.

I grabbed the bucket of threadfin shad in the stern, big metal bucket full of the dead little fish packed in tight with hundreds of dull eyes staring at me. I took two at a time and baited the hooks.

That done, Dad fired up the boat again, headed to a hidden bay. It, too, was thick with underwater timber. We anchored down, baited up with live minnows, and dropped the line. Dad eased back in his seat, his hands behind his head, and glanced at me in the bow where I sat cross-legged staring at my rod tip, waiting for it to wiggle.

"Maw Maw made sandwiches for us," he said. "You hungry?"

I shrugged. "A little, I guess. I can wait."

"How 'bout an apple to tide you over?"

"Okay."

He dug into a grocery sack, tossed one to me. I held it in my hand absently, took a bite and tasted its sweetness, little bit of minnow smell to go with it.

"What's your mama doing today?"

My line started to shift a little and I got excited but realized it was just the minnow swimming around.

"Dunno. Probably still asleep. She'll do laundry and clean later."

We sat in silence for a few minutes, the steady sound of the water chopping on the sides of the boat, wind in my ears and gulls gliding above the open water, every now and then diving down and coming up with squirming fish in their beaks. A turtle popped its head out of the water, then back under.

"Hmm. She sure sleeps a lot," Dad said. "Ha, back when you were younger she joined up on a softball team. Knew I played baseball when I was a boy so she thought she'd show the old man she could do it, too."

I looked at him curiously. Softball?

"About every weekend she'd have something hurt on her. Black eyes, cuts. She weren't no athlete, I can tell you that. Tough, though. She tried."

My fishing line started to move but I didn't pay it any attention.

"Ever see her play?" I asked.

Dad laughed. "Naw. Always said she didn't want me to come watch, said me being there'd mess her up."

He reeled in his line and saw that something stole his minnow and so he put another one on, dropped it down. "Never went. Didn't seem to help her though, near as I could tell."

Doing it slow so he didn't notice, I reeled in my line so that my minnow was just on the surface of the water. Didn't feel like fishing, rather just watch that minnow swim around. Hook through him, still trying to swim though. Must hurt. I took my apple core and threw it hard as I could. It barely missed a tree, splashed down.

"You and Jack get along when he was still with my mama?"

Didn't know if I should call Jack my father around Dad, so I always called him Jack, just like I used to call Dad "Paw Paw" around him. Dad never took his eyes off his rod tip.

"He was no good. Always told your mama that. He never said much around me, just did his work with the rest of the crew. Wasn't around him much."

His hand came up to his rod handle but he pulled it away.

"Glad he's gone. Your mama's better off. And you got me, and that's all you need, huh?"

"Yeah, Dad."

His old blue eyes met mine and he smiled.

"I told her. She wouldn't listen."

I took my line out all the way, took off the dying minnow and tossed it into the water, watched as it tried to swim off. On its side, fins working, then it went still, started to float to the top.

"Dad, Mama never played no softball. Jack was bad to us. Beat my mama, hurt her and she never told you, but how come you didn't ask no questions? I play baseball and I never got no black eye, not once. But you never found out and never took care of my mama. If you knew he was bad, how come you didn't stop it?"

Tried to get more out but couldn't, hurt too bad just saying that. I sat back down, hid my face in my jacket, my baseball cap falling off but I didn't care. He got up, reeled in his line and tossed his rod in the boat, breathing heavy. I heard him say *gawd* under his breath. And we headed back to the dock.

"We going to Mama's house? You ain't mad at her, are you?" I asked over the sound of the motor and cold waves. He just shook his head, held up his hand. A little bit of water was on the corner of his eye but didn't know if it was tears or a splash from the waves.

࿐

It was a quiet ride back in the Chevy, Dad just looking straight ahead, mouth closed and solid-like. Hope I didn't get Mama in trouble. Hope everything was all right.

We pulled up in front of our duplex. Dad owned the whole thing and let Mama and me stay there for free. I ran up to the house as Mama opened the door.

"Baby, why are y'all back already?" she asked but I looked back at Dad and ran past her to my room. I closed the door real quiet, not wanting to bring attention to myself, holding my ear up to the crack in the door above the hinges, little bit of light peeking through, and I could hear real good.

"What?" I heard Mama ask and I could tell Dad was giving her a bad look, only saw it myself once or twice but something's not right when he gives it to you.

"You know what Calvin told me today?"

"No, what?" Voice a little higher now, could hear her being afraid.

"You never played softball, did you?"

Quiet for a while, guessed she was wondering if she should keep lying.

"What are you talking about, Daddy?"

"The softball team, all them weekends you come home with cuts and bruises and you telling me you joined a softball team. Wasn't true, was it?"

More quiet and they moved around a little, floor creaking, and I guessed they sat down. I opened the door of my room. They couldn't see me and I could hear better.

"No Daddy, it wasn't, I was just—"

"That son of a bitch. I told you he was no good. Told you."

"I didn't know what to do!" Mama screamed. "He had me scared, scared for Calvin. I didn't want to see him hurt. He didn't start out that way, Daddy. He was okay at first and then he started drinking and waking up in the middle of the night, yelling about some friend of his in Vietnam. Got worse and worse after that."

"Yeah, well, I told you about him. Told you about a lot of things, but you never listen. Told you to stay in school, told you to quit running around with all those wild people."

"Yeah, you told me, Daddy. You been telling me what to do all my life, try to control everybody, don't you? Even think you can buy Calvin's love and try to control him? So I fucked up with Jack, so I—"

"Don't you talk like that around me."

"I can talk however the fuck I like."

Then a smacking sound and Mama screamed.

"Get out! Get the hell out!"

Shuffling sounds and I heard the door close.

CHAPTER FOUR

MARIAS RIVER WINTER CAMP
JANUARY 1870

Yellow Leaf opened the flap of her lodge and saw that her brother, White Eyes, left a blackhorn robe just outside the entrance. Must have come in the night, she thought, dropped it off along with the meat. Might have cut another track on the way in, and now he goes after it. She grinned, knowing it was not just a kindness to his sister. White Eyes was young, much younger than Yellow Leaf, and he was trying to gain favor with Grey Bear for looking after her. Maybe Grey Bear will choose him in a future raiding party against the Crow, or for something else which might help White Eyes add to his herd.

She stepped out in the half-light of the morning shaking her head at her brother's ambition and, braving the biting winds, wrestled the heavy, frozen hide into her lodge. Out of breath, she peered out again at the sky. Clear, no snow. Good tracking weather, given the snow pack is soft in the hills. And that meant the men will bring back plenty of meat. Her face lightened.

Yellow Leaf had fretted over letting Running Dog go with Grey Bear this time. So cold, she did not remember a winter as bad.

Her great chief, Heavy Runner, said this was necessary, send them all at once, every able man or almost-man. The blackhorn are scarce, he said, and are scattered all through the foothills of the Bears Paw. It will be a good gamble, Heavy Runner said, sending them all at once, because the raiding parties of the Crow and the other enemies will not be out. Cold Maker will keep them away.

Heavy Runner was a wise leader and Yellow Leaf trusted his word.

Still, she worried.

That morning, she tried to put her fears aside and busy herself, taking an empty bladder and stepping outside, cold winds funneling through the river bottoms stinging her face. She broke the river's ice with a rock, collected water. Grey Bear once spoke to her of a man who stepped out into a bitter cold winter day and breathed in the frosty air and froze his throat shut. She hurried back to the lodge.

❧

"Major."

"Alright, Kipp, what do you got?"

"Another band, camped just north of us on the Marias. Went out early this morning and cut some old track. By himself, two horses, one empty, heading into the Bears Paw. Hunting buffalo, I imagine. Gonna be hard doings for them this winter ..."

"Goddammit Kipp, the band. How many of 'em?"

Kipp cleared his throat, looked down and back up at the major. Some major, he thought. Been drunk the last three weeks, and already Kipp smelled the whiskey on his breath. Hell, must have started hitting it soon as he got up this morning. But the winds picked up and it made standing next to him a little more tolerable.

"Oh, 250 or so. Pretty deserted. Most of the men out hunting probably. I know Heavy Runner's band is camped in this area and it may be them. He's a good man, Major. And if it ain't, they looked pretty harmless."

Major Eugene Baker peered at the young scout with bloodshot eyes. Joe Kipp. Goddamn half-breed anyway. His men were starting to stir, huddled in their tents in this frozen wasteland and crawling out, one by one, urinating, cussing, moving slow. He swallowed the last of the whiskey in his tin cup, tossed it in the direction of his tent, and turned to Kipp.

"Harmless, shit. You can tell that to the young lieutenant who was murdered by one of those red niggers, whole goddamn reason we're up here. And Kipp, I'll decide what to do and not do. Not you. You're paid to scout and give me the whereabouts and numbers. Is that clear?"

"Yes, sir," Kipp said.

Major Baker turned his back to him, grunted. "That's all."

Kipp walked away from the major's tent and back to his horse. No snow today, for once, but Lord, how cold. Sweat had formed in the small of his back on the ride in, and the wind was then working its way up his wool coat, chilling his tired body. He eyed the men starting to gather around the cook's tent, the faint smell of coffee and biscuits drifting to his nose as he loosened his horse's cinch.

"Why we're here in the first place," he muttered. Drunken gambling fight, a Blackfoot kills a soldier, and now they have to cross hundreds of miles in the dead of winter looking for his people. Don't make much sense, but hell, Kipp thought, seventy-five dollars a month is what he's in it for, but too much more of Baker and he'll go back to trading and guiding.

Kipp joined the men for what little breakfast there was. His hands, numbed from the cold, tingled as he rubbed them together. Ponsford, a private from somewhere down south, handed Kipp a steaming cup of coffee.

"I heard when we passed through Fort Shaw that it hit forty-four below," Ponsford said through wool collars turned up around his face. "Don't feel too much better than that this morning."

"Yep," said Kipp, surveying the other men. Two hundred in all. All of them cold, tired. Horses not much better, three hundred head grazing on what little grass they can paw up next to the bluffs off in the west.

All over one dead soldier who probably had it coming to began with. He frowned. Of course, Kipp thought, it's more than that.

"Hear me, Joe?" Ponsford asked.

"Huh?"

"Biscuits runnin' low. Better get in there and grab you one 'fore we run out."

☙

Yellow Leaf put the water over the fire to boil. She dipped a cotton cloth in the hot water and ran it along the folds of the hide, gradually softening it and allowing it to open up from its tight bundle. She worked for the next hour, finally exposing half the meat side, and began to de-flesh it with her stone scraper.

She worked a small section at a time, removing all the flesh and fat and thinning the hide so the brains will sink in well and soften it into good leather. Her hands ached, but it helped to keep her mind off other things. Winters past of the men coming in with their fingers frozen and black, or men not coming back at all. But no use worrying.

Yellow Leaf's blade cut into the hide in smooth strokes, thin layers of the milky white skin flaking off. She thought of the meal she'll cook for Grey Bear and her son when they return, boiled tongue or maybe a thick roast, thought of the sounds of them as they sleep in her warm lodge. Thought of Running Dog's laugh, and how he is growing up and in a few winters will be a man.

And then the loneliness hit her. She was one of the few women in camp without children. Having lost two daughters to smallpox, Running Dog was her only one and he was older, wanting to go with his father and not stay behind with her. It was the course of things, but she missed her boy.

The wind had picked up speed, but through its pounding on the lodge Yellow Leaf heard the voice of Bending Reed, sounding excited. She put down her fleshing knife, opened the lodge flap.

There, on the east bluff of the river, were dozens of Cavalry soldiers, the blue-coated Napikwans with whom Chief Heavy Runner had signed a peace treaty last winter. They had dismounted and had their rifles pointed at the camp. Yellow Leaf craned her neck and looked to the west bluff. They had divided their forces to surround them.

Downstream from the river were five mounted soldiers. Chief Heavy Runner appeared from his lodge with government papers and approached them.

They were not far and the wind was at their backs, so Yellow Leaf could hear the mounted Napikwans speak to each other, although she didn't understand their strange tongue. One of them was different. A half-breed maybe, little darker skinned than the others. Dressed different, too. He didn't wear the stripes or the coat of blue. Dressed like the trader she saw to the north in the Always Winter Land where Grey Bear bartered some blackhorn robes for a skinning knife a few winters back.

She closed the entrance flap enough to block out the biting cold, leaving just enough open to see and hear.

"It's Heavy Runner, Major," said the half-breed.

"I don't give a good goddamn," said the Napikwan in the middle, who Yellow Leaf guessed was the Napikwan Chief.

"Got his paperwork, we're wasting our time," the half-breed said.

The Napikwan have come many times and visited with Chief Heavy Runner. Always they trained their rifles on camp, but this did not alarm Yellow Leaf because always they left in peace.

But this new Napikwan kicked his horse closer to that of the half-breed, took him by the neck and whispered something she did not hear. He let go and the half-breed looked very angry. He rode away, disappeared through a draw. This gave Yellow Leaf a bad feeling.

Heavy Runner made a show of the papers in his hand as he approached, waving them in the air, smiling. She heard voices between the Napikwan and Heavy Runner, who could speak the Napikwan tongue, but the winds shifted and she could make out none of the words.

The other women and elderly people peered out from the small openings at their lodges' parlay. Heavy Runner was still talking to the soldiers. He gave the Napikwan chief the papers. The white chief took them with a gloved hand, looking down at the smiling Heavy Runner.

The white chief removed what looked like a flask from his coat, took a drink, put it back in his pocket. He held out the papers, studied them, turned to the others and laughed. He ripped the papers in two, tossed them to the ground. The mounted soldiers pulled out their pistols and fired at Heavy Runner.

Yellow Leaf saw her chief fall to the cold ground, the wind carrying the torn papers away. She screamed, closed the flap, dove to the floor, crawled under a robe and made herself flat, keeping the robe open enough to see out. Her eyes frantically darted about the lodge, not knowing what to do. A hole appeared in the wall. A second later the thunder hit and it didn't stop, a bellowing, incessant barrage from the big guns. She felt the vibration in the ground. All over camp there was screaming, crying from the women and children, wails that could not be drowned out even by the reports of the Napikwans' many-shots rifles.

She buried her face in the earth, wanted to sink into it, disappear. The thunder and screams pounding her ears, the soldiers' whoops. The ground shook and she heard not the screams of many but the screams of one person, two people, then the thunder, then no more screams and she flattened herself more, not knowing, no thought, no feeling.

The thunder again, and this time her ears felt as they would explode. Burning feeling in her stomach. Yellow Leaf crawled out from underneath the robe. The sharp pain came and then blood pooling on the earth. She tried to turn over on her back, but then looked down at the gray coil of an intestine. Holding it in, she crawled outside. Cold winds hit her; thunder was still coming down.

Outside vision was cloudy and darkening, but she turned her head and saw the earth littered with her people, women and children, parts of them strewn on the cold scarlet ground. Her body half-torn and still, Bending Reed's lifeless eyes were still open, vacant eyes that no longer saw, her brown arm outstretched in the snow, open hand reaching out. Beautiful Bending Reed, with whom Yellow Leaf laughed and played when the world was new and they were little girls picking wild onions and swimming in the summer waters of the Marias, with whom she ran in the wide prairies when the wildflowers were in bloom and the sweet smells of the fescue filled the air.

Yellow Leaf thought of Running Dog, sweet, smiling Running Dog. A little boy out playing in the tall grass of the river bottom, chasing rabbits and laughing. Running Dog by her side with a small hand around her knee as he watched the Sun Festival in summer, her hand on his black hair as he cast timid glances at the dancing and singing.

She thought of Grey Bear, of her strong husband's arms cradling her in her warm lodge on cold winter nights, whispering softly in her ears. Of him watching her from across the Marias as she gathered roots along the riverbank, of her sitting with her bare feet in the cool current and knowing he watched from behind the cottonwoods but pretending she doesn't see him.

The world was becoming dark, the sounds of the thunder were far away. She felt the earth shake and saw an approaching horse and rider. A young Napikwan soldier with a pistol in hand, blue eyes bored into her. Yellow Leaf looked past him at the whites of the clouds, the blues of his coat, and reds of the earth. There was only the sound of horse hooves through the red snow, slowing down, a loud whinny. The barrel of the black pistol was trained on her, hammer cocked, then the thunder and darkness closed in.

Up ahead Yellow Leaf saw a whiteness and felt the frigid north winds. The whiteness moved, many grains of white as one. The sting of sand peppered her face and without thinking she walked toward it, trying to mask her face with her hand but it did no good. Her hand was a nothing hand now. The pain went away and the sand could not be felt.

There was a great camp with many head of horses, men coming in from hunts with down meat and women fetching water, fleshing hides, laughing, smiling, readying themselves for a feast. Boys, girls, giggling, playing. Two of them glanced her way, smiled and waved.

Their mother was home.

CHAPTER FIVE

GARLAND, TEXAS

1986

I took my spoon and sliced through the banana, dipped it into the hot fudge, and took a bite, leaned back in the old booth, thinking about what just happened, wanting to relive it. My mother sat across from me in the little downtown drugstore. She was beaming.

"You did it. Can't believe you did it." She shook her head back and forth, smiling.

"Can't either," I said, wiping ice cream off my chin with a wadded up napkin.

"Should've seen Dad sitting in the stands with me," she said. "Watching you out there playing and telling everyone around him who would listen 'That's my boy'. And then when you hit that home run and everybody started cheering, he just sat there grinning and said, 'There he goes' like he knew that's what you were going to do all along."

I spooned up the melted ice cream, mixed a little fudge in with it, and brought it to my mouth. The usual people were in the store, mostly retired, coming in to get prescriptions filled or a cup of coffee. A bald man sat at the counter telling a joke to one of the clerks, leaned over and whispered and I thought about Dad, remember seeing him in the stands watching me play first base.

"How come Jack never tried to stay in touch with me?" I asked her, not sure where the question came from.

Her smile disappeared and her eyes dropped to her half-full mug of root beer float. She picked her spoon up, dug through the melted ice cream.

"I don't know, Calvin. But it's not you, baby."

"I know," I said, not wanting her to be unhappy. We ate in silence for a few minutes, deep chuckling coming from the man sitting at the counter. The clerk grinned, leaned in and patted the bald man on the shoulder.

I imagined Dad in the stands, smiling and chuckling like the bald man at the counter, telling people around him he was my Dad, because Dad will talk to anybody whether they want him to or not. Damn near got thrown out of one of my football games last year because he saw a white woman sitting in the stands with a black man and Dad, being Dad, said, "You don't see a crow and cardinal trying to mate, do you?" real loud to anybody who would listen and Maw Maw told him to pipe down as all the people around him grumbled.

But he was seventy-two, and that's just the way he was brought up, thinking we should all be separate on account of the color of our skin. Scott Sander was my best friend, and he played second base and after the game his dad came up to me and told me I did real good hitting that homer. His *real* dad.

"Okay, kiddo. Let's get going, I'm playing bunko tonight with the girls from work and I need to get you to Dad's."

"I want to call Jack," I said. "How do I find his number?"

My mother hesitated, eyebrows bunched up together, looked down real quick and back up at me.

"Well, you're thirteen now. Figured this would happen at some point. I'll get it from his mother in Fort Worth if it's what you want to do. Now c'mon, let's go."

On the ride over to Dad's and later that night lying on my bed in the back room, I thought about Jack. He beat my mom and was bad to her, but maybe most of that he couldn't help. War messed him up, heard my mama say one time. Said sometimes he woke up screaming and hollering for people who weren't there. Caused him to start drinking more and more and, because he was so drunk, maybe he didn't see Mama anymore, maybe he saw other people and so he beat them not knowing it was really Mama who was getting hurt. And if that was true, I thought, maybe Dad was wrong to call Jack no good. Couldn't help it if he was crazy. Maybe he was better now, and when I call him he'll be happy to hear from me.

Maybe he'll be friends with Mama again and I could go see him and I could have a real dad like Scott Sander.

స్ట్

I turned off the light on the nightstand and lay back looking up in the dark at the ceiling. The television blared in Dad's bedroom; Johnny Carson's on, meant he'll be asleep and snoring soon. Don't know how Maw Maw slept next to him every night like she did.

Yeah, but why hasn't Jack called me? Been eight years and nothing, never talked to Mama or me or nobody, just left and not a word. Could be he just don't care and I'll call and he'll tell me not to call him ever again because he's moved on now. Just be thankful you got Dad and quit thinking about him. So what if Scott has a real dad?

Dad's dog, Charlie, started barking at something outside, a bird or a raccoon maybe. Had a funny bark, like it cuts out halfway before he's done. Him barking made me think of Dusty and I hadn't thought about him in a while. Died last year and didn't think much of it at first because he was old and old dogs die, nothing you can do about it. But then I got real sad because I remembered the times we had, me and Dusty and Ben. Cried a little even.

Charlie was nothing like Dusty, but he was still a good dog. Dusty was his daddy and Charlie was born crippled so he didn't get sold like the rest of the litter, one leg formed different than the other three so he hopped around with a funny little walk. I went out and played with him in the backyard, threw him sticks and tennis balls, stuff like that. He would grab them and start running around but never give them back so I had to chase him down and take them from him.

But then, maybe it won't be like I thought. Maybe Jack'll be glad I called and I could have a real dad. Ain't gonna find out unless I do it.

స్ట్

"Ranger game on, playin' the Orioles today," Dad said, leaning back in his recliner. I was sitting at the kitchen table eating one of Maw Maw's leftover salmon croquettes. I looked over the back of his bald head and saw Cal Ripken squatted down at shortstop, glove opening and closing, blue eyes peering at the batter. I took a last bite and sat on the sofa next to Dad's chair.

"What's the score?" I asked, not really caring.

"Right now it's five-three Baltimore, but Buechele's at bat and they only have one out in the eighth inning." His hand came down on the remote and he picked it up, spinning it around with his fingers. "Bet if you were batting, you'd knock one out like you did yesterday."

I grinned. Yeah, right—I couldn't even see those pitches they were throwing so fast. "Hey Dad, just wanted to let you know that, uh—"

"Strike three," he said, shaking his head. "Do what now?"

"Been thinking about calling Jack. Asking him why he never tried to stay in touch with me."

I watched Dad, not knowing what to expect. He didn't say anything at first, just kept twirling that remote and staring at the television. His face was expressionless, and finally he cleared his throat.

"Don't know why you'd want to do that. Ain't never been around, ain't never done nothing for you."

At the kitchen table, Maw Maw had put her pencil down from the crossword puzzles she was working on, listened to us.

"I know, Dad," I said. "Just gotta find out why, that's all."

"I know why," he said. "He's a drunkard, good for nothing. You're my boy, not his, and you ought to just leave well enough—"

"Ben, if the boy wants to call him, let him," said Maw Maw. "Let him see for himself."

"Well, he'll just find out what I've been telling—"

The front door opened, and my mother called out. "Knock knock."

"You 'bout ready to go, Calvin?"

I grabbed my clothes and got in Mama's car. She stayed in the house for a while and because the front door was still open I knew they were talking about me. Mama's voice got a little louder and then she came out, looking tired with her pinned up hair and sweatpants. She circled around the car and there was Maw Maw at the door, watching us through the screen with a blank stare, her arms crossed.

We were quiet on the ride back to our house until we reached a stop light.

"I called Jack's mother this morning. I got you that number."

My heart sunk. It was real now. Haven't talked to him in eight years but now I had to go through with it. Had to. Had to know.

"Thanks Mom" is all I could muster. I wanted to be alone with my thoughts and not talk about it.

Once in my room I sat down at my desk, pushed some homework papers aside, and stared at the phone. Do it before you lose your nerve. I dialed and it started ringing.

"Hello?"

"Is this Jack?"

"Yeah, who's this?"

"Your son Calvin."

Long silence. Should I say something? Didn't know what to say. Why wasn't he talking? Beads of sweat formed at my brow.

"Hi, son."

"I was just calling to see how you're doing and, uh, was wondering about you," I said.

Another stretch of quiet.

"You know, I think about you every day, Calvin. Wonder how you're doing, what you look like. Never thought your mother would appreciate me contacting you, but you are always in my thoughts."

"So, where do you live?" I started to call him Jack, but stopped short. Didn't want to call him father or dad, but gonna have to figure something out because I can't just not call him anything.

"I'm in Colorado. Got a cabin about forty miles west of Colorado Springs. You'd love it up here in the mountains. I remember you used to love watching Grizzly Adams when you was a little boy and up here it's just like that, and I—"

His words were cut short, like he couldn't talk and I thought he may have been crying but he continued.

"I'd love it if you'd come up to see me this summer, Calvin. If your mother said it's okay, I'll pay your way up here and you can stay with me for a couple of weeks. How does that sound?"

In the mountains with my real dad?

"That sounds good."

CHAPTER SIX

MARIAS RIVER WINTER CAMP

JANUARY 1870

Grey Bear's horse walked more purposefully now, sensing that they were not far from home and a few days rest, its stride smooth, its conformation solid.

It was bitterly cold with the winds funneling through the snake-like canyons and bluffs, blasting their backs. Their clothes, though, dried out the night previous and their fast stride kept their bodies warm. Grey Bear gave thanks to the Below People for the wind as it was at their backs and propelled them home faster. Just the thought of Yellow Leaf, her face when they arrive with meat, her embrace, and her laughter made his heart soar.

They were heading west as the sun came up behind them. Grey Bear recalled the conversations he had with his own father as he thought of the Sun and its force's relation to the origin of it all, the Old Man Napi. According to his father, who was a medicine man, the Sun was the invention of the Old Man, for the Old Man is older than all things. So light, while being all-important, was not of the Sun's origin but of the Old Man, with the Sun delegated by the Old Man as the guardian and provider of this gift. Although Grey Bear had heard among other bands that the Sun and Napi are one, he believed his father.

Grey Bear must sit Running Dog down after they return and talk to him of these things; now that he was older and asking questions, they must have these talks more frequently. He seemed now to be able to digest his father's words. He will tell him of the origin of life, how death came to be when the woman threw the stone in the river, the history of their long-ago people, so many things.

The horse was at full attention, ears pointed toward the southern bluff, whites of its eyes a little too evident. Grey Bear did not see or hear or smell anything, but he raised a fist, and Running Dog stopped.

Taking in every piece of information, Grey Bear stood silent, all senses working together. Something on the bluff. He glanced around for cover and there was none; they were caught in the open with the next cluster of cottonwoods a hundred paces away. He made a downward motion with his hand, and Running Dog moved behind his horse, away from where his father's attention was. Grey Bear did the same, keeping his eyes along the skyline, searching.

The metallic shine from the sun's reflection blinded Grey Bear. He squinted, strained to make it out. His horse was blown back by a shot, whinnying loudly, staggering. Grey Bear back scrambled to get out of the way and tripped on a rock. His horse fell and the booming report from a rifle came down the canyon walls. Running Dog's horse was spooked, passing Grey Bear in a gallop. A second shot and the horse's legs buckled.

"Running Dog! Go!"

Sprinting to the cluster of cottonwoods, Grey Bear's world was spinning. He felt a sharp sting to his head, blood shooting over the hardened snow of the open field. A loud boom and then nothingness.

Sounds were everywhere, strange sounds of men talking in foreign tongues, of hard laughter. Grey Bear opened his eyes and through his blurred vision made out the blue coats of men standing over him. A maddening, sharp pain drummed in his head, coming in a rhythm. The odors of these men wafted down and the smell was sickening; his stomach revolted and he retched, causing more of the coarse laughter. He knew they were deciding his fate. His hands and feet were tied.

"Yep, Jim, you blew his ear plum off. That's got to hurt like a son of a bitch."

"Well, I was aiming to do more than that; wind threw my bullet off a bit."

"We going to take him in with the others or kill him here?"

"I say let's let him live. He's got a good little reminder on him and every time one of them red niggers sees him, they'll think twice about tangling with one of us."

"Okay, hell, take him back then, and I'll move on out. 'Course, him being a buck, slightest bit of trouble out of him I say shoot him and move on."

Grey Bear's vision was a little clearer, although the wafting pain made it impossible to concentrate. He wanted to cry out but held it in, unwilling to dishonor himself in the face of his enemies.

Where was Running Dog? Did he escape? Grey Bear guessed it was so; he did not see his son anywhere. Maybe he watched from the trees.

"Say, you seen a little runt take off when you shot this one?"

"Yep, couldn't hit the little bastard. No sense looking for him, we got to head out. I'm not worried. Little shit'll either starve or freeze to death anyway. He ain't gonna bother us."

One of the men mounted his horse and rode off, then the other took a lariat from his saddle, kicked Grey Bear over on his stomach. The soldier tied the lariat to the rope around Grey Bear's wrists. Turning his head, the sharp pain imploded as his wound scrapped the ground. Grey Bear let out a piercing cry.

"Oh shit, rope don't hurt that much."

The Napikwan unbuckled a skinning knife from its sheath, and cut through the rope binding Grey Bear's legs. The soldier kicked him back over, put his foot on Grey Bear's chest, leaned over, and held the wide blade inches from Grey Bear's face as the soldier's sour breath lingered in the air.

"You just follow along, and don't give me no trouble."

The soldier turned his knife around, blade side out, and popped Grey Bear hard on the bad side of his head. Grey Bear screamed, wanted so badly to reach out, choke him, cut him open and pull his heart out, but he knew that he must do as he was told to keep living because Running Dog was out there and, if he was watching, he will follow.

The Napikwan put his knife back in the sheath and, holding the lariat, mounted his horse. Without looking back, he rode toward the Piegan winter camp. Grey Bear's heart turned to the others, and he frantically worried about Yellow Leaf.

The pain in his head subsided to a dull throbbing with the numbing cold. The winds, always at their backs, pierced his wound and edged down his back. The intense pain and stress caused Grey Bear to sweat until he was soaked, and now the wetness chilled him to the bone.

He willed his legs to keep moving. Grey Bear vowed he will not be outpaced and allow his captor the pleasure of jerking on the rope to make him fall. He tried to block the pain, block this monster in his head, tried instead to conjure up the wisdom of his spirit animal and cried for help from the Above Ones and Below Ones, for vengeance and to keep, if she still lived, Yellow Leaf from harm.

They rounded the final bend in the canyon that opened up to their winter camp. He tried to detect the presence of Running Dog, perhaps keeping pace with them out of sight. Grey Bear believed his son was still alive. After all, he reasoned, would they not show him the body to torture him if they had killed Running Dog? No, he lives. And if he lives, he will follow. But he did not sense his son anywhere. Of course, he did not sense this Napikwan until it was too late.

They closed the distance to the bend and Grey Bear prepared himself. He told himself, over and over, to just breathe, remain calm; do not do anything that will cause these soldiers to kill him because that will be the death of Running Dog, too. No matter how bad it is. No matter if the fate of Yellow Leaf was bad. No matter.

The river bottom opened up. Grey Bear's stomach once again revolted as the stench of burning human flesh reached his nostrils.

There were no more standing lodges. They were all burned to the ground, black circles in the earth. More than a hundred of his people were herded in a circle and surrounded by the mounted cavalry. The bodies of his people lay everywhere. He passed by the great chief Heavy Runner, now almost torn in half by bullet wounds to the chest. On his back, his lifeless eyes open and staring at the sky. His expression a plea for help that will never come.

Beyond were the bodies, all of them women, children, and elderly. Many burned, just blackened shapes of their human form. Body parts of children. A woman with half of her head charred black and steaming, the other half missing, her remaining eye open in her last look of horror, half a mouth still agape.

Grey Bear gazed upon the dismembered corpses, remembered them as they lived. He tried to rivet his attention to those who were living, searching for the slight figure of Yellow Leaf. Where his lodge stood he saw her. Face down. Her body contorted in an unnatural shape. Her hair matted with dirt and blood.

There were no tears, but anger. There was no warning; it was a sudden, insane rage. He could do nothing but look to the sky and scream, for the only other choice was to charge this Napikwan and be killed instantly. So he wailed and the soldier looked back at him with annoyance, but did nothing.

The soldier took him to his people, dismounted, drunkenly untied the lariat and then kicked Grey Bear inside the circle. Nobody acknowledged him. Everyone in a waking death, everyone turned into themselves.

Grey Bear sat, crossed his legs. He wanted to lay on his back and support his aching head but could not with his hands still tied. The rope burrowed into his flesh, the dull throbbing of his wound sharper. But these things were almost a comfort Grey Bear could escape into to avoid the loss of his soul. He kept his eyes down, like the others, unwilling to gaze upon what was out ahead of them any longer.

The Napikwan soldiers gathered around their chief, then mounted their horses. They yelled and Grey Bear's people rose. Day Star, wife of Rain In The Face, was badly wounded, and before Grey Bear could make his way over to her, a soldier rode up, drew his pistol and shot her in the head. Skull fragments and brain matter exploded onto the others. Screams. Grey Bear looked away, senses numbed.

For the rest of the day and all of the next, they were driven in a northerly direction. Grey Bear supposed they were being taken into Canada and released, but this was just a guess. He did not know why they were even being kept alive. He stayed alert for any sign of Running Dog, but he did not show himself. Without hope they walked, walked as living ghosts with everything erased, both past and future.

They had been given nothing to eat and very little water. The first night was unbearably cold. There was no sleep, and they put all their energy into huddling to keep warm. Still, when the morning came there was another dead child, Little Wolf, a boy of seven winters and son to Rain In The Face. Little Wolf had followed Running Dog as they hunted rabbits before the Sun Festival and Grey Bear thought of Rain In The Face, returning from his hunt to nobody now. His eyes lingered on the still, cold little body.

The day's light was almost exhausted when the Napikwan soldiers stopped for the night. The Piegan prisoners were told to sit and two guards were assigned guard duty. They were out in the open prairie with the winds strong and biting. Snow began to fall.

The wound where his ear used to be was raw and tender but the healing had begun. Cold Maker's ice had kept the wound scraped clean and although the pain still pierced, Grey Bear worried less.

They sat together to maximize their body heat, the weakest among them in the middle. Grey Bear was part of the perimeter and the first to see a rear scout appear through the snowy haze with a small figure in front of him.

He hoped against hope but still didn't quite believe what he saw until the scout rode up to the circle. The gaunt figure looked down and, despite everything, smiled. The rider dropped him to the ground, left.

Grey Bear tried to give Running Dog a reassuring smile. As much as Running Dog wanted to hide his emotions, a single tear slid down his face. He gathered himself and joined the circle. Grey Bear yearned to hold him, touch him, make sure he was real.

"Father, I am sorry I failed you."

Grey Bear attempted to reach for him, even knowing that he could not. "Failed me?"

Running Dog moved a little closer, stared at the ground.

"I want you to tell me everything," Grey Bear said. "Tell me where you were. Tell me what you saw."

"Yes, Father. I watched them take you after they shot you. I knew you were hurt badly, because otherwise you would have easily killed both of them. I could see the blood. For a while, after he shot you, I thought you were dead. But then you rose. Because even a bullet in the head cannot easily kill you. They were cowards."

Running Dog struggled with the words, unused to speaking to his father this directly. Grey Bear urged him on with a low grunt.

"I followed you, always staying out of sight in the trees, staying back and off to the side as you would have done.

"When you and the Napikwans arrived at our camp, I saw that everything had been burned. From where I hid across the river I could see our lodge and Mother lying dead beside it. I knew it was her, even from far away.

"Yesterday, I followed our group even though we moved north and away from the cover of the trees. I did the best I could staying out of sight by moving underneath the cover of the breaks and coulees, moving quickly between clusters of brush and staying low."

Running Dog's face tightened.

"I wanted to sneak in that first night and untie your binds, get you away from here so that we may figure out a way to help our people. I thought of everything except how to get past the night guards. I was out in the open with nothing to protect me, Father. And so I waited, doing nothing, waited for a chance when the guards switched, but they always kept a watch on you.

"I followed you today. My eyes grew weary as I had no sleep last night. I fell asleep beside a cluster of sage brush and one of the rear scouts spotted me. He stood beside me and laughed as I slept. I am sorry, Father. I failed you."

Grey Bear's heart was bursting, and Running Dog continued to stare at the ground.

CHAPTER SEVEN

DIVIDE, COLORADO
JUNE 1986

The road wound around the mountains, thick walls of granite shooting straight up on one side of us, on the other side a narrow green valley cut short by the opposing mountain, a near-vertical wall of timber that loomed, the details blurring as we rode past. Felt tight, like the mountains were trying to embrace us, closing in. I was sweating around my neck, my denim jacket too warm with the hot air blowing out of the truck's vents.

"Fishing good here?" I asked.

"Yeah. Got some ponds over by the cabin, eight of 'em, stocked with brookies and cutthroat. There's rainbows in two or three of them. I'll use mostly rooster tails on a light spinning outfit when I go out there, but sometimes I fish salmon eggs. Don't take much. Those stocked fish are pretty easy to catch. You'll like it out there."

I noticed his hand on the steering wheel, amazed at the size of it, veins protruding like angry blue snakes. A hand that could crush rocks. He was dressed in blue jeans and a cotton camouflage jacket. Light brown hair with a little gray sprinkled on the sides. Forty-one years old.

"Never caught a trout before. Fish mostly for—"

"Calvin, look, look."

Big finger pointed across the valley. Three deer, two big ones and a little one, a fawn. They walked to the dense timber, disappeared into the dark woods.

"Those were mule deer. That's what we have up here, in the mountains anyway. No whitetails like you have in Texas."

"I know. Looked them up and read about mule deer and elk and bighorn sheep. All that stuff. Can't wait to see 'em all," I said.

The hum of the heater came back into my ears. Stifling hot but I didn't say anything about it. My father glanced at the mountains that surrounded us, tilted his head a little, stared at the road.

"Well, you can come here anytime you want, stay as long as you want. This is your home too, son."

My home. All the woods I can explore, all the fish I can catch, and I had a father. My real father. Maybe I could call him Dad. And then I thought about Dad back home and felt bad, but I didn't want any bad feelings, so I made myself stop thinking about him. Him sitting in the stands watching me play baseball. Just don't think about it. Jack was driving, staring out at the road and looking like he's lost in thought. Sunlight hit his glasses and the shine hurt my eyes a little.

The valley opened up some and we came to a little town, a few buildings in a row and a sprinkling of houses is all it was, and we passed by a sign saying "Divide Pop: 0".

"Population zero?"

Jack smiled as he turned onto a gravel road heading north. Road was rough and the truck's tight shocks made it tremble and moan.

"Technically, the post office is the town. Rest of it's outside the town, so nobody lives in town."

His soft voice vibrated as the truck whined down the road. The gravel ended, and it was just dirt with bumps and holes, the forest crowding us in again. I tried to spot more deer to get away from the discomfort of not knowing what to say, of making light of things when there was serious questions running through my head, big stuff I didn't know how to go about bringing up. Maybe he'll talk about it soon. Screw it. Push that away too, like Dad back home. I'm in heaven now.

We turned left at a fork in the road, Ponderosa pines and junipers passed in a green blur. Another fork and we were bumping along, distant mountain peaks just above the tree tops. I sensed we were going downhill. We turned off the road and the outline of the brown cabin became clearer as we pulled into a dirt circular driveway.

"This is it," he said.

The cold chill of the wind hit my face; the wetness around my neck sent shivers down my back. The sharp smell of the pines came with the wind, and I took in the earthy odor, feeling alive and light in my feet. For the first time, I heard the sounds of the forest, the nothingness interrupted by a lone squirrel bark down in a draw, the trees as they swayed in the wind, old timbers creaking and groaning, the thermals masking these lesser sounds. Jack leaned against the warm hood of the truck, hands in his pockets and the beginning of a smile on his lips.

"Pretty cool, isn't it?" he said. "C'mon, grab your suitcase and I'll show you around inside."

"Okay, Dad."

It came out without any thought and it felt right, comfortable. He didn't show any expression of surprise, just nodded and turned toward the porch steps. Then something hit me in the gut, real small but I felt it, like I was selling government secrets to the enemy, some traitor doing some underhanded thing to the people who have been loyal to me all my thirteen years. But gotta call him something, right? He was my father.

The cabin was perched on the side of steep, thickly-forested hill. It had a walk-around deck, two-stories with a half-buried basement. I followed him in, looking around. Shoulder mount of a mule deer buck hung over the television, paintings of elk, pictures of rivers flowing through steep canyons, an old overstuffed couch, rustic coffee table made from a hardwood, *bois d'ark* looked like. I knew about that stuff because I saw Dad make a real nice clock out of it.

Dad.

"Let's go downstairs and I'll show you your room, get you settled in," Jack said. I followed him down a narrow hallway and noticed a gun rack mounted on the wall. Double-barreled shotgun with exposed hammers, .22 bolt-action rifle, and then—

"Is that a real M-16?" I asked.

Jack was taking a step down the stairs and, without looking back, said, "Civilian version. AR-15. Colt makes 'em, the good ones, but there's lots of knock-offs, too. Thought maybe tomorrow we could fish, and if you want to in a couple of days we'll go shooting, too."

"Yeah, that sounds great."

We walked down the steps. I studied him. He was thinning a little on top. Still plenty strong, though. Mom said he wasn't a tall guy. Always remembered him being tall but I guessed that was only because I was five last time I seen him. But now he was only a few inches taller than me, five-eight or so.

The basement was an open space, wrap-around bookshelf. Jack walked to a door and it opened to a small bedroom.

"Here you go, son. Why don't you unpack, change clothes if you need to. I'll be upstairs in the kitchen. You like elk liver?"

I set my suitcase down.

"Never had it, but I like regular liver."

"This stuff beats anything from a cow, hands down," he said, walking out of the room.

Walls were bare white save for a framed picture of Jack standing next to a mountain stream. Wind was blowing in the picture, his hair tousled. He wore a brown bomber jacket with a long scarf wrapped around his neck, smiling widely, sun shining on his face.

The window was close to ground level. I stared out at the pine trees looming above like I was buried in a hole, which I was. The image made me a little nervous. The bed was an old twin-size covered with a white comforter that I thought used to be whiter than it was. I unzipped the outside pocket of my suitcase and pulled out an envelope, a letter that Jack wrote to me before I came up. The corners were worn from pulling the letter out countless times to read and re-read it, like looking in the refrigerator after you've looked before hoping to see something new to chew on.

And so I read it again, hoping to make new sense of the words.

April 16, 1986

Calvin,

Thought I'd write you a short letter and tell you some things, things I probably wouldn't tell you otherwise. I'm kind of quiet, don't like to express my feelings so much. I can laugh and cry with the best of them, but sometimes things don't get said what should've been. I've already got so much regret in my heart. I don't want any more.

Hearing your voice again makes me feel alive, like I've finally done something right, something good. I've thought about you every single day, Calvin, wondering how you're changing, growing. I've wondered often about the man you'll become, praying that you'll be better than me. I know you will.

I don't know how much your mother has told you about me, about our problems, about my problems. Don't know how much you remember. Hope you have some good memories, some at least. Most of them, probably, are bad. And I'll have to live with that the rest of my life.

I know I can't ever take that away no matter how badly I want to. All I can do is make it up to you as best I can. I want to be the father I should've been. And I want you to know that I love your mother to this day. I'm haunted by some things, Calvin, bad things I hope you never see or experience. After I left, I went through a real rough time. I guess it'll never completely go away.

I'm counting the days 'till you get here. Looking forward to making up the lost time, fishing, hiking, whatever you want to do. I'm always here for you, and I'll never go away again.

I love you, son.

Dad

I put the letter back in its envelope and stuck it in my suitcase. Outside my bedroom, many books lined the basement bookshelf. A lot of military history, a few westerns, some philosophy, crime and mystery novels. I picked out one about a famous Marine Corps sniper Carlos Hathcock, tossed it on my bed. I headed for the kitchen, smelled the elk liver frying up on the stove. If I don't like it I'll say I do. I'll make myself like it.

ॐ

"Calvin."

The voice came from somewhere deep in a tunnel of dreamless sleep. I stirred, opened my eyes to bright sunlight seeping through the curtains. My father, again in his camouflage jacket and a backpack slung across his shoulder, stood smiling at the foot of my bed.

"Been watching you sleep for the last few minutes. Used to do that sometimes when you were a baby."

I cleared my throat, head felt a little light. Altitude, I guessed.

"Oh?" I said, not knowing what else to add.

"Let's go catch some fish, huh? I packed us some ham and egg sandwiches. You can eat one on the way if you like."

It was only a little way to the ponds, maybe a mile or two down a winding dirt road. They were just like I pictured them, each of them only about an acre or so in size, all except for the first in the string running down the narrow valley. It was bigger, way bigger, covering twenty acres or better, with a little rocky island jutting up in the middle. Its waters edged along the steep mountain opposite us, blanketed in pines which disappeared in a thick, low-lying cloud cover. It was June, but when I stepped out of the truck the chill air hit my neck, ran down my spine. I zipped up my jacket. My father dug in his backpack and pulled out a small tackle box.

"Take a couple of these," he said, handing me some lures. "Sometimes a guy can get hung up at the bottom. Lot of rocks down there."

The lures were rooster-tails, a clump of squirrel tail hair at the end, dyed red and yellow to mask the treble hook, with a silver blade fastened to the front. I put them in my pocket and watched Jack cut a hook from the end of a line and start to thread a new lure.

"Know how to tie a Palomar knot?" he asked.

"No. D ... my grandpa showed me how to tie a clinch knot. That's what I usually use."

I tried to keep an even face. Cold helped.

"Palomar's much easier. Stronger, too. Come over here, in front of me. I'll tell you how while you tie it. First, make a loop in the line, like this."

His hand swallowed mine, deftly taking the end of the line and bringing it around to my fingers.

"Now put the end of the loop through the eye of the lure. Gotta squeeze it tight so you can get it through."

I struggled, but managed to get the loop through on my third attempt. Hands were cold, no feeling.

"Now take your threaded loop and make an overhand knot, like this." Big hands again in mine, warm.

Felt safe out here. So, this is what it is to have a real Dad. These weren't the hands that hurt people when I was little. These hands protect.

Protect me.

I walked down to the bank a few feet from the road, reeled in my line until the lure was at the tip, and gazed at the water.

"Just cast out and let her sink a few feet and reel in, real easy. Don't have any luck there, work your way down, you'll start catching them," he said over shoulder as he hiked off to fish another spot.

I made my cast and the lure arced out, plopped down into the water with a splash. I waited a few seconds, then started to reel as Jack made his way to the end of the pond, to a sloping wall of rocks where it had been dammed up. He stepped onto the rocks, zigzagging his way to the water's edge. Sure-footed, moving like a Billy goat. He cast out expertly, reeling slow.

The winds picked up speed and made my face tingle, little pins and needles on my cheeks. Jack, appearing sad from a distance, a lone figure on the rocks, didn't feel those needles but I thought maybe the needles were jabbing him from the inside.

᠅

"How many you catch?" he asked, leaning against the door of the truck, watching me with a smile as I shuffled up from the embankment.

"Three," I said, showing him the trout in the little canvas pouch he gave me.

"Hmm. Nice little brookies there. Be good eating. C'mon, let's head back."

He got the truck running, the heater already blowing hot. I put my hands in front of the vent and watched them change color. We headed up the road, the cold winds kicking up dust.

"How come you moved to Colorado?" I asked.

"Had an offer to work in the Springs, for one. Could've stayed in Texas. Would've been the same pay, but I like the mountains. Like the seclusion."

I started to say something but he kept talking.

"Been to a lot of places, grew up an Army brat. I was born in California, but we moved all over. Like living in the mountains best. My dad, your grandfather, was pretty strict around the house. I remember once getting hit because one of my socks was out of place in its drawer. Stuff like that happened all the time. He hated sloppiness."

He just stared straight ahead, expressionless, voice soft and matter of fact.

"Anytime we lived near some woods I'd go explore 'em when I could, get me out of the house."

He grew quiet.

"I'm pretty messy with my socks, and just about everything else, too," I said.

"Yeah?"

We topped out on the forested foothill and began down the winding dirt road. I made out the cabin through the dense greens.

"My father was good man. Just wasn't very good to me, or my mother for that matter," Jack said. "Served in both World War II and Korea. Got a Purple Heart in Korea, got shot in the left hand. Couldn't make a fist after that. Too bad he was right-handed."

Struck me as an odd thing to say, and I started to ask what he meant, but then I got it.

CHAPTER EIGHT

Those last four days Grey Bear remembered, and darkness came. His people were eighteen fewer now. The first night took one, the second three, then more and more. As the sun peeked far away to the east, he studied their chests for movement, their mouths for breath. There were many fingers that were black from Cold Maker's painful winds, many noses that suffered the same blackness. Grey Bear looked at them all, counting those who had gone in the night. Five for certain.

Thinking about these blackened fingers, he wondered about his own. The Napikwans still kept his hands bound behind his back and he struggled to sit up. He pawed the snow behind him. The cold stinging his hands like many porcupine quills told him he was well for now.

The Napikwans had been getting colder and more restless. They consumed more and more of the white man's water. Many were ill-tempered, they yelled and flailed their arms about. They staggered into their tents. Their leader, the one who shot the great chief Heavy Runner, was among the worst. He drank all day, quarreled. Grey Bear wondered what they will do with his people, where they will go. Maybe they will all be dead soon. It would be better.

Running Dog's head was against his father's shoulder, sleeping in a fitful doze. The winds swept down on them, his closed eyes squeezed tight. Grey Bear wanted to place his hand on his head, draw him closer and shelter him from Cold Maker's winds. He examined Running Dog's fingers and saw that he was not yet frostbitten, but looked more and more gaunt. His skeletal body was curled up, shaking.

Grey Bear pushed away his idea of death. It would not be better. Not for him. Not now. He prayed to the Long Ago People that, if his people's fate is a bad one, for them to spare his son. And then the anger came. All these things, all the great medicine and the Above Ones and Below Ones and the Underwater People and his bear guide and the Long Ago People were of no use. They had betrayed a good Piegan band who did all the necessary things for their protection and here they were, near the Always Winter Land. Grey Bear wanted to lash out and curse them all, then his anger fell to those who were closer, the Napikwans and their drunkenness. He wanted to take them all, cut out their hearts, hold them high, and curse their god as he cursed his own.

I'll protect you, Running Dog. I'll keep living, for you.

A Napikwan soldier approached on horseback with his rifle up, hat brim pulled low, scowling.

"Get up, you red niggers! Move out!"

Grey Bear rose to his feet, the joints of his weakened knees cracking, and stared at the Napikwan's bloodshot eyes, trying to decipher his meaning. The soldier's eyes shifted to the north and he rode away.

"Son, we must stand."

Running Dog moaned, squinted in the whiteness of the day. He took hold of his father's breechcloth and brought himself up, glanced around, saw the dead and turned away. Horses gathered and rear scouts rode out. The Napikwan leader on his horse, his back to Grey Bear's people, had a finger in the air looking back. Then the group moved, leaving the dead where they lay.

"Running Dog, as you walk, always keep your toes moving, keep your fingers moving. Did you remove your moccasins and rub your feet last night?"

"Yes, Father."

They walked as living ghosts through a blinding white, with the wind coming at them sideways in a single-minded fury. Running Dog shuffled before Grey Bear, his small legs slowly creeping forward. The winds knocked him off balance; he sidestepped, recovered. The old were all gone save one, Kipataki, the old mother of Bending Reed and mentor to Grey

Bear's wife. Her gray hair whipped in the winds and she rubbed her gnarled, dry hands to keep them warm. The winds threw her hair back, exposing her kind face lined with age and hardship and loss. Her eyes focused on the snow before her and she walked with a slow, unsteady pace.

Grey Bear had long since lost all the familiar landmarks, and if there were some they would be masked by the snow. In the four directions he saw nothing, heard nothing. His hunger pangs were gone and there was just the unfeeling void. Remembering the spirits he cursed that morning, he felt a twinge of remorse for they, and Running Dog, are all he had.

There were tingling sensations in his feet as they moved at a quickened pace. They felt of sharp stones and the pain intensified as the numbness subsided. The white emptiness made his eyes ache and so he kept his gaze to the ground, watched Running Dog's moccasins dig into the soft snow. He wondered if this was the way of the Shadow Lands, if, perhaps, he had died and Running Dog had died and this is what it was, a land of nothing, of seeing nothing, of feeling nothing, with no past, present, or future. They just were. He rejected this.

Reverberations of horse hooves in the earth. A Napikwan rider halted a few paces from them. The other riders who were visible through the pelting snow stopped as well. The rider removed two canteens from his saddle bags and threw them at Running Dog's feet.

"Drink up. Last you get until tonight."

Running Dog gave them to the women, each taking a couple of swallows and handing it to another. The last woman drank and gave the canteens back to him. He looked at his father.

"How much is left?" Grey Bear asked.

"Very little, Father."

"Drink it."

Running Dog started to object, then glanced sideways at the women. He tilted the canteen back and drank the rest before giving it to the Napikwan. The soldier reined his horse away and disappeared. They began to walk as the horses ahead moved on.

"Father, you must drink," Running Dog said.

"I have lived a good life. If anyone lives through this, it must be you.

You. Do you understand?"

Grey Bear sensed a change in his son. Some lightness of curiosity was gone, leaving nothing but a pained acceptance on his face.

"I understand."

The muscles in Grey Bear's legs cramped and so he overextended them as he walked. He kept his hands as warm as possible by moving them around and rubbing them together. The blinding snow intensified, falling sideways, and the others struggled to keep moving. He feared that if one of the women fell, she would not stand again.

The idea began to appeal to him. Just lie down and let the darkness close in. But Grey Bear saw Running Dog just a few feet away, a vague slight form in a world of white, head down, walking. There was that nothingness in him, too. Grey Bear used his anger to keep moving.

The sun was in the west, just a faint aura of flaxen through the dense snowfall. Soon they will stop and Running Dog can rest, can hopefully get more water and maybe a bite of food. The thought of food awakened his stomach, thinking of the few handfuls of jerked meat the soldiers threw to them yesterday. He got only a bite of it and Running Dog two bites. Not enough. The darkness penetrated the whiteness and the soldiers halted.

They stood, waited. So many eyes looked not at him but through him. His people stared blankly at the nothingness. The rear guards raced past them, their horses kicking up thick clouds of snow, and joined the other soldiers in a circle.

The leader yelled and then soldiers galloped around the Piegans in a half-circle, stopped, and took their rifles out of the scabbards. One of the rear guards dismounted and approached Grey Bear.

"We're leaving you here, buck. All of you."

Grey Bear snuck a glance at Running Dog who was staring, wide-eyed and alert. The Napikwan had the sharp odor of the white man's water on his breath. Studying his face, Grey Bear knew that this was the man who shot him.

"Now here's the thing," the Napikwan said. "It'd be easy to put a bullet in you right now. Easy for you. You're pretty banged up but you stand the best chance of making it back to your people alive. Better'n all these squaw bitches you're with. And if you do, them other red niggers will take one look at you and think twice about roughing up one of us again."

Grey Bear was not wondering what he said, but why he was saying it. The Napikwan knew that he did not understand. Just drunk maybe. But then the soldier stopped talking.

The blur of a leather fist and then Grey Bear was on the ground, head exploding in pain as he was hit again where his ear once was. Running Dog jumped on the soldier flailing his fists, screaming. The hits just glanced off the soldier's shoulders and head as his hat fell off, then he took Running Dog by the throat and hit him hard once in the teeth, sending him to the ground.

Grey Bear began to rise to kill the soldier and saw the man's fist, then snow and blood. The soldier pinned him to the ground face down. A blade shimmered in the sun. Grey Bear felt a sharp pain in his hand as the blade cut through the binding cords, taking a chunk of flesh with it. He envisioned his hands wrapping around the Napikwan's neck, then an explosion of sharp pain as the fist rammed into his head. Running Dog rose up again, another blow to Grey Bear's head, and then nothing.

☙

The north winds rushed onto Grey Bear's face, cold air spilled into his lungs. He squinted into the whiteness, the flurries of snow falling down on his brow. He gazed into the land of nothingness and the pain it brought. There was a clouded image, a form of a man and a horse approaching.

They were one with the white nothingness, with only their form defining them. The horse was running, kicking up snow in large clumps. Grey Bear saw the blackness of the horse's eyes and the gushing mist of steam bellowing from its nostrils. And through the land of white he heard the horse's heavy breaths.

As they approached, the rider became clearer. His eyes, like the horse's, were the purest black and, like the horse, his eyes were shrouded in whiteness. He rode through the wind like the hawk, seeing, sensing. His stare never wavered from Grey Bear's. He reined the horse in.

The rider's hands were clear like ice. His face white and chiseled, and his eagle feathers clicked against his long white hair. Cold mist gusted out of his mouth with his words.

"You are Grey Bear. You are the one I have come to see. You have strong medicine with your people. Your guide is the great he-grizzly that whispers secrets. He is here, with you now."

The great bear appeared in the distance at the top of a gently sloping snow-covered hill. It turned its dish face and glanced at Grey Bear as it disappeared to the west.

"I am the one called Cold Maker. I bring your people many things, some good, some bad. This time, what I bring for you is something good. I cannot guide you to a safe place, but I have watched you, Grey Bear, and you can do this for them."

Cold Maker peered west where the bear had gone. As he turned, his body made the sound of ancient trees in winter when they strain against the north winds.

"You will head not to the west as your spirit guide goes, but to the southeast. You will take your people down to the Napikwan fort. There you will be safe."

Grey Bear no longer felt the stinging cold as he tried to make sense of Cold Maker's words.

Grey Bear faced Cold Maker, a piece of his white ice leggings snapping off.

"Do as I say, Grey Bear. All of your questions will be answered in time."

Cold Maker then headed north, trotting away, back to the Always Winter Land. He looked back at Grey Bear as he began to fade, the darkness of his eyes staring.

"I must warn you, Grey Bear. Let go of the things you—"

The winds swooped in from the north and carried the words away. Then Cold Maker, like the great bear, was gone.

The cold dullness of ice seeped through the folded deerskin where his wounded head rested, the pain intensifying in Grey Bear's forehead. He strained to open his eyes and saw a world of brightness and whites. A lone hawk in the sky headed east and he thought that this was good, that the hawk was their guide. A face hovered above him, masking the hawk. Falling Leaf, the daughter of Fox Eyes, his great brother Fox Eyes who was now coming home to see his dead wife, Bending Reed. In Falling Leaf's eyes were the eyes of Bending Reed. It felt as though Cold Maker himself was gripping Grey Bear's heart with his icy hands.

Falling Leaf was emotionless as she wiped the blood from his face. Her lips trembled, and Grey Bear was reminded that she was but a young girl barely older than his Running Dog. She had lost her mother, and he had lost his wife, and he knew that her heart hurt as his did. Grey Bear then remembered Running Dog. His chaffed skin and dried blood crackled as he spoke his son's name.

Falling Leaf gestured with her hand. Running Dog stood next to Heavy Shield Woman and looked down on his father. His lips were swollen from the Napikwan's leather fist, and Grey Bear's anger churned again. But he hid it and gave the boy a small nod. Running Dog's face relaxed.

Grey Bear eased his aching head back. All of his people, only fifty or so now, lingered in the bitter cold. Their eyes hollow and lifeless, they stood in the frozen field like the white man's cattle, blindly looking to him to lead them somewhere safe. The sun was fading in the west. Not much time had passed since the Napikwan soldiers left. Still, it will be dark very soon and for this he was grateful.

Grey Bear began to stand, Falling Leaf and Running Dog gripping his arms as he struggled to rise, the many watchful faces surrounding him.

"We will find some cover away from the winds and sleep tonight. Tomorrow we will began our journey to Fort Benton and join our brothers and sisters there. It will take us many moons to reach that place, but we must because this is Cold Maker's wish as he told me through a dream."

There was almost no response. So many frail bodies. No robes, no water, no food.

They made their way through the snow and blinding winds to a coulee that snaked through the open plains, picking their way to the bottom. This was a treeless country, so there was no timber to take refuge in; the last creek that they had crossed that held standing timber was two sleeps away.

Grey Bear came upon an overhanging embankment large enough to shelter them all. They huddled together, wrapping their sparse skins and furs tightly against their chilled bodies. Running Dog and Grey Bear sat outside the circle, backs against the women to shelter them as best they could.

The final light of day was gone; the sun disappeared on the western horizon. Grey Bear was glad because the snows had ceased, the clear night sky revealing Napi's many points of light. The light swirl of wind filtering through the coulee chilled his arms and feet, but with Running Dog at his side he felt the first semblance of warmth in three days. He began to think of the warm lodge but he blocked this out, wanting only to think of now, not then, and not what is to come. Running Dog's eyes were on his father, the beginning of a smile on his face. He pulled out an object wrapped in a patch of torn deerskin. He unfolded it and with both hands lifted it up to Grey Bear.

His knife.

Grey Bear took it from his son, feeling its smooth handle, seeing the glint of the blade. "How did you get this?"

"Father, the Napikwan that hit you. He was the one who shot you at the river."

Running Dog glanced at the women behind him and cleared his throat.

"You do not remember, but that man took all your things while you lay by the river. I watched him do this.

"Today, his mind was not right with the white man's water and with the cold, nor were the other Napikwans paying close attention. These things I saw as he was speaking to you. I saw him take your knife and cut the cords that bound your hands. I saw him put the knife back in its sheath without tying it down.

"I moved so that when I hit him again after he knocked me away, he would turn and face me and have his back away from the Napikwan eyes. Before I hit him, I pulled your knife out of its sheath and dropped it to the snow where it was buried. The Napikwans did not see and after the soldiers left I dug it up."

He finished speaking, unsure that what he did was right. Grey Bear again admired its blade. Holding it in his hands gave him strength, a feeling of something good. He grunted and his son looked up.

"What you did today was a wise thing. I want you to think of this. If the Napikwans had seen, they would have killed us all. But it would have been a quick death. Something better than what faces us out there."

The women slept, huddled together, restless and shaking.

"But that is not what happened. The Napikwans did not see, and now we have a knife. A knife that can bring us food, give us protection from the winds and cold. A knife that can give us fire. You see what you did, Running Dog? You may have saved your people. And even if it had turned out badly, you would have spared them a painful death. Do you understand these things?"

Running Dog's face brightened in the moonlight.

"Yes, Father, I think so."

"What you have done for me, for us, was a brave thing. A thing done not by a child, but by a man and with a man's wit and cunning."

He raised the knife. "This is not a child's knife. This knife has slain our enemies, has butchered many a blackhorn. It is a knife fit for a man. Fit for you, Running Dog. It is yours."

A subtle look of surprise covered his son's face. Grey Bear handed him the knife. Running Dog held it up to the moonlight as he did returning from their hunt, then carefully wrapped it in the deer skin.

"Thank you, Father. Thank you."

"It is I who should give thanks to you, Running Dog. Now let us sleep, for we have to get back to the river and find food and fire."

They huddled next to the sleeping women. Grey Bear gazed up to the stars, wondering what will become of them. Running Dog was doing the same. Eventually sleep took over, a sleep of darkness, of no dreams, of nothing.

Grey Bear woke the next morning to pellets of hard snow stinging his face. He opened his eyes and the brightness burned. Some of his people had stirred, sat up with their backs against the cold embankment, watching Grey Bear with the void in their eyes. Those still asleep all breathed and, for the moment, the darkness was away from his heart. Grey Bear stood.

"We must rise and move south. We are two sleeps from the river, but we must move as quickly as we can."

He heard no voices, only the occasional cough, their frightened eyes and the white mist as they exhaled.

Grey Bear led them up the side of the coulee. The winds drove south and almost knocked him forward. The pellets of hard ice raced sideways, biting him in his neck and head and arms. Several hit his wound and Grey Bear fought back the urge to shout. He lowered his head and began to walk, heard the cries of the women as they, too, felt the sting of the icy snow.

They were walking grouped together, many of them exposed to the wind's effects. Grey Bear thought of Cold Maker, silently cursed him, and wondered of the Below Ones for causing this wind that pushed Cold Maker's wrath upon them. Wondered, too, of Old Man Napi at allowing this punishment of his good people.

Grey Bear shouted, "Walk as one!"

His people formed a single file line behind him.

"Running Dog. The winds are at our back pushing us to the river. This is good, but the winds also make us weak with cold and wet from the ice. So you must lead us, Running Dog. I will go to the end of the line and block these winds from our people's backs."

His son's eyes widened.

"Do not worry. Look back at me if you lose your way. We will talk through hand sign."

"Yes, Father."

Grey Bear went to the back of the line where Falling Leaf was walking behind her grandmother, Kipataki.

Running Dog glanced back at his father. Grey Bear signaled with an open hand and Running Dog began to walk.

Through the fury of white the hazy forms of gently rolling hills appeared, then the distant rim of a far-off coulee to the east. He looked for, but did not see, the familiar image of South Butte.

Falling Leaf was careful to walk in the footsteps of the others, saving her the effort of making her own tracks. The others did the same. It made things a little easier, Grey Bear thought. Maybe they will see their people again.

Kipataki's long gray hair whipped in the winds, her old thin legs plodding forth. She had her arms in front of her, her head down, and her back hunched. A memory came, something so small Grey Bear was amazed he remembered.

Grey Bear was a boy. His father, Rides at the Door, gestured to him in their lodge and Grey Bear saw that he held a pair of moccasins. Rides at the Door told him that this pair was made by Red Paint, as Kipataki was then known. He told him that she used only the hides that she herself had tanned, and for moccasins only hides that had once been the tops of lodges, so that the smoke in the hide would keep the feet warm and dry. She made the best moccasins, his father said.

"Later," he said, "when you choose a wife, make sure she is skilled in making fine hides, for you will always be warm and dry."

Grey Bear did not know why this small memory came to him, watching Kipataki struggle. But the young girl she taught her skills to later caught his eye, and he wondered if his father's words had something to do with it.

Cold Maker's winds picked up speed, a constant push on his back. The cold air penetrated Grey Bear's wound and sent slivers of pain through the hole. He stifled a cry and wanted to scream at the winds, knew he could not because the women would be afraid. They were starving and near death from the cold, but at least they had him, who they thought was strong still. And they had Running Dog, who was now not a boy in their eyes and who didn't let them see his pain, either. Grey Bear thought of when he was a boy named Slender Bow, when there were many blackhorns and the Piegan were a strong people. Not that long ago, it seemed.

I, Slender Bow, walked barefoot on the cold summer earth. I looked back and saw smoke ascending from the many lodges. The women scurried about carrying water and wood in preparation for cooking. Beside me were my father and my brothers and uncles and cousins, the men. I walked with them, proud, my little legs already tingly with anticipation of the cold water. My father, Rides at the Door, walked toward the river. I saw the old scars on his left arm from a war raid on our enemy, the Crow.

I gazed up at his long black hair, the grays mingling with the darks, his kind face with the black, troubled eyes.

"Cold river water is good," said my father. "Make you tough. Make you a better hunter in the winter."

We men threw off our blankets, ran to the Marias riverbank and jumped in, yelling, laughing. The cold flowing water hit my body and I felt as though Napi himself had sent many strikes of lightning through me. My head broke the water's surface and I shouted. My cousins were grinning and pushed me, so I shoved them back and we all laughed.

Still damp, I walked into our lodge and my father sat, then I sat, and my mother was hunched over cutting freshly boiled meat. My mother, Day Star, wore her soft elk hide dress with her beloved beads that my father got for her trading with the Canadian Napikwans. These colorful beads ran the length of her dress and shining white wapiti ivories were sewn onto the front. Her hair was carefully braided and she smiled at my father, handed him the meat in a bowl of clay. I was amazed at how much my father eats: three, four pounds of boiled blackhorn rump, silently feasting as the juices ran down his content mouth.

When we finished eating, I went outside and felt the thumping of the earth. I heard the whoops of the young men and the whinnies of the many horses, spilling into the valley through the narrow draw. Horses, hundreds of them. They filtered in, the pintos, the piebalds, the sorrels, the bays, the grullas, the blacks, the whites. The buffalo runners came first: bigger, stronger horses that were smart and agile. Then the others, the travois horses, used for carrying our things when we moved, and mounts for boys and young men who have not yet counted coup.

My father gathered his things and the men left to go hunting. There had been no blackhorn herds sighted and so they hunted the wags-his-tails, the prairie runners, and the wapiti, the great horse deer with shiny ivories and the sweet flesh. I lamented my youth, that I cannot go, and contented myself with rabbit hunting with the other boys along the river bottoms.

Toward the setting of the sun, the men returned, bringing many carcasses for the women to butcher and prepare. Many calls for feasts were heard throughout camp. My father shouted for a feast as well, inviting his old friends Otter Belt and Two Moons.

I sat away from them, watching, listening, as they gathered around the fire. It was an honor to be in my father's presence for the feast and I was proud because these two men, Otter Belt and Two Moons, have counted many coups between them, and have honored themselves in battle and the hunt. Both had strong medicine not only in our band, but the tribe. They regarded my father as a superior who was to be accorded respect.

My father did not eat with them, and when they were finished, he lit a pipe and passed it to Otter Belt on his left. Otter Belt drew in the pungent smoke, passed it to Two Moons. My father cleared his throat, began to speak.

"You are brave men, just in from a hunt. You, Otter Belt, have seen your father join the Long Ago People in the Shadow Lands. And you, Two Moons, have seen your brother join him last winter against the Crow. I will share with you a story of two other men, both good Piegan."

Otter Belt and Two Moons sat in respectful silence as my father inhaled the thick tobacco of the pipe. My mother sat opposite me and stopped fleshing a hide to listen.

"These two men were called Wolf Calf and Black Robe, both strong warriors, but Wolf Calf was the wiser. They went to war against our hated Crees to avenge the killing of one of our braves and many stolen horses. They tracked the Crees for many moons until their horses gave out and so decided to go home.

"As they traveled they wandered into the Sand Hills. They soon discovered a fresh travois trail. They followed it until Wolf Calf saw that it was leading north, not to the southwest where they belonged.

"Wolf Calf said to Black Robe, 'Why follow this any longer? It is just nothing.'

"Black Robe said, 'Not so. These are our people. We will go and camp with them.' So they continued to follow this trail until they came upon a dog travois and a stone maul. Black Robe picked up these things and admired them.

"Black Robe said, 'Look at this. How lucky we are! I will take these things back to our camp.' He packed them on his horse and they journeyed further up the trail until they both tired and made camp.

"They woke the next morning to the sounds of an active camp. They heard young men calling out war cries, women chopping wood, men calling for feasts and all the different sounds of the camp. Wolf Calf and Black Robe looked all around, saw nothing, and became very frightened so they covered themselves up with their robes and shaded their eyes from what they dared not see."

My father inhaled more of the tobacco and cleared his throat. Otter Belt and Two Moons sat transfixed and leaning forward.

"Some time passed. Wolf Calf and Black Robe became curious and so looked again. The sounds of the camp stopped. They saw nothing, heard nothing.

"Then Wolf Calf said, 'Over there! There is my father running black-horns!' Black Robe looked where Wolf Calf pointed and saw a lone brave on a white horse. They watched the brave kill one blackhorn. Wolf Calf and Black Robe walked to where the brave was butchering the animal.

"When Wolf Calf and Black Robe came closer, the brave looked to them, got on his white horse, and rode off. Instead of a blackhorn the two men looked down on a dead mouse. And next to it, Wolf Calf saw an arrowhead.

"He picked up this arrowhead and said, 'This is my father's.' Wolf Calf moved his hand closer to show Black Robe and when he opened his palm it was not an arrowhead but a blade of spear grass. Confused, Wolf Calf put the grass into his medicine bag. They mounted their horses and left.

"When they arrived at camp, they turned their horses out to graze with the rest of the herd. Black Robe's wife boiled a pot of blackhorn tongue for him. The smoke from the fire rose up and Black Robe inhaled its sweet smell, then he fell down and died. His horse, grazing with the others in the deep grass, also fell down dead. You see, the shadow of the person who owned the dog travois and the stone maul was angry that Black Robe followed him, and so sought revenge.

"Wolf Calf enjoyed a fine meal. Before he lay down on his robe next to his wife to sleep, he looked into his medicine bag. He saw that every-thing was gone, including the blade of grass. Instead there was only his father's arrowhead."

Otter Belt and Two Moons sat back. Their eyes never left my father's. The pipe was once again passed to my father. He paused before inhaling the tobacco.

"The arrowhead was the only thing Wolf Calf kept in his medicine bag from then on and he prayed to it daily. It brought him great fortune, luck in battle and down meat, and he lived to be a very old man."

My father, Rides at the Door, then took a last draw on the pipe, rose and knocked the ashes out in the fire. He turned to Otter Belt and Two Moons and said, "Kyi."

The two men stood, nodded to my father, and left the lodge.

CHAPTER NINE

DIVIDE, COLORADO

JUNE 1986

Jack sat on an old wooden rocking chair on the front deck, looking off to the north, as the sun peeked over the mountainside. It was a cloudless morning, the outline of Pike's Peak distinct, a massive wall of white against blue.

I saw him from behind the kitchen counter through the glass door. He didn't hear me creep up the stairs, and I didn't think he was aware of me. He held a mug of coffee, its steam spiraling up, swirled away. I watched the side of his expressionless face, just staring at the mountain, at the horizon, and I wondered what he was thinking.

Sliding the door open, I felt the cool blast of the morning wind. The dew on the deck chilled my socks as I slid the door shut. Jack's gaze never left the mountain.

"Mornin'," I said.

"Good morning, son," he said, shifting his weight in his chair and bringing the hot mug to his lips.

"Come out here every morning," he said. "Even before I go to work. Helps."

Feet freezing, I wanted to go back in and put some shoes on but decided not to. I sat on a wooden bench next to the railing, folded my arms, gazed at him.

"Must be a long drive everyday," I said.

"Yeah. Don't mind, though."

He set his mug down on the end table next to him and crossed his legs.

"See deer once in a while. Couple of weeks ago seen a buck. They're in velvet this time of year, you know."

Thoughts pelting my brain like hail in a blizzard. What can I say?

"Ever get lonely out here?"

His chin tensed in thought, eyes still on the horizon.

"Sometimes. Work a lot though. Try to stay busy." He picked up his coffee again, no longer steaming, took a sip and cleared his throat.

"I know I told you about some of this in our letters this spring, but can't remember how much. After I got out of the service in '68, I did quite a bit of moving around, trying to figure out where to call home. Lived in Jackson, Mississippi for a while, then headed north to Ohio, came to Texas where I met your mother. Did a bunch of odd jobs, photographer, cook, roofed houses for your grandpa. Always liked working with my hands though, liked fixing up old cars and building things. Liked what I did in the military, patched up Huey choppers. Mostly."

I wiggled my toes as I listened, tried to warm them up, felt like a hundred needles in them. Out of the corner of my eye I saw the sun coming up over the eastern hills, wished it would hurry.

"Anyway," he said. "I stayed in Dallas after I left you and your mama. Went to work for Texas Instruments. They sent me to school for engineering, and I got transferred up here to build missiles. Working on a new one now. It's all black box, that type of thing."

Jack stood up, mug in hand, and walked up to the railing next to me. Didn't look at me, though. Why? Shame?

"Fish a lot on weekends, doesn't get lonesome too often," he said. Glanced at me. "Gotta work tomorrow, so we better get moving if we're going to get some shooting in."

His hand reached out to touch my shoulder but missed.

"Bring the bolt back and release just like that," he said. Before I could say anything, he fired off three shots, sharp piercing sounds that came so fast I heard them all at once. My heart was beating in rhythm to the echo and my ears whined. He shot that rifle with one hand. Now he's going to expect me to shoot it with the same kind of calm he did. Don't show anything in your face, I thought. Just be cool.

"Okay, yeah, I get it," I said.

He handed me the rifle, the AR-15, the black barrel shroud and pistol grip warm to my cold hands. Heavier than I thought it would be.

"Round in the chamber," he said, with the beginning of a grin.

We were parked in the middle of an open meadow in the bottom of a narrow draw. Jack set up a coffee can where the timber began to run up the hillside, maybe forty yards out. I sat down on the blanket he spread out, nestled the butt of the rifle in my shoulder and lined up the open sights. Jack chuckled.

"You shoot left-handed, like your old man," he said. "Remember, make your body tight. Breathe in, start to squeeze the trigger and let the shot go as you exhale. You should never know when the rifle is going to go off."

The recoil jolted my body back, the crack of the .223 not near as piercing as those first shots. I looked behind me and Jack was studying the can with a pair of binoculars.

"Dead center, son. Perfect shot. Bullet went straight through."

"Really?" I asked before I catch myself. Not supposed to act surprised. Supposed to act like it was on purpose. But then, the wind shooting down the narrow draw changed course. Not in my face anymore. It was coming at my back and a smell came from somewhere close. Something I haven't smelled in a long time. Sharp, like the crack of that rifle. Whiskey.

Jack was still peering through those binoculars so I looked behind him and saw a big black plastic mug with a lid on it.

He sat down behind me, drew his knees up to his chest.

"Aim for the bottom," he said. "Make that baby jump."

Pretend you don't know. Just don't pay any attention to it and keep shooting and smiling and having fun. Doesn't mean anything. Wasn't the whiskey made him mean to me and Mama, just that he was going through a bad time. It's not a bad time now. Everything's good. Got my dad back.

"All right," I said.

I shut the heavy door of the Ford, and Jack cranked the ignition. The big 460 fired up and we were back on the dirt road. He had the windows up and the liquor's smell hit my nose again, powerful and burning. I started feeling a little queasy, snuck a glance at him and he met it.

"Big guy can haul some ass. Want to see what it can do?" he asked, eyes bloodshot and a grin on his face.

Say something. And don't act scared.

"Yeah."

He punched it, a wall of dust shooting up behind us, engine so loud it hurt my ears, trees beside us became a blur and he started chuckling, real slow, almost under his breath. My chest felt funny like my heart's trying to leave through a back door I didn't know about. Sharp turn coming up fast and he ain't slowing down, going faster. Everything fuzzy, even him laughing with the mug of whiskey between his knees. Turn was on us and he stepped down on the brakes; the big truck lost its grip on the dirt and I felt it spinning around, whole world spinning, me and my dad and the whiskey.

The truck stopped but the dust kept going, shooting over us like a cyclone. Jack broke out in laughter, a whiny, sinister laugh that just trailed off.

"Look a little pale, son," he said.

I made myself smile. "Yeah. Fun, though."

We parked in front of the cabin and I busied myself grabbing the rifle cases from the bed of the pickup, watched him out of the corner of my eye as he pulled the front seat forward. I caught a glimpse of the bottle he took out. My shoulder still hurt from shooting his old shotgun, double-barrel with two triggers. He told me to squeeze them both at once and then laughed as it bucked me back on the grass. It was all right, though. I would've thought it was funny if it wasn't me.

I got the cases out of the bed and walked up the wooden steps to the deck. He was sitting at the kitchen table with that bottle and glass with ice in it, taking a drink and staring out the window.

"Just put 'em in my room. Worry about it later," he said, never taking his eyes off the window.

Dull pain shot up my shoulder and I winced. Wasn't expecting it and wanted to cry out but caught myself.

What do I do? Go sit down at the table with him? Go to my room, leaving him alone? I stood there for a few seconds, not wanting to do anything. Heart started feeling funny again, like I was in a truck going too fast. But it was okay. Just go in there and sit down. Going to my room would be rude, and what if he came looking for me?

His back turned to me.

"Better shut the door. Starting to get cool out."

The shadows under the pines got bigger, winds picked up. Smelled fresh, the pine and wood and dirt. Kind of smell that'd wipe away that burning whiskey. I just wanted to walk outside, close the door behind me, and disappear. I didn't though. I took a last look around and closed the door.

All the lights were off in the cabin except the little one above the kitchen sink. Shadows were in here too, then.

"Come here, son. Sit down," he said.

Stared at me with the bottle of whiskey between us, and I didn't look at him or the bottle, instead my eyes darted around the room. Maybe I'll find something to talk about, make that quiet go away.

"When was that taken?" I asked, pointing to a small framed picture of Jack and a couple of other men posing with mule deer bucks. Looked like they were out in the middle of a desert.

"Couple of years ago," he said. "Guy on my left is Lee, good friend of mine. Hunt elk together every year, met him in the Springs."

He took the bottle and poured himself another drink, reached over and took the picture from the kitchen counter.

"Was a good day. Got to hold on to your friends, Calvin. Get fewer and fewer as you get older."

I nodded, not knowing quite what he meant. I felt my stomach start to rumble. Been hungry for a while. Hadn't eaten anything all day. Jack didn't say anything about it this morning. We just left.

"I was stationed in the Philippines for a couple of years. Was a good gig there. Eight hours working on chopper engines. Rest of the time could go do what I wanted. A group of us ran together, all of us Air Force mechanics, started learning martial arts."

Another drink, hardly no ice in his glass. Just straight whiskey. The air starting to get thick, made my head hurt.

"I took a karate class last year," I said. "I made blue belt."

"Oh yeah? Maybe your old man can show you some moves. C'mere," he said. He took a big swallow of whiskey, got up from his chair.

Pain in my head came in waves making it hard to think. Maybe good, though, maybe I don't want to think. Legs felt a little funny, weak. Jack took his shoes off, kicked them to the corner of the room. He picked up a newspaper from the coffee table and rolled it up tight.

"Lots of folks don't know that a newspaper is a weapon," he said. "You can break a man's ribs with one if you know what you're doing."

I took a step closer and didn't say anything. The air was thick, beads of sweat on my forehead.

"Now c'mon Calvin. Come at me with everything you got. Hit, kick, whatever."

He started moving to the side, slow. Just act like I'm having fun, that's what I should do, it's what he's doing, just having fun, ain't gonna do anything to really hurt me. Yeah, just have fun. Know my head hurts and I'm tired but just ignore it and it'll be over and maybe I can go to my room.

"What's the matter, son? Just a newspaper. Go on, let's see what you got." Half-smile on his face.

I lunged at his chest with my fist and then just a blur. I was on the floor, my ribs hurting. Sharp, constant pain. I couldn't move or I would cry out, had to hold it all in. I felt a tear form in my eye, and I rubbed it off with the carpet.

"See? Exposed yourself. Gotta protect those ribs, son."

He was circling me with that same half-grin, big blue veins in his arms and fast feet.

C'mon, get up, I told myself. I got up slow, legs so tired, my ribs throbbed like they were going in and out, pain shooting through and another tear came so I winced, forced it to go away. I was protecting my rib, arm covering them up, stepping away from him, but he moved forward. Couple of drops of sweat on his t-shirt, and the whiskey made it hard for me to breathe.

"Try again. Come at me hard this time. Thirteen years old, I know you can hit harder than that."

He chuckled, and it reminded me of the truck heading straight at a curve when I knew we couldn't make it. I was scared to swing at him with my right hand because I had to protect my ribs. I came at him with my left, aimed for the stomach, my fist making contact. He grabbed my arm, spun me around, hit me in the side of the head and I went down again, ear screaming. I yelled, covered my ear, and didn't want to look up again. Did though, and he was shaking his head from side to side, putting the newspaper back on the coffee table.

"Ever hear of Aikido?" he asked me, like we was still on the front porch enjoying the sunrise, like he was still my dad.

Ear hurt so bad I had to tilt my head to one side, kept my hand on it.

"No," I said, and looked at him. It's like I wasn't even there, like he was talking to somebody else far-off.

"It's all about defense, about manipulating a person's joints to render them helpless. An interesting art form, really."

Casual as that. The pain wouldn't go away, and I couldn't do anything, but I wasn't afraid as much and started to get mad. He moved sideways again.

"No newspaper this time. Come at me again."

I'll hit him in the face this time. Right across the jaw. Yeah, that's what I'll do. Ain't got nothing to lose. I swung as fast as I could. His hand gripped my arm, and again I was twisted around. With his arm around my neck, I fell backwards, everything spinning, his legs locking around me. I couldn't breathe, sucked in a big breath but nothing came out. Tried to yell but still nothing. He pulled tighter, and everything got fuzzy but he didn't let up. Blackness closed in.

He got up and smiled, and I tried to breathe. It didn't sound like me but like an old man, deep and hoarse. Gotta keep my face down. Don't cry. Can't cry. Words came from somewhere.

"Got to be faster than that, son."

"Okay," I heard myself say. "Tired. Go to my room?"

I looked up at him, and Jack slowly shook his head back and forth, grin on his face. He poured another drink and sat down with his back to me.

I rolled over on my side, still breathing heavy, chest pounding. I struggled to get up. My legs felt like they were someone else's, no feeling in them. I made myself walk quiet, sideways like he does, and watched him. Walk on the sides of your feet, Jack said when we was shooting. Put your heel on the ground and roll. That's how Indians moved through the forest when they were hunting, he said. I shut my bedroom door slow, got in bed with my clothes still on and pulled the covers over me.

In a safe place then so I cried, trying to keep the sobs quiet. The brass doorknob shined, and I wished it had a lock. Head started pounding again. Tried to keep still and maybe it would go away, then my stomach started to growl. So hungry, but the only food was up there with him.

I heard music playing. Old jazz stuff. Mama never listened to that. Dad neither. Dad always listened to old country songs, and sometimes when I was spending the night with him I would sneak into Dad and Maw Maw's bedroom and sleep with them when I was little. Used to curl up against Dad's back where it was warm and they always played the radio low when they slept. I'd listen to that until I fell asleep. A mistake to think about that now. Then more tears because Dad was far away and couldn't save me here.

The music stopped and I heard his voice upstairs. My watch glowed in the dark: three in the morning. Pain in my stomach, and I thought about that egg sandwich I ate, when? Didn't know.

He talked, sometimes loud, sometimes quiet.

❧

Been an hour, no more sound. I thought about food, about sneaking up to get some. I heard a scream, his scream, but sounded like a far-away animal caught in a trap. Felt like I was in the trap, like I fell in a pit trap, looking up at an animal screaming. Is he mad? No, not mad. Scared. He stopped. Should I go look? No, couldn't ever go look. Didn't want to see.

❧

I felt a pain in my head, and opened my eyes. Sun came through the window and I reeled back. Had to go to the bathroom. It was noon. Had to pee real bad, aching. I sat up and put my hand up to my ear. Dull pain shot down my neck. Had to go upstairs. He was at work, and that meant everything was okay; I could go upstairs and pee and get something to eat and it was okay then.

Walked up the steps real slow, old wood creaked under my feet, opened the door and looked down the hall. He was on the deck sitting in his chair, back to me and looking out at the mountains. Still there. Bathroom was just across the hall, though, and I went to pee which took some of the hurt away but then I was real hungry. Second day with nothing to eat. If I went to the refrigerator he would see, but didn't care anymore so I walked quiet like an Indian, opened the refrigerator real slow, looked inside. Nothing but a bottle of ketchup and a jar of mustard. A half-froze steak thawing in the sink. I felt his eyes on me, peering at me through the glass doors, and I knew I had to go out there.

"Hi, son. Sleep good?"

He sat in his chair, only this time with a footstool in front of him, his sock-covered feet propped up. Thinning hair a little unkempt and eyes bloodshot, short-sleeve shirt unbuttoned. Air was cool but it didn't seem to bother him any. Like the cold wasn't there, or last night either.

"Yeah."

"I was just reading this book about Buddhism," he said, holding it in front of me. It had a picture of an old Chinese man on the faded paperback cover, sitting in front of some kind of temple. "Reading about Oneness. Studied it a lot when I was younger. Learned to focus the mind through meditation. Know about any of that stuff?"

"I've heard of it," I said, even though I hadn't.

"I once went to a place in the forest where nobody was around. I like quiet places like that, sat on a blanket underneath a ponderosa. I shut my eyes and built a log cabin in my mind. Saw every detail, saw me picking up an axe and imagined the splinters of wood flying from the bark with each chop. Saw me piecing it together, every bead of sweat, every pain in my body. I imagined it all until it was done."

He paused and I should've thought of a response but didn't have one, too busy thinking about that steak in the sink, so hungry.

"Sat out there for two days. Day or night or what time it was, didn't matter to me. Wasn't really there anyway."

His eyes returned to the mountains again.

"No work today?" I asked.

"No, not today," Jack said. "I've got to go to town for a while. Why don't you take the rod and that creel and go fishing? I'll be back in a couple of hours."

Before I could say anything, Jack walked into the cabin with me following, not knowing what else to do. He put on his shoes and pointed to the gear in the corner.

"You can take my box of lures with you."

He looked at me expectantly, so I picked up the rod and tackle box as he grabbed his keys next to the almost empty whiskey bottle. I followed him outside and he locked the door behind him.

"See you in a couple of hours." He walked down the steps to the driveway. And then he got in his truck, left.

Asshole. What, this supposed to be some kind of a lesson? Trying to make me tougher or something? Or does he just not give a shit?

I sat the fishing gear by the door and thought about going around to the front of the deck, but no, didn't want to be anywhere that reminded me of him. I poked through the fishing gear looking for a lighter. Maybe if I caught a fish I could make a little fire and eat it. I got that image in my head of cooked trout and it was all I could think about. No lighter though. I kept looking, hoping one would appear, but it didn't. I took everything out of the box, found an old wooden match stuck to the corner. Didn't look like it was any good and I didn't know if I could walk that far anyway, so tired.

Just going to get out of here. Walk a ways in the woods. Maybe I'll meditate like Jack. Only I'm not going to build a cabin. Maybe I'll cut his down.

☙

A bead of light shot down on my face. I woke up and didn't recognize anything. Rolled to my side and a pine needle pricked my arm. On the side of a hill, pine trees growing thick and crowding out the light. Then I remembered: I was just a couple hundred yards downhill from the cabin. Lot more shadows then. Five o'clock, not long before dark. Had to get back, didn't want to be out here after dark. Really? May be safer out here, but he'd come looking for me. I started doubting that, too. He hadn't even thought about feeding me. Who's to say if he'd notice if I were gone? But I was just tired and not thinking right. Needed to get moving while I had a little energy.

Light ran out fast. It was going to be dark in just a few minutes, only light then coming from the cabin. Jack's truck was parked in the driveway and he had taken the fishing gear back inside. I couldn't think about anything but food then so I didn't care what he said.

Perched on the couch with a new bottle in front of him, just a little gone out of it. Kitchen light was on, but it was dark in the living room. Didn't want to, but I closed the door behind me. He watched me, expressionless, something missing in his eyes.

"How come you didn't fish?"

Almost like he had his feelings hurt.

"Just wanted to walk in the woods," I said. That steak just twenty feet from me, I could taste it. Just wanted to eat and go home, all I wanted to do. He didn't say anything, though, just went back to his world, wherever that was. Didn't know or care, just so long as I wasn't there with him.

"Anything to eat?" I asked.

He filled his glass, took a swig, shuffled to the kitchen.

"So you're hungry, huh?" he said.

Don't say anything. He'll hurt me bad this time. I'll just do what I got to do to get out of here. I sat down at the kitchen table facing him, legs burning with tired. He grabbed a plate from one of the cabinets, knife and fork, put the steak on the plate. He turned around and set it down in front of me.

I looked down at it, blinking.

"Raw?" I asked.

Jack ambled back to the couch, sat down with his drink, stared back. "Raw," he said.

Just do what you got to do. So I cut it up and ate it.

Jack said nothing as I ate, just drank. I took the last bite, chewing the rubbery flesh, and put the plate and fork in the sink. I kept the knife. Ran the blade under my sleeve and held the handle in my palm, sat down. Felt better.

"Ever seen a plastic pistol?" he asked.

"Like a toy pistol?"

"No," he said, walking into his room and returning. He threw something heavy and black at me. It hit me in the chest, fell in my lap.

"You're dead," he said, hovering over me.

Just don't make any sudden moves. Act calm. I picked it up.

"See that little black button on the side where your thumb is? Push it."

I did and the pistol's magazine fell to the table, the sudden sound making me twitch.

"Glock came out with these babies last year. A nine-millimeter with a polymer frame."

Hollow-point bullets. Knew that because I had seen them in hunting magazines. Jack took the pistol from my hand, picked up the magazine, locked it back in and went to the couch. Took another swig.

He's going to kill me. Maybe he didn't like to think about the way he treated us. Killing me would make it go away. My fingers rubbed the wood handle of the kitchen knife in my palm. Lot of good that'd do. Even without that pistol. He could take that knife from me and slice me up into a million pieces before I knew what happened.

I glanced out the window, but there was no help there. Nothing but black past the glass door. No stars even, so I guessed it was going to rain or maybe snow. He sat there, glass of whiskey in one hand and the Glock in the other, his index finger moved along the trigger guard.

"Got to hold on to your friends, Calvin," he said. "Get fewer and fewer as you get older."

Quiet for a few minutes, the amber disappearing from the bottle.

"Didn't have any friends growing up, moved around too much," he said. "Mostly kept to myself. Didn't make friends until I went overseas. Picture you saw with the deer, didn't want to get into it but that's not Lee next to me. It's his brother, lives down in Arizona. Looked him up a couple of years ago."

Quiet again. I glanced back at the picture on the kitchen counter. A younger man than Jack, blond hair, broad smile. Not Lee.

Looked like all the blood left Jack's face, just turned white like some monster was in front of him. His eyes welled up and a tear streaked down his cheek, but he was still quiet. Looked scared, more scared than I ever seen Mama or anybody.

"See the same thing every night," he said, words coming out fast. "Did three tours in Vietnam. I was an M60 gunner and Lee and I were in the chopper waiting on the pilot. He's playing around on the gun aiming at some water buffalo grazing in a field. I dared him to take a shot at one and he said no, that he's not going to shoot a fucking cow and get his ass chewed. I called him a pussy and laughed. He looked at me, about to call me something back, and his head exploded. I've got his brains all over my face, skull cut me up. Head's gone, just gone, and he dropped out of the chopper. Never had another good friend like him."

He said it real fast, hard to understand. Then he groaned, not loud, just under his breath.

"I'm sorry, son," he said.

In one motion he chambered a round in the Glock, put it to his head and squeezed the trigger.

Not a loud sound, just a pop seemed like, a spray of blood on the wall behind him. He exhaled a deep gush of air and his body leaned to one side. It's like I wasn't even there, like I was watching all this from somewhere else. I walked up to him. One of his eyes had come out and I screamed. Ran out of the cabin, dark, couldn't see anything, felt the cold rain hitting my face. I ran into the woods, ran until I couldn't anymore, crawled underneath a big pine tree.

Old country music playing on the radio.

Dad's warm back.

Dad help me Dad help me.

CHAPTER TEN

SACRED BUTTE
JANUARY 1870

As he marched in the blinding white, Grey Bear sensed it getting colder, the winds a little more forceful. He continued to wonder about the blade of grass and the arrowhead his father told those men about so many winters ago, wondered if Running Dog will one day find an arrowhead of his and keep it in his medicine bag. He wondered if he, too, as a shadow, will mask this arrowhead to others as a blade of grass. It did not matter now. Think about now, not then, or even when. Now.

The light grew dim. Grey Bear could not see Running Dog through the thick snows and so he whistled. His people stopped their slow walk south. Running Dog's hands and legs shook, his face gaunt, his dark eyes hollow. Grey Bear took his son's hands and saw that two fingers on his left hand were black from the cold. He cut a strip of his breechcloth and wrapped them.

"We must find a place away from the winds and make camp," Grey Bear said.

Running Dog's trembling lips tried to form words, but nothing came out. Grey Bear peered around, searching the landscape for any depression, coulee, break. Cold Maker still pushed his wind south. Toward the Sacred Butte was a south-facing outcropping.

It was too small to shelter them. Grey Bear's eyes strained against the icy winds through the sideways snow. He stood this way a moment, changed positions, looking. He made out the skyline of a small hill, steeper than the others, steep enough to give his people some protection.

"We will go rest now," he said.

As he led his people east through a gentle valley, the snow became deeper, so he tried to cut a trench so that the women did not have to raise their tired feet so high. Grey Bear felt the muscles in his legs that had seen thirty-five winters stiffen up. Despite the bitter cold and the winds, sweat poured down his chest and face, the salty liquid freezing to his leggings and breechcloth.

The hill upon them, he cut a big swath through the snow to its base, advanced up where the snow was shallower and the winds less. His people lined up, those at the end invisible through the mist. Running Dog directly behind him, eyes to the ground, mouth hanging limp, and for the second time Grey Bear saw the nothingness in him that he saw in the others and was afraid.

A scream echoed through the narrow valley. "Grey Bear! Come fast!"

He motioned for those close to him to clear the area and make camp. The snow kicked up with his feet and the winds sprayed the cold ice on his face. A group of women circled around a figure in the snow. There, with eyes half-closed, lay Kipataki. Her long hair of black and gray strewn in the snow, her hands limp at her side. He kneeled down and her eyes shifted from the sky to his face. Her lips parted in a half-smile.

She strained to reach up and he leaned closer.

"Grey Bear. My legs and my heart are no more. My time has come."

She saw his struggle, and her dark eyes softened.

"You will take me away from our people a short distance where I will rest and then join my father and mother in the Shadow Lands as I sleep."

Grey Bear knew there was no other way.

"Kipataki, I will do this thing as you say. It will be an honor."

Falling Leaf's tears flowed down her face. She knelt down to Kipataki and they embraced.

Running Dog sat with the others, huddled against them in the dug out snow.

Grey Bear took Running Dog's knife. "I might need this to dig out the ice to make a place for Kipataki to sit."

Running Dog glanced up from the ground, gave his father a slow nod.

Grey Bear picked up Kipataki, surprised at how light she was. She wrapped her arms around his shoulders, her dim, tired eyes looking into his.

He carefully placed his feet into the tracks of others where the snow was packed down. She said nothing during their journey, her eyes shut. The sporadic snowflakes tumbling on her face and melting, the water sliding down the lines in her cheeks to the ground.

The first outcropping was near. There were no tracks to follow, so the going was slower. Grey Bear's arms ached and his legs cried out to stop. He wondered if the muscles will pull and not work anymore, but they kept going.

The outcropping blocked the wind, a peaceful place for Kipataki to rest. He set her down gently and dug a hole in the snow just big enough for her to lay down. He struck hard ice and removed it with the knife, knocking it out in chunks. Kipataki stared at the hills, mouthing soundless words. Then there was just a patch of dirt surrounded by a wall of snow. It will be good. He stepped out of the hole, squatted next to her.

"You were such a smart boy growing up," she said. "I remember this about you. You have made yourself into a fine man, good warrior and hunter. You have made your people proud, Grey Bear."

He did not know what to say and so just nodded. She leaned closer. Her eyes moist, she put her hand on his.

"You have brought me here to die like I have asked and I am grateful. But there is one more thing I request of you."

"I will do anything to help you."

Kipataki gazed at her hand on his, the lines on her face deepening.

"I am an old woman. We have walked a long time and I can walk no more. My legs will not allow me to continue as they are useless now. I know I must die here. But I know also that I might live through the night."

A tear fell down her face, and the wind took it away.

"I want to die a quick death. I do not wish to see the light of the next day. Take the knife, Grey Bear. Take the knife and end my suffering. Allow me to go now and be with my people."

He felt her pleading stare as he studied the ground. How can she ask him to do this thing? But of course, she may live another day. She will suffer more. It was the right thing to do. But can he do it? Will he be banned from the Shadow Lands? Surely not. The Above Ones and Below Ones could see it was right. Kipataki was a great woman who deserved a quick death, a dignified death. Not at the hands of the Napikwan or even Cold Maker.

Grey Bear raised his head, met her stare. She turned her back to him. "Please, Grey Bear."

The knife still in his hand, he stared it at, pondered it like he had never seen the thing before. He gripped it, pointed it at the base of Kipataki's neck, the place where there will be little pain and an instant death.

Cold Maker's winds picked up force and the darkness closed in. Grey Bear drew the knife back as he stared at the back of her head. The winds pushed her hair forward, exposing her neck and she sat still, waiting.

He brought down the knife with all the force he had, the blade stopping at her neck.

Grey Bear cried to the Above Ones and Below Ones and the Underwater People. He screamed at the bear and Old Man Napi and all those who put him there, for this.

"I cannot do this thing you ask, Kipataki."

She looked back at him, startled.

"If you do not, I will die a slow death here. Please, Grey Bear, I do not wish to do this."

"I will go back to the people and we will pray that you go to sleep and not wake up among us. What I cannot do, Napi will. He will listen to our prayers, Kipataki. He will listen because we are his good people and have endured much."

Opening her mouth, her tired face loosened. She cast her eyes away from him and then turned them back.

"You do not have it in you to give me an honorable death. So be it. You say to rely on Napi and Cold Maker and the Above Ones to let me die, and so I will. And in my prayers I will ask that our women be kept safe. Do not fail them, Grey Bear."

She crawled into the dugout and lay down, curled up, folded her arms into her body. Grey Bear gazed down at her, cursed himself.

He went back to Running Dog and the women.

The clouds cleared, the moon coming up, Grey Bear found the women huddled in their little mass under the cover of the hill. Running Dog, despite the cold and black fingers, was seated on the outside, protecting them, shivering, looking blankly at the vast, snow-covered hills and prairies.

Some were asleep and so Grey Bear woke them to tell them about Kipataki. They must pray, use all the medicine they have as he will use his, for her to go now to the Shadow Lands and be with her people.

He lay next to Running Dog as the women drifted back to sleep, the winds dying down to a gentle push and Grey Bear shivered with the sweat that had yet to dry.

Grey Bear, so honored in battle and a provider of much meat for his people. Many coups have been counted and much medicine has been deemed his. A warrior, a hunter, and he could not even kill an old woman.

He listened to the strained breath of his people and wondered who will be next.

He heard the howls, one howl at first, then two, then the rest. Then their sharp barks. Wolves. A pack of wolves.

And then Kipataki's screams came at him through the valley.

CHAPTER ELEVEN

GARLAND, TEXAS
SEPTEMBER 1990

Y ou know what he did?"

I stood between my mother and Dad in his kitchen, my back to them, staring down at the old four-burner stove, hands clenched.

"Just him and some boys out drinkin', is all," Dad said.

"And you came to bail him out of jail right when he called, didn't you?"

"Well, sure."

"Why didn't you call me?"

"I figured he would tell you about it this morning."

The night before, some buddies and I drove to the lake after a ball game. I knew an old Pakistani guy that ran a liquor store in downtown Dallas who wasn't real particular about whom he sold to, so we bought a keg of beer from him. A few hours into the party, the cops showed up at our little shoreline campsite. Four hours later, I was in Dad's truck going to his house. Didn't remember much of that.

"No, no, no. You're not getting my point, Daddy," my mother said, voice raising a little louder. "You buy him anything he wants, bought him a truck, paid for all the speeding tickets, now you bail him out of jail and don't talk with me first? He's not your son, he's your grandson and in case you forgot I'm his mother."

"Yeah, I know, I know."

"You know, it was bad before, spoiled him as a baby, but after Colorado it's like you think you can buy that pain away from him, protect him from everything."

She paused, drew in a deep breath. I felt like I had my back to a bomb about to go off.

"How am I going to teach him any responsibility? How am I going to teach him to be an adult when you buy him every goddamn thing he wants and bail him out of jail?"

Her voice broke and she swallowed a sob, just a whimper. I glanced at her and quickly shifted my attention back to the white porcelain of the stove. My mother stood there in the kitchen, in the house she grew up, arms at her side, hands out, eyes moist in front of Dad with his mouth set and hands in his pockets.

"Never could do much for you when you was growing up," he said, matter of factly. "Now that I have it, want to do what I can for my boy."

I watched her face out of the corner of my eye, changing color, her eyes narrowing.

"He's not *your* boy. He's *my* boy, and you're ruining him!"

She took a step toward him. "That's your idea of love, isn't it?"

Both of them stared, quiet. Dad's mouth began to tremor. Mama shook her head back and forth, tears falling down her cheek, crossed her arms.

"Love. Just give him anything he fucking wants, shelter him from everything. Nobody can take away what he went through, not you or your money, so just forget that. That your idea of love?"

"No, no."

"Bullshit!" She burst out crying, brought her hands up to her face, back quivering. She turned away, facing a kitchen cabinet opposite of where I stood. She slammed a fist against the oak cabinet, turned back around.

"You've never even told him you love him!"

With my head down, I began to cry, tried to keep it down but couldn't. They were quiet for a few seconds and I wiped a tear from my face, looked up at Dad. Hands in his pockets, he took them out and they shook, his eyes away from us. A couple of steps toward the living room, and he looked across at Mama, tear streaming down his face.

"He knows I love him!"

And he turned and walked away.

॰ঌ

"Heard about last night," Ivey said.

The creek's current flowed faster than usual, runoff from a recent rain. Not pausing for a response, Ivey picked up another smooth rock, flicked her wrist and watched it sail over the water's surface, creating a line of delicate splashes as it skipped along and quickly disappeared beneath the surface.

"Yeah. Was fun until the cops showed."

She raised a critical eyebrow.

We met when she moved in a block from Mama's, and then later in World History class. Didn't think much of her at first. A gangly girl with freckles, shoulder-length dirty blonde hair a little unkempt. Pretty blue eyes, though, and when I saw her one November day shivering, sitting across from me, I offered her my jacket. She wore it all day. Funny thing is, I never noticed how unhappy she was until I saw her smiling that day. Been friends since.

"Funny how that works," she said. Some strands of her hair, wet from creek water, clung to the side of her face.

"You've been going out a lot lately," Ivey said. "Seems like we don't hang out as much these past few weeks. What's up?"

It was my turn to pick up a rock. I had walked to the creek from Dad's house, further away than the normal quarter mile journey from where Mama and I lived. As an afterthought I stopped by Ivey's.

Felt the chalky surface of the rock, turned it over in my hand.

"It's just that when I go out and have a few beers, seems like some of the bigger stuff goes away."

I thought about this.

"Maybe not go away. Hides. For a while."

A familiar sliver of anger in her eyes.

"That's what my mom's boyfriend said last weekend. 'Lets him forget his problems,' he said. One of the few things I could make out between screams."

"So what are you saying?" Calvin asked,

She stared back, crossed her arms.

"Just that you don't want to end up like him. Every time I think about what happened to you, it pisses me off all over again. I know your grand-father feels that way, but he buries it deep down, doesn't talk."

A half-submerged boulder on the sandy bank, Ivey sat on it, flipped her hair back.

"It's not good," she said. "And it's not good to think you can escape it through beer and idiot friends, either."

This put the picture back of Dad crying and saying he loved me. Never heard it before. Had to push that away.

Still wearing the T-shirt and jeans from the night before, I smelled faintly of stale beer and smoke from the fire we built, all mixed with sweat. Felt a little sick. I plopped down in the sand, the constant ripples in front of me, the old lean-to I built as a boy nestled in the oaks and buffalo grasses just beyond the opposite embankment. As a boy. Was I still a boy, after all this?

"Kinda weird. After I got back to Texas, I couldn't sleep nights, for months. Wouldn't talk about it, though. Figured my mama was going through enough. Every little sound, every little shadow, was him. So I'd keep a light on, any little thing and I'd be checking it out, telling myself it was just the wood creaking in an old house, or the gas heater hissing, or whatever it was. Making it real. Make it safe, you know?"

Ivey picked up a dried up oak leaf and, with her head down, began picking it off down to its stem, watching the snakish fiber dance in the light breeze.

"Make it safe," she whispered.

Flipping a pebble at her, bouncing off her leg, she glanced up at me.

"And then, one day, it was gone. He was gone. Creaks and moans became wood and metal again."

The sun kissed the tops of the bare mimosas to the west. Despite the coolness, I wiped the sweat from my forehead on the back of my hand.

"Not really gone, I guess. But hiding, like I said. And that was good enough."

Ivey released the bare stem, watched it twist to the sandy ground.

"C'mon goober. Let's hit the trail," she said. "Gotta start heading back."

I scrambled up the steep embankment, Ivey extending a hand as I pulled her up. A small patch of hardwoods, with a thick cover of browning buffalo grass, gently rose higher until it plateaued out at the unseen winding road. The receding sunlight pored through in thin vertical beams, delicate transparent walls.

A game trail wound through the crowded grass and we followed it, hopping over exposed rocks and roots. I caught movement above. A gray squirrel darted across a twisted limb, paused, disappeared behind the trunk. Nearby, another one barked and then it too was gone.

"Why did he come back?" Ivey asked. "From hiding, I mean."

Took a moment for the words to register. I paused, looked back. Started to answer, but my breath left. The sunlight cast a glow from her skin, clinging cotton blouse. And then the question brought me back.

"I don't know."

Turning around, I began to walk, not wanting to think.

"How long have we been friends?" Ivey asked.

Without stopping, I said, "Couple years. Why?"

The contours of the woods began to level off, the shadows casting longer, darker. A spider web spun between the dead branches of a mimosa, vibrating, vacant. What is the fate of those prisoners whose captor has died?

"Remember when you lent me your jacket?"

"Yeah. And I remember you wouldn't give it back all day, you little shit."

"Know why I didn't?"

"Dunno. Probably just to piss me off, I guess."

The gray of the road ahead. Mama was back home, probably, unless she went out a while to calm down. Doubtful, though. Hopefully she was asleep. Just wanted to make a sandwich and…

"It's because I liked you."

"Well, I like you, too."

"You know what I mean, you ass."

Her blue eyes boring into me, I glanced away to gather my thoughts.

"Really, Ivey? You couldn't have maybe told me about this, I don't know, earlier?"

"Why not now? I notice how you treat me around your friends—who are not really friends, by the way. You pretending to look down on me like they do."

A timid step forward.

"I just want you to be honest with me, that's all."

The shadows of the hardwoods merged, winds picked up. Ivey caressed her bare arms, waited.

"Don't know, just thought we were friends and…"

"It's because of my mom, isn't it?"

"Your mom?" Calvin said. "What do you mean?"

"Because we're poor. Live in a shitty house. Not good enough."

I glanced at the road through the trees. Starting to get cold, and dark besides.

"Ivey, I'm your friend. Always have been."

The wind blew strands of hair across her eyes and she brushed them away.

"Guess that's where the line is."

"Line?"

"Yeah, the line you don't step over with trash. You can be friends when the need arises, but nothing that would put you out in public with them. The trash might rub off or something."

The whites of her eyes reflected the dying light as moisture welled in them. A little waiver seeped into the sarcasm. Bad as I wanted to get home, the exchange took my thoughts off worse things, and immediately a pang of guilt.

"Ivey, we're not exactly rich," I said, and then wanted to take it back, with her mom's drinking and going out, live-in boyfriends doing odd jobs during the week and disappearing for days at a time, occasional police cars parked in front, her mom yelling as they handcuff her for who-knows-what-this-time.

The anger flowed across her face.

"Hey, no," I said.

I walked up to her, inches away. She didn't meet my gaze. Ran my fingers through her hair, down her soft cheeks, her neck.

"What can I say? What can I say to fix it?"

"You can't," she said. "Can't be fixed."

I held her, feeling the moisture from her tears on my shirt, ran my hands down to the small of her back, her lithe figure smooth, comfortable. The spider web came back. Two little insects caught in its snare, still alive, groping for possibilities. Except the spider was dead. My spider. What of hers?

"Anything you want to talk about, you can tell me, okay? Here for you."

She pulled away from me, wiped her eyes.

"I miss you, that's all," she said.

CHAPTER TWELVE

SACRED BUTTE
JANUARY 1870

Grey Bear bolted to Kipataki on the cut trail. Snow kicked up around his face, the bitter cold freezing it on him. The barks and growls and her screams echoed through the open valley. He bellowed the old war cries, screamed the names of his dead children, the names of Yellow Leaf and Running Dog, then her name and he did not call her Kipataki but her name of his youth, making it echo back, again and again.

"Red Paint! Red Paint!"

The moon cast light down on the sloping snows and Grey Bear raced toward her.

The images came through her wails. The wolves bit her, chewing, dragging her across the snow leaving a blood trail. Her eyes then of white. The knife in his hand, a flash of fur and teeth. Grey Bear lunged at the beast, plunged his knife deep in its throat as it sank its teeth into Grey Bear's flesh. He held the knife in and twisted, tearing the muscles and tendons. Hot, foul air released from its neck and its grip on Grey Bear's arm relaxed. He threw the dead wolf to the earth.

With a high moan, she stared past him into the valleys south with wide eyes. Her innards strewn on the earth, the wolves stopped feasting to circle Grey Bear with angry yellow eyes.

He filled his lungs, released a horrible screech of hate, and charged the nearest. The wolf snarled, showing its teeth, and took two steps back. Grey Bear saw the pronounced ribs and the vacant look in its eyes, the red teeth and the foam spilling from its mouth, and the hate rose again. Another wolf pounced. He spun, jamming the knife into its stomach. The wolf's teeth found his wounded head. Grey Bear rammed the knife harder into the wolf's abdomen. It fell to the ground, the head coming up once, twice, the roar dying to a low guttural sound.

"Grey Bear."

He jerked up to see her lost eyes on him, and they went blank.

The rest of the wolves backed off and circled wider. He picked the closest one and charged. It growled and then stepped back as Grey Bear plowed through the snow. Another step back, then the wolf turned, darted off. He went after them, running, screaming a war cry, willing Napi to power him onward. The wolves disappeared over the rise of a distant hill, their barks and howls dissipating.

Grey Bear knelt beside Kipataki. Gone. Her eyes stared into the night air; her mouth open in a silent last scream, almost torn in half by the starving wolves. Grey Bear buried his hands and knees in the snow and rested his head on his arms, contemplated the cold earth. The sky began to clear, the snow less heavy on his back, nothing then, only the silence, only the dark. He wept.

A swift wind shot through the open valley and gained power through the narrowing draw where the outcropping began. Cold Maker's sharp stings raced up Grey Bear's back.

Grey Bear rose, his breath leaving his lips in a white cloud. He saw her next to him, her hollow eyes, the tears on his face frozen.

The dead wolves' blood blanketed the soft snows. He picked up a handful of the red coldness, rubbed it in his hand, dropped it. One wolf's hot steam of breath just a whisper, a thin willow of whiteness against the black sky, but still alive.

A paw quivered, its eyes open and turned to him. The yellow anger gone, no longer the wild eyes of hunger but of surrender, light fading, tongue flat, faintly panting. The breaths came in short, slight bursts.

Grey Bear's hands glided through its thick coat and felt the hard ribs. He lifted the wolf, brought it close, felt the heat from its body. The wolf's ear twitched. Its head was too weary to turn, a single eye on him with only a trace of fear.

The moon cast its light onto the many contours of the hills and coulees and prairies; the brilliant rays cut through the falling snow and made the ice on the earth reflect back at the dark sky.

His hand found the wolf's cold nose and gripped the back of the head with the other. Grey Bear exhaled, twisted.

A brief whimper, a dull crack.

He turned from it, unthinking, and made his way back to Red Paint. He carried her up to the highest point of the outcropping and gently set her down on the smooth, icy rock. Grey Bear knelt before her and silently wished to give her something of comfort so that she may journey to the Sand Hills in peace. He had nothing, no robe, no water, no beads or moccasins. He placed his hands on her chest and prayed to the four winds and the Above Ones and Below Ones and the Underwater People, prayed that she will soon be with her people, safe and warm in her Shadow Lodge, tanning her robes and laughing. Grey Bear left her in peace, as she looked beyond at things more real.

He took the knife and cut a hole through the leg shanks of the two wolves, pulling them along as he returned to his sleeping people and Running Dog.

ॐ

Their huddled mass appeared as he approached, the silence broken by their low moans. Sitting at the bottom of their sleeping bodies, and crouched in a tight ball, was Running Dog. He said nothing to his father, but a hint of light appeared in his weary eyes when he saw the two wolves. He felt his son's shivering body. Running Dog asked no questions, spending all his energy staying alive.

Grey Bear gripped the wolf and pulled the hide from its body, the skin making a smooth tearing sound. His hands weak from the cold, their grip was not sure.

He shook the blood off the hide as best he could and quickly wrapped it around Running Dog, the big wolf seeming to swallow his frail body. Lips trembling, almost blue, he spoke no words. His eyes no longer following his father, they gazed at the unseen horizon.

Grey Bear cut the wolf's windpipe, pulled out the entrails, then tore away the morsel of tenderloin lining the spine. Long and stringy, not much meat. He cut it in half and placed it under Running Dog's nose.

"Eat."

Running Dog opened his mouth, took the meat from his father's hand, chewed. Grey Bear reached back into the carcass and cupped a handful of blood. Running Dog began to drink, a thin line of red spilling down his chin.

Grey Bear quartered the wolf, severed the head at the top of the neck, cut the carcass in half between the ribs, chopped into the spine to separate the front quarters from the hind. He sliced a chunk out of the flank and ate it, the first meat that had touched his lips in three days. It was strong and tough, but he swallowed it and longed for more. He placed the quarters next to his sleeping people so that they may wake and have food, along with the other wolf. That one had not lost much blood and so he did not skin it, better to keep it intact so that the women will have as much nourishment as possible.

Running Dog slept sitting upright wrapped in the wolf hide. Grey Bear examined his son's face. A natural color began to return to his lips. Grey Bear relaxed and he momentarily forgot the horrors of Kipataki, glad that his people had some meat and two extra skins for warmth. It was not much, but it might be enough.

The exhaustion came over him and he positioned his back against the warmth of Running Dog's wolf hide.

There is nothing but a land of white that is one with the sky; I see no horizon. I feel tiny stings all over my body. I am cold and know that it should be the snow and ice that pains me. My hands embrace my arms, I expect them to come away wet, but they are dry, dry and coarse. My feet are unsure as they move forward, going nowhere, but I know they must move. The stings are on my face and I bring a hand up to shelter my eyes. I look down and see the tiny grains of sand that are stuck to my palm. Sand, then.

I look to where my mind tells me the horizon is. The cold is penetrating my skin; my body shakes and my lips tremble. I fight to look ahead at the unseen horizon; I fight to keep moving, one step at a time, the small grains of sand flying sideways in my face.

I see a swirl in the distance; the sand moves in circles faster and faster and the cold winds blow harder, the sands are unbearable. I crouch down, cover my eyes. I look through my fingers. I see first my hands, and they are not my hands. They are the hands of a boy. I look down at my body and I see the body of a child. The circle is moving blindingly fast and it takes the shape of a warrior. I see his headdress and breechcloth as he dances. His form is now solid, his back is to me. He dances and chants:

Kiaayo Ninaa Yaapi
Kiaayo Ninaa Yoohto
Kiaayo Ninaa Yaapi

I see the strands of gray hair in the black; I see the scars on his arms. He looks upward, his arms outstretched, palms up. His voice booms through the nothingness as my heart breaks. It is my father.

His image becomes hazy and then there are only the swirling sands.

Women screamed. Grey Bear's eyes opened to the brightness of the sun. A hand gripped his arm.

"Father, please."

Grey Bear sat up, Running Dog's lost face turned away. The women, only twenty of them, huddled around the many dead. Falling Leaf cried over Snow Bird, wife to Grey Bear's friend Black Arrow, who waged war against the Crow by his side, and Grey Bear remembered Snow Bird's smile. His eyes moved over the dead, these many faces of comfort and food and laughter, Sleeping Fawn and Prairie Flower and Stays At Home and My Heart. These many sisters, these many lovers and wives.

He glanced at the wolf in the snow that he did not skin. Could he have saved one of them? Yes, he could have saved one. One of them died from Cold Maker's snows because he chose unwisely to save the wolf's blood for nourishment.

Running Dog gave his wolf skin to Spider Woman, who clung to it as she wailed for her sisters. So it had come to this. The son protected his women better than the father. Spider Woman's face was gaunt, sunken in, her voice cracked as she wailed, her bony hands weakly resting against the cold bosom of Rabbit Child.

"We are two moons' walk from the Marias," said Grey Bear. "It will be cold and the winds fierce. I will ask you to do something and you will not question because this is what Napi himself commands."

He drew in a breath and looked each one of them in the eye. Their lips trembled.

"I want you to look at the dead not as your sisters and friends, for they are now in the Sand Hills with the Long Ago People, their mothers and fathers and those who had gone before. Napi will provide for them, and we can use their clothing.

"So, all of you, remove their clothes and wrap yourselves in them so that you may live and that we may all meet our brothers and sisters at the Benton's Fort. We will carry our dead to the hilltop where we will pray and Napi will guide their journey."

Running Dog peered at his father questioningly and Grey Bear's glance told him to remain quiet. Grey Bear prayed Napi will forgive him for this lie.

The women knelt to undress the dead, with no words, just low moans and stifled sobs that faded into the winds. They finished and brought the bodies, seventeen in all, to the top of the hill and lay them side by side with their feet toward the Sand Hills. They prayed and trudged back to the bottom.

Grey Bear pointed to the ground for them to sit and they did so without words. He opened up the second wolf and felt that the blood was still warm.

"Come," he said. "Drink."

They circled around, Falling Leaf, Strong Deer, Sight Of Day, Calf Mother, and the others. They dipped their hands into the warm cavity of the wolf, sipping the salty blood. This done, Grey Bear finished skinning and quartering it.

He handed the knife to Running Dog. "Feed them."

Running Dog cut flesh from the hindquarters and gave each woman a bite. The women chewed slowly, painfully, staring at the ground. Grey Bear turned his back to them, toward the South and the Marias. The morning had been dry and cold with only light snows coming from the north, but then they came heavier, the winds moving faster. He peered at the unseen horizon in the distance and thought of the Marias in the spring, lush with bunch grass and cottonwoods. The wags-his-tails bounding through the thick brush along the water's edges; the prairie runners peeking down from the bluffs; the cool, gentle waters stirring slowly eastward, and many fish rising to the water's surface, sipping at the hatching insects. Grey Bear watching through the cattails, past the riffles, across the river, at Yellow Leaf sitting on the bank with her bare feet in the cool water and her eyes on him. She smiled.

Grey Bear blinked, his moist eyes once again on the vast white hills and coulees.

Running Dog worked on the last front quarter, taking the shreds of flesh in his hands and giving it to trembling fingers.

"Running Dog. Strip some cloth and strap a hindquarter to your back," Grey Bear said as he gestured toward the first wolf. "I will carry the other one and give those two front quarters to Falling Leaf and Strong Deer."

Running Dog, his frail little body beneath a second layer of clothes, began to walk and the women followed. With an open hand, Grey Bear gestured to the South veering west. Running Dog's cold feet picked up and disappeared into the snow drifts.

Grey Bear followed Falling Leaf, her soft black hair blowing past her and wafting in the sideways ice. He positioned himself to block these winds. Winds, always at his back, always pushing them to south and to home, never shifting. Cold Maker's doing. He willed them to live.

The drifts deep, they struggled through, the women gasping as they lifted their tired legs again and again. Sometimes Grey Bear sensed it was too much for Spider Woman and so he called to Running Dog, held a fist in the air, and they paused. But never for long.

They marched through the drifts and skidded down the bluffs and climbed back up, the ice penetrating their meager clothes, freezing their skin. They marched, planting their feet in the steps of those before them.

Running Dog kicked up clouds of snow as he cut the trail. His small feet dug in until the compact snows held, and then he took another step, another kick, and the women trailed behind.

Grey Bear willed the winds to hit his back and shelter them. They moved through a narrow draw, the snows piled high, and Falling Leaf faltered. Her knees buckled, hands digging into the snow. Grey Bear wrapped his arms around her, lifted her up. She looked at him with red eyes, frozen tears, turned and marched again, her head down. Her shoulders quivered under the falling snows.

The sideways snow more forceful, the white horizon darkened to a hazy gray. The shadows of the hills and bluffs through the mist, the land took them in, held them in its dark grasp. The muscles in Grey Bear's legs tightened, old tendons straining under his weight, threatening with each step. The wolf's hindquarter bones shifted and dug into his back; he rolled his shoulder to readjust. He felt the frozen sweat through his breechcloth, on his back, his chest. Small slivers of pain needled his cold, wet feet.

The many shapes of the land were as one, the shadows longer, merging. The blackness of his hair whipped before him. The cold winds whistled past and he heard their whispers, their underneath words.

The whiteness grew dim. Napi's sun made its last peek before dipping down into the earth through the dark ice. Grey Bear searched for shelter, for another outcropping, another steep hill. A bluff loomed to the southeast, and Grey Bear signaled his son to head for it.

The women huddled together under its protection, kicked away the hardened snow and stomped a circular pattern until the frozen dirt was flat and smooth. Spider Woman and Falling Leaf took pains to clear a comfortable place for Running Dog and Grey Bear, digging down to the earth at the foot of the circle and then with their palms packing in the walls of snow.

Grey Bear searched for any trees, any wood. He breathed out sharply at seeing that Spider Woman has laid down a cloth for him to sit on. Grey Bear untied the hindquarter from his back, tossed it next to the women, and sat down to lean against the cold wall of snow and faced them all. He rubbed his hands to bring the warmth back and stretched his aching legs.

The muscles pulled tight, then relaxed.

One more day's journey, Grey Bear thought. Then they will be at the bank of the Marias. There will be wood and fire, food. And no more death.

Running Dog gave his knife to Strong Deer and she removed the flesh from the bones, separating the muscles from the connecting tendons, then slicing each muscle into smaller pieces. The rest of the women huddled, their whispers lost to Grey Bear in the winds. Running Dog sat next to Strong Deer. She gestured toward Grey Bear and Running Dog picked up a portion of the meat.

"For you." He tossed the meat in the snow in front of his father.

Running Dog returned to Strong Deer. His words drowned in the winds but Strong Deer's face grew stern, then Running Dog became angry.

"It was me, not him!"

"What goes on here?" Grey Bear asked.

Running Dog's narrowed eyes turned to his father.

"If it was not for me, we would have no knife, no food. And I lead the way home, me, breaking trail for everyone and making it easy for the rest to walk. I saved our people and Strong Deer should not ask me to bring food to you."

Running Dog took a step forward.

"I should at least be served as you are, and maybe first because—"

The back of his hand struck Running Dog's cheek. He slipped on the ice and fell on his back, looked up at Grey Bear in horror and the child returned. Running Dog turned away, hiding his tears. Grey Bear's lips parted to shout but he heard the women's gasps. He glanced at them and they lowered their heads.

"Eat your food and rest. We will march to the river tomorrow."

Grey Bear sat down, picked up a piece of the meat and ate, staring at the flakes of snow that blew into his dugout and watched as the winds moved them about.

CHAPTER THIRTEEN

Is Ivey home?"

Standing on the concrete porch, a crack in the middle working its way through like a jagged river cutting through limestone, old beams of oak beginning to rot, curled paint giving up its fight with the oppressive sun. I stared down at Ivey's mother, Eileen, dressed in a blue bathrobe, a hole from a cigarette burn in the breast pocket. Hair pinned up, tufts jetting out of the top of her head, last night's mascara running wild.

"Yeah, Calvin, c'mon."

On a threadbare corduroy couch on the stained carpet of the living room slept Eileen's boyfriend, three days' growth of beard, arms outstretched, mouth ajar. His face an angry red, the color abruptly ending in the middle of his forehead where it transformed to a pasty white from wearing ball caps out in the sun all day. The house, as always, smelled of stale beer and cigarettes.

"She's in her room playing with her paints," Eileen said, lighting a fresh smoke and waving her hand. "Want something to drink? Got tea, water."

"Yeah, sure. Tea, thanks."

I walked to the open kitchen, a small pile of dirty dishes in the sink, the uneven floor straining under my feet.

"Hear you're going to college next year."

"Yes, ma'am, I'm..."

"Ivey talks about it, you know. Just don't think we can afford it. Better for her to get a job around here, maybe take a couple of night classes."

She handed me the glass, her loose robe revealing the top of a rose, faded red and outlined in black, just a couple of petals of it, on her left breast. I wondered how far down the stem extended.

"She goes on about her art, doing that and all. Ain't no money in it, though. All that fluffy shit. Maybe you can give her some direction, talk her into something that'll make her something."

Walking on the sides of my feet like an Indian, I slowed my steps, wincing at the inevitable creaks of the aged wood floor. At the door, I peeked around the corner. Ivey had her back to me, headphones on, blonde hair spilling down her back. A canvas of pastel color in front of her, a field, or perhaps just a collage, of flowers: dandelions, daisies, jasmines, lilies, laurels. No roses, though. I smiled.

Entering the room, I slowly stalked, right behind her, ran a finger down her arm. She let out a stifled yelp, jerked her head around, eyes wide.

"Jesus, Calvin!"

"Didn't think you'd freak out that bad. What, your mom never comes in your room?"

"Yeah, but, I don't know. Just surprised me, that's all."

The color coming back to her face, I nodded my head at the painting. "What's this?"

"I call it 'Memory,' like Minestrini's, but not of childhood, like his. It's a memory I'll have when I'm old."

"When you're old? Why not a memory now?"

She dipped her brush into a glass of stained water, carefully mixed colors, leaned closer, added the brush stroke.

"Because I don't have it yet," she whispered.

"We've seen lots of flowers in the woods."

"They're not flowers, Calvin. They're feelings."

I nodded my head as though I understood, picturing her as a flower. A beautiful, exotic flower in a field where she didn't belong.

"Your mom said you should do something that makes money."

On her bed, I lay down on my stomach, propped my head on a pillow, studied her. Ivey, mouth tight, brow tense, carefully applied a swath of azure to the contour of a petal. My gaze shifted about the room: an old second-hand dresser, bare, cracked mirror, and then Ivey's paintings, landscapes mostly. I focused on one, a winding dirt road in the foreground, snaking into the background of a swaying field of grass interrupted by a lodge pole jackleg fence, the gate shut. Beyond, the road shrunk into hazy hills, disappearing through a distant valley. I cleared my throat.

"Hey, I noticed that the gate on—"

"Jesus *Christ*, I'm up!" Eileen's boyfriend's voice was distinct through the walls.

"'Bout time. You need to get your ass out of the house and look for a job," Eileen said. "Haven't done shit for a week."

"Just shut up and give me an aspirin. Head's pounding," he said.

"Good. Told you not to open that second bottle."

Footsteps. Shuffling. Cabinet doors shut.

"Give me a light," he said, coughing.

Rising from her chair, Ivey quietly stepped to the bed, laid next to me. Her body was warm next to mine, fragile. She rested her head on a pillow, peered at me with delicate blue eyes through a veil of blonde hair. I tilted my head toward the wall.

"Where did this one come from?" I asked.

"The usual," she said. "Bleacher's Bar. He's been around a couple of weeks. Name's Steve. Does drywall. Guess the boss ran out of work for him."

An oily, pungent odor wafted in through the door's crevices. The marijuana reminded me of last weekend's party after the ball game, and a hint of nausea began to well up in my stomach.

"Getting an early start, I suppose," I said.

"No, that's usual, too."

Inaudible conversation. A sharp banging of glass against wood.

"Look, get off my ass about it. I got bills, too, you know."

Ivey touched my shoulder, ran her fingers up my neck.

"C'mon. Let's get out of here," she said. In one motion, she jumped out of bed and scurried to the window, unlocked the latch, and with a swift motion lifted it up and hopped out. Her face peered at me from outside, cool air spilling in. She smiled.

"What are you waiting for, wienie?" I got my feet over the side, strained to reach the window to close it.

"Steve, get out. Just get the fuck out!" Eileen screamed at her boyfriend.

With a grunt, I shut the window tight, jerked my head around and Ivey was running, wild hair bouncing in the wind. I chased her, the cool breeze on my face, a blunt sting, the aged houses and cracked sidewalks blurring, gelling together and dissipating. She moved effortlessly, bounding over curbs and weaving through parked cars. With labored breaths, I followed.

The houses around us abruptly ended and the storefronts of downtown began: the hardware store, a women's apparel chain, a Mexican restaurant. We came to the town center, a square block of a cemented pond, jets of water shooting up in the air through an underwater compressor, concrete steps leading down to the water's edge. A flock of mallards erupted as we arrived, Ivey jumping two steps at a time. When she got to the water, she stopped, sat down, glanced back.

Out of breath, I walked the last few steps, plopped down next to her, stretched my legs, my feet dangling over the foamy water. Ivey sat Indian-style, her hands propping up her head, staring down at the many coins that glimmer on the porcelain of the pool's surface. Her eyelids at half-mast, small beads of sweat on her forehead, strands of hair adhered to her skin. She began to laugh, a muted giggle.

"What?" I asked.

A sad smile, slowly shook her head.

"Fuck my life," she whispered.

Running my fingers through her hair, I rubbed the nape of her neck.

"It'll be okay," I said. A bead of sweat ran down my cheek, and I swiped it clean.

"Nothing I do is right with her," she said. "Thing is, nothing she does is right, either. Like she's blind to that, though. Because anything I say to her is ignored. It's always gonna be like this, Calvin. I feel like my life is just a predetermined pile of shit."

The image of my father came, a deep, resounding, ancient pain. A dull ache in my bones coming on with the cold. *No toys, Calvin.* A raw piece of meat, detached eyes peering across at me.

Too much. Don't want another bite.

"She's not you," I said. She folded her arms, gently rocked to and fro.

"You aren't her. She's not you." A single tear dropped down her cheek, spilled onto her bare leg, snaked its way down, losing energy.

She turned and we embraced, Ivey burying her face in my chest, her back quivering, bronze skin warm, smooth. She pulled away, stared up at me. Tracing the outline of her lip with my finger, I leaned in, kissed her soft. Her hand moved up my neck. The sweet warmth of her tongue. She pulled away, gazing up at me.

"I love you, Calvin."

The words sounded comfortable. Like home.

"I love you, too."

⮞

His old hickory cane, always within arm's reach, leaned comfortably against the oak gun case next to the recliner. Everything about him weathered save his eyes, sparkling brown bright with long-held mischief.

"Would be up in those river bottoms every week when I had my dogs," Uncle Calvin said. "Now, it's just me and Duke out there."

Dad, Ivey, and I made the trip from Dallas to the little rural town of Carnigie, Oklahoma, the night before, school letting out and Ivey and I in the brown Chevy with Dad, driving and telling stories about his brother, and my namesake. Glancing out the window, the lone black and tan hound lay on his side, body motionless, ears twitching to ward off the flies.

"Can I go out and pet him?" Ivey asked.

Calvin gave her a toothless smile.

"Sure, little lady, go on ahead."

Ivey smiled back, freckled and child-like, clapped her hands quiet and was out the door. Duke's eyes perked, lazily he rose and hobbled to the chain link gate, greeting her. I watched through the window as she talked to him, inaudible but the soft sounds of her voice, the dog's tail wagging in delight.

"Best hold on to that one, boy," Uncle Calvin said. "She's a good one. Knew it when she walked in the door."

Before I could respond, Dad cleared his throat.

"Sure enough. That's my girl there. Her folks aren't very good to her. She's a tough one."

Calvin's expression didn't change. He crossed his legs, his worn Dickies overalls hiking up, his bare shins pale and hairless.

"Like us," he said.

Dad walked over to a chair, an old oversized Adirondack, sat, took a sip of the iced tea in his hand, wiped his mouth.

"Yep."

Setting the glass down on an end table, Dad said, "Course, with eleven of us, guess daddy had to be a little rough."

Calvin stayed silent, just nodded his head.

I strolled around the room, perused the photos on the wall. Many were old, framed, but with the frayed edges of being stowed in a box too many years. I spotted one of Dad and Uncle Calvin, young men, their wide-brimmed hats concealing their eyes, mouths set, crouched over a half dozen raccoons, a redbone hound in the background sitting next to a thick cluster of hardwoods. I looked back to see both of them gazing at the picture, too.

"That was after you up and moved to Texas," Calvin said to Dad. "I remember you came back and we had some sport over that fancy tie you wore."

Dad chuckled.

"Yeah. Thought I was gonna impress all of y'all. Never much liked to wear 'em, really."

He paused.

"Been hunting those same bottoms a lot of years, huh?"

Calvin glanced up in the air, doing some invisible math.

"Fifty-six years. As of this spring."

Calvin peered over at me.

"How 'bout we all pile in the pickup and go have a look at it? I think your girl would like it."

"Sure, Uncle Calvin. I'll tell her."

❧

We passed through the middle of town on the way. An old town square surrounded by emaciated storefronts, old trucks parked in front, the few people we saw in overalls and jeans.

"Has it changed much, Uncle Calvin?" Ivey asked.

Calvin put a plug of tobacco in his cheek as he waited for the lone red light.

"Naw. Maybe not as many people now as there was in the old days, you know, with the oil boom come and gone."

His eyes turned to soft focus as the light changed.

"Sue sure loved that store there," he said, pointing to an old fabric shop. "Spent many an hour there picking out the right colors for her dresses. Wasn't a seamstress just for a living, but loved doing it, too. Course, I was the same. Love woodworking. Gotta do what you love, you know."

Ivey glanced up at me, a knowing smile. Uncle Calvin lowered his voice.

"She passed last year. Leukemia."

"I'm sorry," Ivey said.

The residential area gradually gave way to farmland, and soon just the sporadic house set back from the road, aged pine front decks, rusted iron rockers sitting empty and lonesome. The road rose, then spilled out into a massive valley of soybean and dormant corn fields, and a wide swath of hardwoods, oak, ash, cherry, cedar, cutting through its center, the thin strip in it hinting at the river snaking along its bottom.

"There she is," Calvin said. "The bottoms run along for miles, thousands of acres. Lots of coon, of course. But there's whitetails, bobcat, coyote, turkey. You name it, and it lives there. Haven't messed with that other stuff for years now. Like running my dogs too much."

I glanced at Ivey, her eyes wide and fascinated.

We turned off the pavement and onto a dirt road, the occasional rock shooting up from the tires, banging against the chassis. The open fields of corn gradually gave way to the timber. Twisting oak, maple, poplar, the forest floor littered with dying and dead wood, switch grasses, grama grasses, bluestems, penetrated through. Dad rolled the window down, the cool air of the river bottoms whipping in. Through the wooden matrix ahead the wide river appeared, running flat and slow, murky red.

The road abruptly ended at a two-track pathway that paralleled the water. Calvin turned the truck around and backed up to the water's edge. We got out, Dad grunting as he swung his legs over. Calvin lowered the tailgate, opened the cooler of fried chicken and coke. I leaned against the tailgate, Ivey in front of me staring down at the cool water. My arms folded over her chest, she cradling her head against me.

"So peaceful," she said. "Even better than our creek, I think."

Her hair tickled my chin.

"Yep. Better. Wanna move?"

She looked back, grinning. A playful slap on the leg. *No.*

Dad and Calvin busied themselves setting up their folding chairs and plating up chicken, the fizz of their Coke bottles hissed as they opened them.

After we ate, Calvin gestured for Ivey and I to follow him. Dad leaned back in his chair, arms folded, half-asleep.

"C'mon," Calvin said. "Show you something."

He walked precariously up the narrow two-track road, his cane gingerly negotiating exposed rocks and roots and tall bunch grasses.

"Stay behind me so I can watch for tracks," he said.

His head slightly bent over, eyes moving along the muddy rut.

"There," he said. "See that track picking up and following the road? Buck whitetail. Big one, too, from the looks of it."

Ivey bent down, traced the outline of the distinct pattern with her finger.

"How can you tell it's a buck?"

"Size, mostly," Calvin said. "That one's well over four inches. Does are three or less."

He walked further up the road.

"Okay, now look here. Hog track."

Ivey bounded up to it.

"They all look alike to me," she said.

"Ha, I guess they would, little lady."

He set his cane down in the grass, slowly got down on his knees, his stubby, brown finger pointed.

"See the ends? Lot more rounded off. And it's harder to find clean prints, too. They step in their own tracks a lot more than deer do."

"Oh, I see," Ivey said, genuinely fascinated.

"Out here when I'm hunting or just looking for 'em, you learn the little things about sign. Little details. Get an eye for 'em. You notice hair on grasses, broken twigs, slight differences in walking patterns. Get to where you see just about everything."

Calvin strained to rise, and I quickly supported his arm to help him, reached down, handed him his cane.

"I thank you, Cal," he said. "Getting too old to be messing around out here, I suppose."

We hiked back to the truck, Dad in his chair, cap brim pulled down, mouth partially ajar. Calvin chuckled as he hobbled up behind him.

"Hey, old man."

Pushing his brim up, Dad glanced around at him.

"You get 'em squared away on finding critters?" he asked.

"Good as a Seminole," Calvin said, sitting down next to him.

Ivey and I perched in the grass on the riverbank beside them. They were silent for a few moments. The sun eased its way down, only half exposed over the looming oaks on the opposite side of the river. The light cast an orange hue on the water's reddish surface, illuminating the edges of the forest. Way off in the distance, a flock of geese made their way to the adjacent fields to feed and roost, their honks barely perceptible as they appeared as one, a darkish triangle in the dying light.

Calvin shifted forward in his chair, rested both hands on the cane, watched closely the school of bream rising to the surface, feeding on mayflies and the occasional grasshopper. Dad glanced at him.

"When do you go back for another round of chemo?" he asked.

Calvin picked off a blade of buffalo grass, tossed it in the midst of the feeding bream, watched as they momentarily disappeared, then reappeared, gave it a nibble, then went back to their mayflies

"Quit going," he said. "Cancer spread to my pancreas."

Dad rubbed his lips, eyes back on the river. Ivey's hand covered mine, squeezed. Dad cleared his throat, his face searching. Maybe, I thought, looking for answers somewhere along the riverbank. Perhaps he wanted life to backpedal. Just for a little while. The echo of a dozen hounds hot on the trail. Calvin's powerful legs racing after them, yelling with excitement. Later, he and his brother at the bar in town, cold beer and stories, laughing. When the world was new.

"How long?" Dad asked.

Calvin set his cane down in the soft grass, leaned back.

"Three months. Give or take."

CHAPTER FOURTEEN

MARIAS RIVER
JANUARY 1870

He woke from a dreamless sleep to look into a wall of white glinting from the eastern sun. Grey Bear's back numbed, he found Running Dog was gone. The women began to wake from their fitful slumber and Grey Bear spotted his son, drawn inward and sleeping next to Falling Leaf.

The muscles in Grey Bear's cold body ached. A sharp pain shot up his leg and he rubbed the sides of his knees. One more day to fire, to warmth. The thought filled Grey Bear with joy, and then he thought of last night and Running Dog and the pain came to his throat. He choked it down.

Grey Bear swallowed a handful of snow to quench his thirst as he waited for the women to ready themselves. So many moons of coldness and discomfort in their eyes. The wrinkles deepened around their mouths. Running Dog roused, gave his father a quick glance, and climbed out of the hole. The women stared intently at Grey Bear.

"We will walk today to the river and tonight we will have fire and be warm. I know you are weary, but we must not stop until we reach the woods. We will be safe once there and that will give us strength to make the journey to Benton's Fort. You will all soon be with your people."

Their expressions did not change, but Grey Bear saw a light in their eyes. He gestured to Running Dog who came and stood in front of his father with eyes downcast.

"Running Dog, you will lead them once more." Grey Bear pointed to the southeast, to a draw that climbed, then flattened. "We will come out of that draw and the snows will not be as deep." Grey Bear met his son's eyes.

"Yes, Father." Running Dog walked away, his back to Grey Bear, glanced at the others and they followed. Grey Bear turned from the flowing blackness of his people's hair in the winds to the sky above. The clouds had moved on, the heavens a pale blue. The snows kicked up around their feet and the flakes in the air lingered, reflecting sunlight.

A hawk high above appeared, hovering, and Grey Bear tried to see what it saw, their dark figures forming a line of the walking dead in a sea of white. He tried to know what it knew, to look at them the way it did from a vantage far away and above. He could not.

Running Dog led them to the crest of the bottoms and up the narrow draw. Falling Leaf's delicate feet picked their way up the rock-laden depression, falling in step with those in front of her. They reached the butte's rim and Grey Bear heard their shallow breaths. Cold Maker's winds picked up again and worked under his half-frozen robes.

Sage all around, Grey Bear's people weaved through the sharp-smelling tangles of ice. They began to make good time. The hawk dove, its dark wings tilting to the right, and then it disappeared below the butte's horizon leaving only the open blue.

Grey Bear's mind wandered. He thought of the wolves that fed and clothed his people, of the hawk that watched them, of his father. And he remembered. It was a story that his father, Rides At The Door, told him long ago when he was just past a boy, just a few winters older than Running Dog.

❧

My father sits on his robe smoking, the smells of tobacco and boiled wapiti linger in the summer night air. I chew the sweet meat and study him, watching him as his mind drifts. His eyes meet mine and he begins to speak. My mother, as always, stops stitching her heyoka moccasins to listen.

"Slender Bow, as we returned from the Bears Paw two moons ago I saw you looking at Yellow Leaf as she took the wapiti hides from your hands. Soon you will be honoring yourself in battle and not many winters from now you will have your own horses and lodge and will be looking for a wife."

My mother regards me with a hint of a smile and I look down, embarrassed. My father continues.

"There was once a man with two wives. These women, unlike Yellow Leaf, were bad. The man thought about his problem for a long time and decided to move his lodge away from his wives' band, to a place where there would be no other people and then, he thought, he could teach them to be good. So, he told his wives to pack their belongings and he moved their lodge to a far-off place in the open prairie.

"To the west of their camp was a high butte, and every evening close to sundown the man would climb this butte and look out to the four corners for sign of blackhorn and approaching enemies. There was an old blackhorn skull where he stopped to scout, and he would sit near this skull to rest. Meanwhile, the women would stay at the lodge.

'I am very lonely here,' said one woman as they sat in the lodge one day. 'We have no one to talk with and visit.'

'We must go back to our relations,' said the other. 'We must kill our husband.'

"And so the next morning, when the man rose and went to hunt the blackhorn that he had scouted the night before, the women snuck off and climbed the high butte. They found the blackhorn skull that the man had spoken of and they dug a deep hole. They covered it with sticks and dirt and smoothed it all down, then they carefully placed the blackhorn skull on top."

I watch my father's lips move, his eyes not on me but gazing at the shadowy walls of the lodge with its painted figures of the wapiti and the many birds, figures seeming to dance in the firelight. My father cocks his head as he contemplates these things and continues.

"In the afternoon, the man returned from his hunt with a heavy weight of meat. The women took the meat and cooked it for him. After the meal, the man climbed the high butte and scouted the four corners. He found no sign of either blackhorn or enemies. He knew that the blackhorn would return to the grasses of the prairie, that his family would not go hungry in the meantime, and that they would be safe from nearby Crow. He walked to the blackhorn skull to rest and watch the sunset. The man stepped on the cover of sticks and dirt which gave way, and he fell into the pit.

"The wives could always see the man as he sat on the buffalo skull, and that night they watched even more closely. When he came to the skull and disappeared from their view, they knew he was trapped and would die. They packed up the lodge, loaded all their belongings on a dog travois, and walked back to their family and friends. When they were close to the camp, they made a special effort to cry and wail so that their brothers and sisters would hear them. Their people rushed to them.

"Why do you mourn?" they asked. "Where is your husband?"

'Six moons ago he went out to hunt and never came back,' they replied. 'He is dead.' And at this they cried and wailed louder still.

"This man, it was true, fell into the pit, but he did not die. He was hurt with a badly bruised leg, so that he could not stand, much less jump out of the pit. So he sat in agony staring up at the night sky.

"When the sun came up, a hawk flying over the butte spied the man and told his friend the wolf. The wolf ran to the high butte and he saw the man looking back at him with pained eyes. The wolf took pity on the injured man and began to howl.

"Soon other wolves came to see what troubled him. Kit-foxes, coyotes and badgers came and also took pity on the man.

'You can all see,' said the wolf, 'that here is a fallen-in man. Let us dig him out of this pit and I will make him my wolf-brother.'

"The other wolves, coyotes, kit-foxes and badgers all agreed that the wolf spoke well and true and so began to dig the man out. Once they had dug down to him, he was silent and very ill. The animals dragged him out.

"The wolves gave the man a liver to eat, and when he was able to walk they took him to their den. Here lived an old, blind wolf that possessed powerful medicine. This old wolf cured the man and made his head and hands into that of the wolf but left the rest of his body unchanged."

My father brings his pipe to his lips. He exhales a streaming cloud of smoke that meshes with the smoke from the flames. He turns away from the many animal figures on the pis'kun walls, his gaze settling on my mother. Her dark eyes focus on his, her black hair casting a shadow over her cheek. His attention returns to the figures that dance in the shifting lights and darks.

"Back in those days our people did as we sometimes do now when animals come to steal food; they made holes in the pis'kun and set snares. The coyotes and wolves were caught by their necks.

"One day when the wolves went to do this, they approached the meat that was laid out. The man-wolf said, 'wait here. I will trip the snares so that you will not be caught.' He sprang the snares and all the wolves and coyotes and badgers and kit-foxes came and took meat back to their dens for their families.

"The man-wolf was glad to do this thing in repayment for the kindness his wolf-brothers had shown. This took place for several nights thereafter, and the people were astonished that each night the meat was stolen and the snares were sprung but nothing was ever caught. The elders of the camp discussed this and decided on a plan.

"When the wolves went to the pis'kun to again steal the meat, they found only a small, rotting chunk of an old bull blackhorn. When the man-wolf saw this, he cried out, 'Bad you give us! Bad you give us!' The people heard him and the elders' suspicions proved to be true, it was a man-wolf.

"The next day the elders placed pemmican and a nice chunk of fat back in the pis'kun. That night the wolves again came, and when the man-wolf saw the good food he rushed in to feast. The elders caught him with ropes and took him to a lodge. The fire's light gave them a better look at this man-wolf.

'You are the man who was lost!' cried one.

'No, I was not lost,' said the man-wolf. 'My two bad wives tried to murder me. I was scouting for blackhorn when I fell into a pit trap they dug, and I would have died had my wolf-friends saved me.'

"The elders became angry and asked the man-wolf how he would like them to punish the bad women. The man-wolf thought about this for a moment and then told them: 'I give those women to the I-kun-uh'-kah-tsi; they know what needs to be done.'

"And after that night the two bad women were never seen again."

My father finishes his story and places his pipe down. With a grunt he lies on his robe, the strands of his gray hair mingling with the darks. His eyes linger skyward for a moment, his hands on his chest, and then his eyes shut. I hear the low rumbling of his breathing as he falls into a slumber.

With the sun at its center, Grey Bear's people approached the opposite rim of the high butte. The wind remained strong at their backs, the sky clear. Grey Bear looked to the southwest. Running Dog and the women turned to each other with smiles that Grey Bear had not seen in many moons. South Butte in its beauty loomed over them, where many men had gone to find their spirit animals, whose vantage point had revealed many an enemy, whose presence always hovered within their home on the Marias. Grey Bear's heart sang.

Running Dog needed no further direction, beginning the steep descent down the draw to the open prairie. The women picked their way down, an occasional foot lost its grip on the shifting snows. Grey Bear admired Falling Leaf's sense of balance. She glanced at him, her lips smiling, eyes bright.

They reached the bottoms and, without pause, Running Dog worked toward the eastern side of South Butte. Cold Maker's winds stayed at their backs as if Cold Maker himself shared their longing for the Marias.

Grey Bear felt the soft crunch of the bunch grasses beneath his feet and thought of the spring and of many grazing blackhorns. He thought of the sweet backstrap chunks that he and Running Dog shared on the Marias on that day which seemed so long ago. His stomach responded to these thoughts and he pushed the hunger away.

He thought of his father and the story of the man-wolf, of the high butte and the wolves. What did the wolves call this man? A fallen-in man. Yes. A fallen-in man, saved by the wolves and the coyotes and badgers and kit-foxes.

Grey Bear scanned the sky for the hawk but did not see him. Instead, he looked to South Butte again, tried to imagine the opens beyond it, and home.

But then, that home was just a dream. There was only the river, and no home. A dream. Just like his children, like Yellow Leaf on the banks of the Marias in the summer splashing her feet in the cool water and watching him in the cattails.

A dream, just like the one two moons ago. His small hands on his face and the sands and then his father, dancing and staring to the heavens, chanting and seeing things far-off, unreachable, and crying out to them.

Bear Man Sees Bear Man Hears

The sound of his father's voice lingered in his mind. Grey Bear could not make sense of these things and pushed them away. South Butte loomed larger to the west and Running Dog walked faster, his small legs kicking up the shallow drifts of snow.

There was no pain in Grey Bear's legs but a dull ache throbbed in his hips. He worked his hands, closing his fingers and opening them, the tiny sparks of pain ignited as the numbness left. The sun began its descent into the west and he worried about making the river before nightfall.

They marched, and South Butte's towering presence shifted to the north. Then Grey Bear saw at the horizon's edge that the land was no longer barren. A rough outline of trees.

"I see the river's edge," he shouted. "Soon we will have fire and food!"

The women chattered and pointed at the horizon; they cried with joy and shrieked with delight. Their pace quickened, and South Butte's presence became smaller behind them.

⟿

Cottonwoods stood tall against the fading light of the sky. The women walked around them, their moccasins making soft crunching sounds on the frozen bunch grasses. Running Dog squatted against a tree trunk, his knees folded against his chest and his arms wrapped tightly around them. The voices of the women lightened, an occasional laugh, smiles more frequent.

Only Running Dog did not smile. Grey Bear had not often hit him, only twice before, and then he quickly shook it off. It was not so then. Maybe because boys were supposed to be punished in this manner, but not men. And Running Dog, rightfully maybe, no longer thought of himself as a boy. Maybe Grey Bear was wrong to strike him in front of the women.

Maybe he should not have struck his son at all. He should have talked to him. Like a man. Running Dog sat apart from the women, his face blank and staring through the thick clusters of cottonwoods at the river.

Maybe there was something else.

Strong Deer spoke with Spider Woman about the Benton's Fort and their relations there. When Grey Bear approached, they stopped talking.

"Give me the sinew from the two wolves," he said to Strong Deer. "We need to rest here before we make the journey to the Benton's Fort. Gather the women and find a good place to make camp. Have them collect wood, and we need a fire pit."

Strong Deer called them together and they searched for a good clearing. Falling Leaf began to follow them but Grey Bear gently took her by the arm. He held up a hand and looked to his son still seated by the tree.

"Running Dog!" Grey Bear called.

His son's eyes reluctantly turned to him.

"I want you and Falling Leaf to set out traps. Take these." He handed the sinews to Falling Leaf. "Use them for snares. And Running Dog, set up some deadfalls, too. Work until you can't see the tracks, then come back."

Falling Leaf nodded. Running Dog's head was down but he began to follow her.

"Running Dog," Grey Bear said.

He faced his father.

"Take the knife."

He absently took it and walked away. Grey Bear watched until they disappeared into the cottonwoods and alder brush. When Running Dog returns, father and son will eat together, Grey Bear thought. I will tell him I was wrong to strike him.

Sounds of the women carried through the woods, talking and laughter and the breaking of branches. Grey Bear followed the voices until he came to camp, a small clearing surrounded by tall cottonwoods on three sides and a wall of alder brush to the south.

Spider Woman brought stones to place around the fire pit. He watched her lay them out.

His eyes weary, he sat down against a thick cottonwood. The women blurred as he began to doze. When he awoke, the sun had disappeared behind the rocky breaks to the west. The women huddled around the fire and stared intently at the flames.

"Where is Running Dog?" he asked Falling Leaf.

"He said that he would set up a few more deadfalls under the moon's light and gave me his knife so that we can use it in camp," she said.

Her eyes turned downcast. Something wasn't right. He shifted his weight and gazed into the flame as it flickered and smoked.

These ghosts that are forever doomed to wander here, they can talk, Running Dog.

Grey Bear jumped to his feet, disappeared into the darkness of the woods.

CHAPTER FIFTEEN

GARLAND TEXAS

1991

How far is Lubbock?" Ivey asked.

At the combination pharmacy/ice cream parlor downtown, Ivey, dressed in her favorite denim skirt, tan arms propped on the table, looked small sitting in the massive red booth. She sipped her root beer float, wiping the cream from her lips. My usual banana split began to drip. I spooned a mouthful, thought.

"Don't know. Four hundred miles, maybe?"

Her forehead furrowed in concentration.

"That's too far."

"You're not locked down here, you know," I said. "The college has a great arts program, and you could get all kinds of student loans and grants."

"Where would I live?"

I smiled.

"They have dorms there, too, you dork."

Ivey twirled the straw around her drink, gingerly sipped, eyes cast away.

"Look," I said. "I know you talked about junior college here in town. But it would mean another two years of living with your mother."

She still wouldn't look at me.

"Don't you want to get out of here?"

"It's not that simple, Calvin," she said. "I don't know if she'd do well without me. I'm like her mom. Get her out of bed. Make sure the laundry is done." Ivey raised an eyebrow. "Weird?"

"Yeah. But I know that's how it is. Can't go on forever, though. When does it end?"

She shifted in her booth.

"I don't know. When she gets her shit together. If."

"Ivey," I said. "you can't—"

The bell hung by the front door of the parlor jingled. Derek, Matt, Michael. The guys I got drunk with at the lake.

"Oh great," Ivey said under her breath.

Matt was the first to see me, a sly smile appearing. Dressed in his pizza delivery uniform.

"Seven o'clock," I said. "aren't you supposed to be working?"

"What's up, Cal? They let us go early. Who's this?"

Ivey glared at him.

"I go to school with you, moron," she said.

Derek and Michael chuckled.

"So," Matt said. "Your name is?"

Ivey looked exasperated.

"Seriously?"

She shot me an angry look.

"You didn't tell them about me, Calvin?"

She had me. But not for the reasons I knew she was going to assume. Just didn't want to share her with anybody. She always seemed … above them. I looked around at the guys for help, but they just gave me a collective bewildered expression, shrugged their shoulders.

"You didn't," she said. "you really didn't."

"Whoops," Michael said.

"Why?" she asked.

I calculated how much grief I would get from the guys if I told her the truth in front of them. *Forget them. Just tell her the truth.*

"Don't know," I said. "Just never came up."

She let out a little cry, like a puppy trapped in a hole it can't crawl out of. I quietly cursed myself. She shoved her half-full root beer float at me, the cold cream spilling down my shirt, pooling up in my lap. Soaked in through my jeans and shirt, the guys cackled with laughter, curious stares from the men and women at the counter.

My eyes shifted up to Ivey, her head lowered, lips quivering, arms folded.

"On that note, fellas," Matt said.

"Yep," Derek said. And they walked out the door.

"Ivey," I said. "I didn't mean ..."

Seething, she picked up a wadded up napkin, hurled it at me, got up from her seat, turned and left. I watched her through the parlor's windows, the wind lifting her hair as she ran away.

The television blared in Mama's room as I quietly closed the front door, faint smells of an hours-old supper of pork chops and cabbage in the kitchen, the quiet hiss of the gas heater. Creeping through the small duplex, I entered my room, shut the door. Gently lifting the window curtain, I gazed at the outline of of Ivey's house a block away, looking unusually peaceful for a Friday night. Typically three or four cars were parked in the front, the music audible even at this distance, the voices of Eileen's friends rumbling in the undercurrent of the rhythm.

When they arrived a couple of years ago with a long-departed man from Alabama, Dad lamented the downgrade in the neighborhood. An older couple lived there before, moved away to be closer to their grown children. An old man who perpetually tended the garden that had lined the front of the house, sweating in the sun, wearing a safari-style hat. A reclusive old woman that never seemed to leave the house.

"When the trash moved in," Dad said of the recent arrivals, shaking his head, his mouth set and grim. I watched nonchalantly, until I saw the petite blonde bounce out of the old Dodge pickup, uncertain pale face glancing around her new environment. Dad, of course, didn't notice my interest, instead continued shaking his head and mentioning something about property values.

Feeling eyes on me, I turned to see the door partially ajar, my mother peering in.

"You okay?" she asked.

"Yeah, why?"

"It's just you usually tell me when you're home."

She glanced around the room, probably looking for something to chastise, usually involving cleanliness.

"Everything good with you and Ivey?" she asked. For a while, Mama and I had an unspoken agreement not to tell Dad about my friendship with her, until one day Ivey showed up at his house looking for me. To my surprise, he instantly adored her, calling her henceforth "his girl."

"Just a little misunderstanding, that's all."

Tried to think of something to add so she'd change the subject.

"I'll talk to her about it tomorrow. It'll be okay."

She nodded her head.

"Well, all right. You're in for the night, right?"

"Yeah. I'm tired."

"Okay. See you in the morning, sugar."

⁎

"Calvin."

My mother's voice rolled in from far off, over the rhythm of the electric fan in the darkness. Wasn't completely dark, though. Through the curtains, a vague redness flashed, amber, then red.

"Yeah?"

"There's something going on at Ivey's house."

I sighed.

"It's Friday. Always something going on over there."

"Think it's worse this time."

Fear in her voice.

"Okay."

The wind bit my skin through my shorts and T-shirt. At the end of the block, a paramedic ran around an ambulance, jumped in the driver's seat. It raced past us, lights, siren blaring.

Mama and I eased up the sidewalk, closer to the small crowd of police officers, neighbors. Amidst the shouting and frightened faces, I saw Eileen gesturing wildly to an officer. He scribbling notes as she rambled. Steve sat on a curb next to a patrol car, handcuffed, his body unsteady, staring nervously across the lawn at Eileen.

Not fully awake yet. Eileen and Steve. Who the hell was in the ambulance? Where was Ivey? I inhaled the night air, shiver running down my back. Glanced at my watch, saw it was 1:21 a.m. I crossed the street, Mama followed, tentative. A handful of neighbors stood in silence, in bathrobes and T-shirts, unkempt hair, lined faces, arms folded. I stood behind them, listened.

Eileen had stopped shouting. Her face was pale, her mouth moved with quiet words. An officer strode over to Steve and lifted him up. He barked commands, Steve silent, eyes unfocused. I heard the words "under arrest" and then he was in the back of the patrol car, speeding away. Eileen was escorted to another squad car, got in, left in the direction of the ambulance.

I glanced back—my mother behind me, her eyes red from the wind. She turned to Eileen's next door neighbor, an elderly Hispanic man in a flannel shirt, his black hair disheveled, head down, shaking.

"Jorge, what happened?" my mother asked.

Jorge gave her a timid glance.

"Eileen told the officer she woke in the middle of the night to crying. She found Ivey badly beaten. Barely alive, she said."

Searing wave of ice through me. Couldn't feel my legs.

Jorge cleared his throat, an apprehensive look at his wife.

"Said that man raped her, and when she fought back ... that's when it happened. The beating. *Tal un Ángel*, Ivey. *Sería matarlo*."

Words came from somewhere out of me. Like I was talking underwater.

"Hospital. Mama, we have to go to the hospital."

Mama's face rigid, she squinted intently at the road ahead. Ours was the lone car on the street, a light fog settled comfortably above us, a gentle mist peppered the windshield. Mama reached up every few seconds, flipped the washer on, wiped it clean. I shivered. The heater in the old

Cutlass always took its time to blow hot. Hard to breathe.

She turned onto the road leading up to visitor parking, another turn. Eased the Cutlass into an empty parking space, killed the engine. She exhaled deeply.

"You ready for this?" she asked.

None of it. Ready for none of it.

"Yeah. Let's go."

The automatic doorway opened with a swoosh; the crisp, sterile air hit my face. A few people were in the waiting room, grimly thumbing through magazines, sagging faces. I recognized a few of our neighbors, Jorge, his wife, and an older couple. I nodded as they turned their heads. A small child lay asleep next to his mother, oblivious.

Shuffling back to the rows of cushioned chairs, we sat in a corner. Stacked on an end table were perhaps a dozen magazines. The walls adorned with paintings of idyllic fields. I spotted one, a mosaic of flowers. And I couldn't hold back. Hiding the tears with my hands, I doubled over, nauseous. Mama's hand rested gently on my back.

"Hey, she's a tough girl. She'll be okay."

We sat for a few minutes, me still bent down, hands covering my face. Didn't want to think, so I focused on getting rid of the knot welled up in my chest. On breathing. In and out. And then, finally, I did want to say something.

"She thinks I'm ashamed of her," I said.

I didn't uncover my face. There was no answer for a few seconds. And then Mama cleared her throat.

"Why would you ever think that?"

So I told what happened yesterday at the ice cream parlor. And then I told her why I said what I said.

"I imagine she's had to deal with that her whole life," Mama said. "She just expects it, that's all."

"But it's not her fault," I said.

"Doesn't matter. Ivey, I expect, found that out early. Older you get, the more the baggage accumulates. Ivey was born with it."

I wiped the dampness away from my cheeks, sat up. The neighbors

were across the room from us. Jorge's wife rifled through an old issue of
Redbook, her house shoes tapping the white tile. Jorge had fallen asleep,
his mouth partially ajar.

"Wish she could let that go. Not have anything to be embarrassed
about."

"Maybe one day she can," Mama said. "People have many lives, in a
way. This Ivey, maybe, can one day just be somebody she used to be."

Not really understanding, I just nodded my head. A wave of fatigue
swept through me, and I leaned back, closed my eyes, my mother covering
me with my jacket.

≈

Voices. I roused, momentarily confused as to where I was. The neighbors, Mama at the admitting counter, their backs to me. Jorge and his
wife slowly turned around, left. Mama lumbered back, her head lowered. I
wiped my eyes to clear my vision. She got down on her knee in front of me.

"Calvin?"

"How bad is she?"

The color was drained from Mama's face.

"Calvin. She's gone."

No thought. I rose.

"Gotta go."

"Where are you going? It's the middle of the night. C'mon, let me …"

"No. I just have to go."

Spinning around, I dashed out the door, Mama's voice trailing after.
The night air hit me hard, a thousand tiny needles pricking my face. I
picked up my pace, breaking into a jog, then into a run, the wind whipping
against my jacket, the fog wet against my forehead.

The damp sidewalk a blur beneath my feet, I hopped over curbs, scurried
past streets. The occasional headlights of cars whizzing past. The hardware store. The bicycle shop. Like everything's normal. Like nothing has
happened. The world, exactly the same as it was before. A grain of anger
in me, growing, rising.

Clothes clinging against my damp body, I reached my street, veered off and raced toward the bend in the road. Jumping into the grasses, I sprinted toward the creek's edge, dropped down the embankment, the moist sand engulfing my feet. The moon's sapphire light glimmered off the sand encasing my ankles, tiny dull sparkles, air motionless, thick. Nothing but the black water, bumpy, constant flow. Tears ran jagged down the creases of my mouth.

Her hair, moist and clinging to her bronze skin. I reached for her and there was nothing.

I scanned the creek floor for rocks, picking out the smoothest, flattest of stones, chalky white. Six of them then, slippery in my hand. At the water's edge, my feet sank smoothly in the shallow current, the chilled wetness penetrated my shoes. Leaning close to the riffles, I tossed one, spinning it with my index finger, the smooth disc skimming over the surface, disappearing in a dark vortex at the base of an embedded boulder. And then another, still not far enough. Another. Abandoning this, I let the last three sail higher over the water, lodging in the thick mud opposite me.

I cried out. All the sound, all the air, left my body and echoed through the winding bottom. My vision clouded from the murky water, my focus was back on the timber, watching the swaying shadows. A form moving through the looming hardwoods, ambled, weaved in the midst of the matrix.

A bear.

Heart sinking, I wiped the moisture from my eyes, but he was gone.

Dropping to my knees, the icy water drenched my clothes, stung my thighs. My hands ran through the current. I dipped my head in it, rose up, gazed through the timber on the other side.

Flowers, I thought. I'll hike to the meadow behind the old lean-to and pick some flowers for Ivey. All colors, all kinds. The world for her.

CHAPTER SIXTEEN

MARIAS RIVER
FEBRUARY 1870

The moon's light penetrated the tangled branches. Grey Bear trudged through the tangled timber, keeping the river in sight. The sharp branches raked his bare arms and face, a trickle of blood inched down his cheek, blending with the cold sweat. He stopped and listened in the half-light. Nothing but the gently flowing current and sharp moans of the trees as they shifted in the winds.

Grey Bear came out of the alders and stood in the shallow snow, his eyes scanning the woods for movement. He saw the clouds begin to mask the moon's light.

"Running Dog!"

There was no answer from the forest ahead, or from the river. He advanced, fifty steps, a hundred.

"Running Dog!"

The winds brought biting flakes of ice that fell from the branches, stinging his head. Grey Bear willed his ear to hear but the winds came stronger and caused the live timbers to moan their resistance, the grinding of the live trees against the leaning dead, and the leaning dead against the fallen dead.

The winds pushed but he struggled forward. Shadows moved, shifted on the forest floor. Biting pellets of ice glanced off his injured ear, sending splinters of pain through his head and down his neck.

Grey Bear kept the subtle sound of the Marias within earshot. The winds blew faster in his face. The shadows around him darkened and expanded. His feet shuffled, the blowdown timber was thicker here and caused his pace to slow as he stepped over and around them.

Grey Bear lifted his leg over another log. He began to take another step and caught his foot on an unseen exposed root. He fell, the side of his face hitting the cold hardness of a down cottonwood. He cried out, rolled on his back, his hands covering the injury. Groaning and writhing in the snow, blood oozed down his neck. With a last grunt, Grey Bear brought himself to his feet.

"Running Dog! Come to me!"

No answer.

Running Dog tried to shame his father in front of the women, spoke as if he was a man, and now this. Running Dog will pay, Grey Bear thought. This time, he will give his son a real beating.

Grey Bear kicked a log, snow collapsing around his feet. He hiked another hundred paces, listened for any sound, searched for any movement. He peered into the thick brush, saw the softness of the moon penetrate the dark clouds and cast a half-light on the small sliver of water running through the middle of the river between thick, uneven sheets of ice.

With his back to his father, Running Dog stood by the river's edge. He was still, riveted, hands by his sides. The moon's false light revealed Running Dog's face, colorless. He stood in his tattered buckskin breechcloth and leggings, his thin moccasins wet on the slick surface. The winds cut through the openness following the path of the current, his hair swaying.

Grey Bear's anger built and the wound on his face throbbed, making the dried blood crack. He worked his way to Running Dog, the tiny branches of the alders whipping his face. He stalked through the tangled mass and wiped the stinging wetness from his eyes, peering at Running Dog with fury. Across the river, he saw the object of Running Dog's gaze and Grey Bear's knees dropped to the ground.

The moon's dim light illuminated her bronze face as she crouched by the bank. Her lips whispered beneath the winds. Her long black hair swept sideways to reveal the soft skin of her bare arms and face. She wore the dress with the many wapiti ivories. Her bare feet stepped onto the ice. As Grey Bear crouched in the tangled alders, she smiled, reached out. Yellow Leaf.

Running Dog stepped onto the ice. He moved forward, tears falling.

She laughed the laugh that Grey Bear knew when he watched her play along the Marias.

The crack was sharp. Running Dog dropped as the ice broke. A brief whimper and then just his arms and head were out of the water. Grey Bear burst through the alders. On his stomach, he crawled toward his son. Running Dog's face turned and was again that of a lost child, his eyes wide.

"I'm coming, Running Dog!"

Sharp ice dug into Grey Bear's elbows and hands. He moved carefully, listened for cracking ice. "Take my hand!"

Running Dog's face white with fear, his lips trembled. He extended his hand as far as he could.

Grey Bear grabbed it. "Your other hand, Running Dog! Grab onto me!"

He squeezed his father's wrist but the current's force sucked him down and pulled Grey Bear forward. Grey Bear brought a foot down violently, digging into the rough ice. Running Dog was pale, his face pained, his mouth open and gasping.

Grey Bear's foot slipped. Running Dog's grip on his father's wrist loosened. Grey Bear screamed and tried to pull the boy from the current, his son's body refusing to budge.

Running Dog gasped and released a hand. It fell limp into the water. The current pulled him in and Grey Bear's hold on the ice weakened. Running Dog's head was just above the water's surface, the current splashing over his face. Grey Bear dug in and pulled, grunting, sweat running into his eyes. Running Dog's body started to rise out of the water but then Grey Bear's foot lost its grip.

Running Dog stared into his father's eyes and Grey Bear saw the fear and light leave. The boy looked away, released.

"No!"

His head disappeared and Grey Bear gripped his limp hands, then the current pulled harder, his grip slipped, and he was gone.

Grey Bear plunged his arm into the hole and groped through the cold water. Nothing.

He crawled back away from the hole and, still lying on his stomach, buried his face in his arms. The winds rattled the cottonwoods, making them creak and moan. Grey Bear stared into the dark ice, his hot breath spilling over the frozen surface.

Somewhere in the recesses of his mind he remembered Yellow Leaf and craned his neck to look where she stood. He screamed, scrambled back toward the bank.

The clouds had moved off and the moon's light illuminated the monster of winter. Cold Maker took a slow step toward Grey Bear, the ice groaning, small chunks of white fletching from his arrows shattering on the hard river. His eyes bored down on Grey Bear, eyes of the blackest black in a mountain of white. He glanced to the heavens and the winds ceased.

Grey Bear scuttled back further.

"He is mine now, Grey Bear," Cold Maker said.

Grey Bear stood, heart pounding. Cold Maker loomed over Grey Bear whose eyes strained against the moon's reflection on the light blueness of aged ice.

"If you had proved worthy I would have let you have him, but you did not hold on to what you love. I watched you with Kipataki and watched you shame Running Dog. It is he who has guided your people here with the aid of my winds. He saved your life, and your people. Now he will be my son."

Anger stirred in Grey Bear's hollow heart. "You deceive my son with the ghost of my wife, and so it is you who is shameful. You are nothing but a cowardly old coyote."

He turned his back to Cold Maker, his eyes resting on a rock half wedged in the riverbank. He kicked it free and charged Cold Maker. His war cry echoed through the open valley and he hurled the rock as hard as his arm would throw.

The rock struck Cold Maker's chest. A chunk of blue ice exploded and he jumped back, shattering the ice beneath him. His legs were immersed in the open current. He roared, shaking the frozen cottonwoods.

"Otahkoissksisi yoohkiaayo omahkinaa i'nit!"

His words thundered through Grey Bear's heart and Cold Maker lunged forward, his great fists slamming down on the rough river ice and spraying white chunks in Grey Bear's face. Grey Bear fell into the water as the surface gave way and felt the pain of a thousand needles as the current tried to take him under.

He swam for the bank, found an exposed root, and crawled up the edge. Cold Maker's black eyes narrowed and he let out another horrific roar. Grey Bear found another rock, this one smaller. He began to stand and Cold Maker leapt from the middle of the river to its edge, frigid water splashing into Grey Bear's eyes.

The water knocked Grey Bear down and Cold Maker jumped up to the bank. His ancient face hovered over him, cold, black eyes burning with death. Grey Bear cocked his arm to hurl the rock. Cold Maker's hand reached up behind his back, his body of a thousand winters whining, the ancient ice falling off and new ice forming in its place.

A high-pitched sound rang in Grey Bear's head and Cold Maker pulled out his knife not of tempered steel, but of azure blue ice. He held the blade to Grey Bear's neck. Grey Bear dropped the rock and felt the ice-knife against his cold skin. His flesh began to freeze, first a horrific throbbing pain then a cold numbness. Cold Maker's breath began to freeze Grey Bear's hair and face, leaving him unable to move.

He stood that way for a moment, watching Grey Bear with contempt, before pulling back the knife and returning it to its sheath.

"No, Grey Bear," he said. "You will live."

Grey Bear lay motionless, his body paralyzed, eyes twitching. Cold Maker walked back into the river. He became hazy, a spinning cloud of white, and then was gone. The winds returned and the frozen cotton-woods groaned.

The newly freed current of the river flowed and water spilled over the break's edge. Across the river and up the bluff was a looming blackness outlined only with the sky's lighter shade of darkness. Something was on the ridge. A lone form moving west. It stopped for a moment and seemed to turn, then moved on, disappeared.

Grey Bear's eyes were half open and looking past the winding alder branches at the black, starless sky. He forced his weary legs to keep moving, his feet to keep stepping over down logs.

He saw the flickering flame, a blinding flash of light in a world of darkness. He weaved through the tangled mass of wood and ice. Upright forms moved around the fire. The women were all still awake. He emerged from the woods and they spotted him. Their many high-pitched voices all questioned why Running Dog was not with him. Grey Bear looked at the fire beyond them and kept walking, their many hands on his shoulders and arms, soft, comforting.

Spider Woman scurried to lay a wolf hide on the ground by the fire and Strong Deer told Calf Mother and Falling Leaf to prepare food. Falling Leaf went to collect bark from the cottonwoods and paused to give him a fearful look.

Grey Bear sat on the wolf hide and stared into the flames with no thoughts or feeling. Strong Deer brought him river water in the dried bladder from the wolf. He ate the roots Calf Mother had prepared and the bark Falling Leaf collected. The bark was sweet, and as he chewed his eyes never left the flames. He drank from the bladder; the water was warm from sitting next to the flames. His wet garments began to dry.

Grey Bear's eyes were weary but he looked to Falling Leaf at his side, who met his glance and quickly looked down. Her delicate hands clutched her dress. Strong Deer watched with a worried look.

"Running Dog is dead," he said. "He fell into the river and drowned."

The wails from the women echoed through the valley, and Grey Bear let them wail. He lay back on the robe and the last vision he saw with half-closed eyes was Falling Leaf.

She stood with the knife by the fire, staring at the river, cutting off her hair. The blade sliced and black strands formed a pile on the white snow.

CHAPTER SEVENTEEN

GARLAND, TEXAS
1992

D ad's in the hospital, why don't you drive down?" is all she said early on Thursday morning. I had class, but figured I could skip it and get the notes later. My mother didn't say what was wrong and I didn't ask. She didn't want me worrying while driving all that way, I guessed. Always protecting me and freaking out about the least little thing. I was nineteen and you'd think she'd loosen up a little, but no.

Probably nothing, I decided. Miles of mesquite brush were whizzing past as I tooled down Highway 20 heading east to Dallas. In the distance were little chopped up squares of pasture and cotton fields ending with a flatline horizon that seemed to wave under the sun's heat. Yeah, it's nothing. Probably his diabetes acting up again, may have to change his diet. But why would my mother ask me to come home for that? Never did before, not for something that minor. Don't matter, though. He's tough.

I flipped through the radio in my little Mazda pickup and it was nothing but static. One little old time country station came on, but it was far-off and mixed up with a signal from some Mexican station down south. Sounded funny. An old gravelly voice and a steel guitar interrupted by a riled-up deejay speaking rapid-fire Spanish. Two different worlds battling it out in space somewhere and neither knew it. I turned it off.

Last year Dad drove with me down this road when I first left for college. Need someone to help get settled, he said. Truth is, I think he just wanted to see those dorms for himself and make sure there's no monsters there to get me.

We stopped in Abilene at a little barbecue stand and had chopped brisket sandwiches on an old picnic table. I remember it was breezy that day, lots cooler than West Texas has a right to be in August.

"Have you decided what you're going to study?" he asked.

"Journalism," I said. I had told him this before.

"A newspaper man. Be a good job. Always said I wanted to live long enough to see you graduate. Looks like I might make it."

❧

The sliding doors of the emergency room opened, the sterile air of the hospital rushing into my face. A middle-aged black woman sat at the reception desk and stared at me impassively.

"I'm here for Ben Nichols," I said. Crowds of families sat in the waiting room thumbing through magazines and watching the television mounted in the corner. I suddenly remembered the last time I stood in this room, and then a flash of Ivey's porcelain neck, the subtle perfume. No. Not now.

"Room 228," she said. "Through those doors and to the left."

My legs were a little stiff from the long drive. My stomach felt empty but I knew I wasn't hungry. Everything was white. The walls, ceiling, the tile floors. Hurt my eyes. I made the turn and my mother was leaning against the wall at the end of the hall. She walked toward me. I expected her to smile but she didn't. Her hair was tied back in a ponytail and her eyes were red, a little mascara streaking down her face.

She hugged me, her back muscles tense.

"Glad you're here," she whispered.

"Yeah, me too," I said. "What's wrong? He gonna be okay?"

She pulled away but kept her hands on my shoulders. She looked at me, then down at the white tile floor.

"Well, we don't know. He had a stroke. Pretty bad one. Can't move his right arm very good and he's not thinking straight."

"I want to see him," I said. Her grip tightened on my shoulders.

"He may not know you."

No, it's not that bad. Can't be.

"He'll know me."

I peered into the room with a white tag on the door that said "Nichols." Maw Maw was sitting next to him in jeans and a light blue blouse thumbing through a magazine, not really reading, just scanning the words, fingers clumsily turning the pages. Every few seconds she glanced at him, quickly going back to her magazine.

Dad lay on the hospital bed, the aluminum rails up on both sides. He was dressed in a blue hospital gown, an IV tube taped to his tanned, age-spotted arm. His eyes were closed in a fitful doze, his mouth opening and closing. He looked fragile. Never thought I'd think that about him. Handle with care, like an antique teapot.

The skin of his bony arms looked almost gray, hanging from his once powerful biceps. I stared at those arms. Holding me high as a baby. Throwing me countless footballs and baseballs. Bringing up fish that I caught. Now they were still, his right hand contorted into a claw-like shape. Only his chest moved up and down in short, shallow breaths.

Maw Maw put her magazine down on an empty chair when she saw me. It slid off and fell to the floor but she didn't notice. She stood up with a sad smile.

"Hey, you."

"Hi, Maw Maw."

She wrapped her arms around me. I returned the embrace and we stood like that for a few seconds, saying nothing.

She raised her head up slowly and whispered, "He's going to be okay."

The knot in my stomach wound tighter and I fought with everything I had to not cry. I finally managed, "I know."

"He's just resting now," she said. "Would you like to talk to him? It'd probably be good for him."

I put my hand on his chest. I could feel the warmth of his body through the cold gown. He stirred and looked up at me in a disoriented, cloudy gaze. Then, a spark of knowing.

"Hi, Calvin."

ॐ

Maw Maw sits at the kitchen table working her beloved crossword puzzle, her lips pursed in thought, the rise of an eyebrow, the quick pen filling in letters with careful precision. She smiles as I walk in carrying a small cooler, the ice shifting in rhythm with my steps.

"If you're going to the backyard to clean those things, you better take *him.*" She gestures with mock animosity toward Dad. He's sitting in the den in his old recliner watching a baseball game. I give Maw Maw a knowing wink and grab the knob on the back door before turning to him.

His bald head is visible above the cushions of the recliner. I see the familiar tan, the age spots, the wisps of white hair. His feet are propped up and his right hand holds a remote control. He's watching a Ranger game. His favorite player, Pudge Rodriguez, throws a baseball to the pitcher and then squats down, adjusting his face mask.

"Dad!" I say.

His head turns and he peers at me out of the corner of his cloudy right eye.

"I'm going out back with a mess of crappie," I say.

He coughs and clears his throat.

"I'm coming," he says.

He pushes the handle of the recliner forward with his unsteady hand and the footrest comes down.

I grab the folded aluminum walker leaning next to the cabinet. He looks up to me and extends his hand. I help him get up as he groans in the effort to stand. I grip the back of his arm as he steadies himself.

Maw Maw opens the back door. I lead him, careful that his feet find firm ground on the steps. I walk with him to the patio. His feet shuffle forward, the walker grinding and creaking as it hits the hot pavement. He stared with concentration at the ground in front of him, taking in a couple of feet at a time. We reach the table on the patio and I pulleout one of the plastic chairs for him. He shifts his feet around and sits with a grunt.

"I'll go get the gear," I say.

Dad nods, breathing heavy. Maw Maw is at the door with a bowl of water in one hand and a fillet knife wrapped in a towel in the other. I take the knife and bowl, grab the cooler, and walked back. Dad is sitting under the shade of the pecan tree he planted fifty years before. He stares at the kennel with old, lost blue eyes, his shaking hand resting on the cedar table.

I gripped a crappie's mouth, pinching it with my thumb and forefinger, and set it on an old wooden cutting board. I make a vertical cut just behind the gills, then cut back to the tail. Dad watches, his hands in his lap.

"Where'd you go this time?" he asks.

I finish separating the thin white meat from the skin and drop the fillet in the bowl of water, watched it drift to the bottom, trailing a wisp of blood in its descent.

"The east bay next to Dalrock," I say, reaching for another fish.

"Oh, yeah. Good spot. Good spawning ground all up in there."

Dad leans back in his chair, crosses his legs, let his arms dangle loosely off the plastic arm rests. A warm spring breeze whips through the branches of the old pecan tree and brings the smell of the grasses and sprouting leaves in the neighboring yards. The faint smell of fresh fillets rises from the cutting board.

"Boy, me and you sure had some fun out on that lake, didn't we?" Dad grins, a little spark coming back into his eyes. I smile as I drop another fillet in the bowl.

"Yes, we did."

He gives me a playful hit on the arm. "You remember, oh, you was twelve or so, me and you was out running trotlines by the dam, up in that cove, uh …"

"By the Mimosa campgrounds," I say, knowing the story well.

"Yeah. You started hollering and yelling. That big 'ol hook went plumb through your hand." He chuckled. "I remember at the hospital I told everyone I went fishing and caught me a hundred pounder."

"And told everybody after that for the next two years." I shake my head in mock exasperation as I wipe my hands on the towel.

We sit in silence. I let the breeze dry the perspiration on my forehead, he taps his fingers on the rails of his walker and stares at the blue Texas skies with searching, misty eyes. He shifts his gaze to me and then returns to the sky beyond the shifting branches of the neighboring magnolia trees.

"I sure wish I could've gone with you today," he says.

CHAPTER EIGHTEEN

MARIAS RIVER
FEBRUARY 1870

Falling Leaf." Strong Deer placed her hand on Falling Leaf's closely cropped hair. The girl's eyes opened as she woke.

"Go check the snares you set last night."

Falling Leaf rose and wandered off into the thick cottonwoods. Some of the women were rousing from their slumber. Grey Bear lay facing away from them sleeping. The winds blew his hair away from his face, revealing the patch of black where his ear once had been. Fresh wounds marred his face with dried blood. His hands, too, were deeply scratched.

Strong Deer thought of Running Dog and her heart sank. She crouched by the fire pit and moved the dead ashes aside, finding a smoldering ember and isolating it with a stick. She collected a handful of small twigs and bunch grass stems to place around the live ember, leaned in, lightly blew under the cluster. A light wisp of smoke wafted up and dissipated in the swirling breeze. She stacked the small bits of wood on top of the flame and the fire grew.

Her breath was visible in the crisp morning air. Her eyes wandered to Grey Bear and the blood and she wondered what happened.

Strong Deer stood, picked up the two bladders and gestured for Spider Woman to follow her to the river.

They walked in silence, weaving their way through the tangled alders, and came to the hole Grey Bear had broken in the ice. It had re-frozen, so Strong Deer broke it open with a rock and filled a bladder full of water. Spider Woman took a drink, her eyes on the bluffs across the river.

Strong Deer filled the second bladder and brought it to her lips. She took a long drink of the icy water, the cold chilling her bones. She cradled the bladder in her arms and glanced at Spider Woman.

"Only a day's journey to the Benton's Fort now."

"Yes," Spider Woman said. "Only a day's journey." Spider Woman stared at the bluffs. Her eyes narrowed, and a tear fell down her cheek.

"Come. Let us go back. Grey Bear will be rising soon," Strong Deer whispered.

All of the women were up and moving around, Forest Water, Calf Mother, Sight of Day, and the others. Grey Bear had risen and moved to the edge of the clearing where he sat against the trunk of a cottonwood and he blankly stared at them.

Strong Deer knelt down beside him.

"Grey Bear, please, drink," she said, offering him the bladder.

He brought it to his lips and took a swallow. Strong Deer studied his tired face, the lines around his mouth and eyes ran deep, the gray in his long hair as the light breeze blew it across his shoulders. Last night's blood was still thick on his face. She moistened her fingers with snow and gestured with her hand so that she may clean the blood. Grey Bear brought his eyes to hers and relaxed as he again looked at camp. She ran her damp fingers across his face, wiping the blood away.

Falling Leaf appeared out of the woods carrying three snowshoe hares and a pine marten. Strong Deer stood.

They gathered around the fire, Forest Water, Calf Mother, Sight of Day, Falling Leaf, and Strong Deer, and skinned the animals, Forest Water and Calf Mother fleshing out the hides with sharp rocks and braining them to soften them. Strong Deer cut the meat and handed chunks to Sight of Day and Falling Leaf who roasted it over the fire. They placed the cooked meat inside of a bladder so it may stay hot.

They labored wordlessly, each glancing at Grey Bear with questions on their faces. Spider Woman and the rest were doing the same as they returned from the river and whispered in hushed tones. Strong Deer continued to slice the meat and noticed Forest Water watching her with her tired eyes.

"It doesn't matter how it happened," Strong Deer said. "Running Dog is dead."

Forest Water stretched a hide, frowned, and put the hide down.

"You know it matters," she said. "I mourn Running Dog, but Grey Bear may have disgraced himself and may bring the wrath of Napi and doom us, after all of this."

Forest Water gestured to the north where they came from. "We do not know. But we do know that Running Dog had angered him."

Falling Leaf picked up the bladder of meat and walked toward Grey Bear. Strong Deer dropped the knife, peered at Forest Water.

"Grey Bear is a great warrior who would never disgrace us. He struck Running Dog and he was right to do so but now he mourns his son, and if you think that Running Dog has died by his hands, it is you who disgraces us, and you who will curse us."

Strong Deer chopped more forcefully. Forest Water glanced down at the hide in her hands.

"I never said that he killed Running Dog; I only say that—"

Falling Leaf screamed.

"I do not want any food! Feed the others!" Grey Bear bellowed.

His voice boomed through the valley and every head jerked up startled. Bits of cooked flesh were strewn over the snow. Falling Leaf cried and scurried to pick them up, crawling from one chunk to the next on her knees.

"You will all eat as we walk," he said. "Let us move on now to the Benton's Fort." The anger dissipated as quickly as it came. He faced Strong Deer.

"You will lead them."

He disappeared into the alders, towards the river. Strong Deer glanced at the others and they began to walk.

She led them into the cottonwoods heading east and southeast and following the river's flow. The winds were light and in her face. They were only a hard day's journey from their people and she thought that this moon would be their last on foot. This lightened her heart. The journey, although long, will be easy as they travel though the sandstone cliffs sheltered from the biting winds. She saw the looming cliffs, gave them thanks for this last protection. In the sky there were no clouds, no storms on the horizon.

This, too, gladdened her heart.

Strong Deer stepped over the blowdowns and heard nothing but the crunching of the feet behind her on the snow and the light breeze shifting the frozen woods. She thought of the absence of the slight figure ahead, the figure of a lone boy braving the biting winds and deep snows, and the pain found its way back into her heart.

Strong Deer remembered the springs of her youth, the morning sun shining down on the light sandstone, its rays glimmering off the smooth surface, running through the deep grasses of the riverbank in the morning, the fresh dew on her feet. She remembered Yellow Leaf, her constant companion with bright eyes of eight winters laughing. Her little fingers were stained with the colors of choke cherries and service berries and camas bulbs they picked and brought back to the lodges. Cool breezes blew off the river as she raced to the lodges, her small feet bouncing off the cool earth like the wags-his-tails and the rabbits bounding through the thickets. Yellow Leaf ran to catch up, her laughter in Strong Deer's ears and the whipping of her black hair behind her.

Strong Deer blinked, icy snow from the branches falling into her eyes. Behind her were the many faces hardened by struggle staring at the forest floor, each of them lost within themselves. Grey Bear walked apart from them, his head turned to the sandstones, his face hardened like the others but different somehow. Strong Deer looked ahead as the current's flow made its slow arc to the southwest and the mother river.

CHAPTER NINETEEN

CRIPPLE CREEK, COLORADO
1996

We drove down the two-lane highway in silence, both of us lost in thought. I glanced over at the game warden in his jeans and boots, tan western-style shirt and Fish, Wildlife and Parks baseball cap covering a mop of graying brown hair. His mustache covered most of his mouth. His eyes were trained on the road. I shifted in my seat next to him in the big truck.

"I appreciate you letting me tag along with you. I learned a lot. It'll make a good story," I said.

"Yeah, well, the real story will be when all these Californians move in here and they start butting heads with the bears. We need that spring hunt, if anything else for the sake of all the bears that'll have to be transplanted or put down because they got in too much trouble." He glanced sideways at me, the wrinkles around his eyes deepening. "People don't know any better. Hell, they'll feed the sons of bitches to get them to come in every-day. Then they wonder why their homes get broken into and demolished."

I took note of his words, thinking I could paraphrase him in the article I was doing about him and the move to eliminate the spring bear hunt in Colorado.

I had gotten offered this job at a small newspaper in rural Colorado when I finished college. The publisher decided to take a chance on me after I submitted my writing samples, and I was grateful. It was good working around and writing about what I love, the mountains and wild animals and fish. I glanced out the window at the imposing mountains looming straight up from the side of the highway and then shooting down to the canyon below. We headed west from Colorado Springs to the small community of Woodland Park, where my newspaper was based.

The paper serves many of the surrounding communities, Divide, Victor, Cripple Creek, all small mountain towns of a couple hundred people or less with the exception of Cripple Creek, which flourished as a gambling town. But even the people of Cripple Creek hunt and fish. They cared about how elk herds were managed and habitat preservation, about water purity in streams and rivers and how it affects the trout.

The narrow canyon that the warden and I were driving through opened into a small valley, the houses and businesses appearing all of a sudden, condensed, seemingly crammed together by the surrounding mountains. We drove down the main drag of town.

The warden pulled his truck into the gravel parking lot of the newspaper office, a small three-room building with a faux log cabin exterior and a canopied front deck. I opened the truck door. "Thanks Dave. I'll do a good job on this."

Paula, the editor, was busy piecing together articles and ads on the large drawing board she used to lay out our paper once a week. She arranged small pieces of paper, fitting them together like a jigsaw puzzle. She looked like an editor, a middle-aged woman with short, graying dark hair and glasses. Her expression told me something I didn't like.

"Hi, Calvin. You need to call your mother, she's trying to reach you."

"Oh?"

"I tried Dave's cell but it must've been out of range."

I thanked her and sat at my little desk in the middle room, picked up the phone.

"Mom."

"Calvin, we took Dad to the hospital yesterday with pneumonia."

"Pneumonia? What, he decide to go ice fishing down there?"

She drew in her breath.

"Is he okay?" I asked, the pit of my stomach starting to burn.

"He died this morning."

I said nothing, feeling everything wash away.

"Calvin? Are you … are you okay?" She was crying.

"Let me call you back. I'm all right."

"I gotta go," I said to Paula. She just nodded, the color leaving her face.

I headed west, the opposite direction from my apartment and the highway to Texas. Needed to get back to the woods for a few minutes, get away from people and phones.

I saw the little post office in Victor, saw the little tavern across the street. I pulled my truck into the driveway. The cool air hit my face, the smell of pines wafting down with the thermals, the sharp, pungent aroma enveloping my senses.

The bartender, a kid with long blond hair and a stocking cap, said hello. I sat on the barstool and ordered a whiskey-Coke. He asked me what brand and I said I didn't care.

I guzzled it down and ordered another one. I'm going back to Texas. Have to go back. Not just for the funeral. Dead. I remembered when I was a kid hearing him tell somebody that if something ever happened to me he would just lay down in the coffin with me. If I died he'd have no more reason to live, no reason to be here. Well, Dad, it works both ways, you know? What am I going to do without you?

I took the second drink and moved to a table next to a window, my back away from the bartender. My stomach turned inside out, heart exploding. I began to cry, a crying I had never done, pulled from deep down, always held in, an old stagnant hurt that came up and peeked out for the first time.

The bartender was moving behind me, reaching down on the table with another drink.

"This one's on me, man."

CHAPTER TWENTY

FORT BENTON, MONTANA
FEBRUARY 1870

Lone Fox gazed into the bright embers of his dying fire as he chewed the last bite of dried pemmican. The camp dogs barked outside his lodge and he looked around. Others emerged from their own lodges, their heads turned to the northwest at the shadowy figures beginning to appear out of the darkness. His wife, Spotted Rabbit, had set down her fleshing stone and deer hide. Lone Fox held a finger up and then closed the hide entrance to the lodge. He trotted up to the dark figures with several of the braves in camp.

A woman led the small group with twelve others following in a slow moving line, all women. Lone Fox looked behind them at the fort in the distance. The lights of the worn down structure shined through its artillery holes and the sentry guards paced along its edges. His ear listened for any sound, any shouts, but he heard none. They had not seen this group approach. The woman leader stopped in front of him.

Lone Fox's eyes widened with astonishment. Strong Deer, a distant relation of Spotted Rabbit who he had seen in winters past at the Sun Festivals with Heavy Runner's people, stood before him. She was tired and thin and looked much older than he remembered.

"Why do you and the others come to us in the dead of winter looking so weak?" he asked. "Where are your people? Has something happened to your great chief Heavy Runner?"

The young braves who had followed Lone Fox circled the group of women who huddled close to each other behind Strong Deer with unbelieving eyes.

Strong Deer's lips quivered.

"Our great chief Heavy Runner is dead, Lone Fox. Murdered by the Napikwans."

Lone Fox's heart tightened. The braves sucked in their breaths and whispered to each other in anger. Lone Fox knew that their anger would grow stronger, and it would not be long before he heard war cries.

"Brothers, we will not speak of this until we have heard everything. Hold your tongues and take your thoughts away from your knife and bow for now. Do you understand?"

Plenty Hawk had joined them and for this Lone Fox was grateful. Plenty Hawk was highly respected, an old warrior with many coups who the braves would listen to and obey. Lone Fox turned back to Strong Deer.

"Did the men fight the Napikwans who did this thing? Where are they now?"

Strong Deer said, "Our men had gone away to the Bears Paw to hunt the blackhorns as we were out of meat. There were no men in camp, save the chief and a few of the elders who could no longer hunt. Our men will hunt for many moons until they find enough meat for us to last the winter. They, I think, have now returned to camp and seen the dead and will track down the Napikwan soldiers. The snows were heavy, though, and I fear they will not succeed."

Strong Deer looked into the open plains behind her and the blackness.

"There is only one man with us. He and his brave son were captured as they returned early from the hunt. It is Grey Bear."

Lone Fox listened to her words but his eyes were distracted by a shadowy movement behind the women. A lone figure appeared out of the darkness. The braves whispered as they recognized him. Grey Bear stopped next to Strong Deer.

Lone Fox stepped back. This man could not be Grey Bear, with whom he had waged war against the Crow in winters past and who had counted coup on four different braves, each time holding the scalp high and bellowing a piercing battle cry. Lone Fox had seen Grey Bear acquire many fine horses, riding off in plain daylight on Crow lands. He had big medicine, a powerful medicine bag and a ghost bear that watched over him. The young braves were a little afraid of Grey Bear.

Grey Bear was gaunt, the once powerful muscles in his arms withered and slight, eyes sunken in and downcast, many lines etched into his face. Grey Bear the warrior was gone, Lone Fox thought. Here was a fallen-in man.

"Come," Lone Fox said. "We will go to my lodge and feed you and give you a warm robe. We will then meet with Chief Old Man Coyote in his lodge."

Grey Bear looked up, his eyes not meeting Lone Fox but turning to the Napikwan fort and then to the barren hills past it.

Plenty Hawk eyed Grey Bear with a fearful expression. Lone Fox grunted, gestured toward the camp. They walked toward the lodges surrounded by the curious women.

∂

Spotted Rabbit placed a robe around Grey Bear's shoulders, and stacked fresh logs on the dying fire and he stared into the flames as they built. The warmth surrounded his cold body.

"Spotted Rabbit, go kill one of the young dogs so that we may have fresh meat," said Lone Fox. She left the lodge. Lone Fox pulled out a chunk of dried pemmican.

"Here," he said, handing the meat to Grey Bear. "Eat this and warm up. Spotted Rabbit will be back shortly and then you will feel stronger."

Grey Bear bit into it, the sweet flavors of pounded service berries and dried blackhorn meat reawakening his taste buds. He grunted in appreciation.

They rested in silence for a moment, Grey Bear chewing the pemmican as they sat across from each other. Lone Fox's mind had many questions, but he respectfully waited.

Spotted Rabbit returned with fresh puppy meat and placed it in a pot to cook. As the water over the fire boiled, the smell of fresh meat wafted through the lodge and awakened Grey Bear's stomach. Spotted Rabbit removed the tender flesh, folded it in a swath of deerskin, and handed it to Grey Bear. He ate in silence, the meat juice warm in his hands and mouth.

When he was done and the bones were clean, Lone Fox rose and gestured for Grey Bear to follow. They left the lodge and walked toward Chief Old Man Coyote's lodge, lit up and alive with men inside.

The elder braves Plenty Hawk and White Arm were seated around the blazing fire. Grey Bear looked to Chief Old Man Coyote who was seated apart, dancing shadows partly obscuring his welcoming face.

"Come, Grey Bear, sit with us. We will smoke and listen to the story of you and your people," Old Man Coyote said.

Old Man Coyote lit his pipe which was decorated with symbols of his spirit animal and an eagle feather that danced with his movement. He held this pipe above his head with both hands and the men sat in silence.

"I welcome my people to my home this day and to Napi, overseer of all things living and in the Sand Hills, I speak. I wish that my people reach the next winter in safety. I wish that my children multiply and when my sons go to war, I wish that they return with many coups and when they hunt, may they always have the wind in their faces. I wish that the blackhorn may return in numbers and the plants and cherries thrive and be plentiful, and that no illness befalls us."

Old Man Coyote held the pipe higher still and closed his eyes.

"I say this to the great mountains and the big rivers and little creeks, smoke. I say this to the Above Ones, smoke, and to the Below Ones and to the Ones Beneath Water, smoke. And I say to the Winds of the Four Quarters, smoke. I offer smoke to all of these beings who watch over us so that they may aid us in our decision about this great wrong committed by the Napikwan. And I say to these beings, if we wage battle to avenge those who have been murdered, may we all blacken our faces in token of victory and may the hearts of the murdered ones gladden as they watch from the Sand Hills."

Old Man Coyote opened his eyes and brought the pipe to his lips. He handed it to Grey Bear, seated to his left, and the pipe was thus passed around.

"And so, great warrior Grey Bear, how did our people come to be murdered so?"

Grey Bear exhaled as he passed the pipe to White Arm, who took it solemnly. Grey Bear told them how he and Running Dog were captured and how they saw the many charred bodies of their people in the burned camp and about the Napikwan soldiers who were drunk with the white man's water and who led them to the Canadian border only to release them for no reason.

Grey Bear told the men of his people's journey back to the Marias, how many died of thirst and how many froze to death in the middle of the night as they slept.

The pipe was passed to Grey Bear. The food and the warmth and the smoke made his eyes grow heavy and he fought to keep awake. He did not tell these men what became of Kipataki nor of his early vision of Cold Maker nor how his son died. Surely they had heard already through the women's talk about Running Dog's bravery getting back the knife from the Napikwans. These men questioned nothing and Grey Bear was grateful.

They sat in silence for a moment after Grey Bear finished speaking, each taking the pipe when it was passed to him. The air was stifling with the smoke and Grey Bear's stomach turned. He swallowed hard.

Old Man Coyote cleared his throat. "The great chief Heavy Runner has been murdered along with many of our women and children. For this we must have vengeance. The Napikwans are never to be trusted, this we all have known. But this—"

Old Man Coyote grunted.

"For five winters the Napikwan soldiers have made this fort their home. Before this, for many winters Napikwan trappers traded their furs when the beaver were still plenty. These Napikwans were mostly good. And until today we allowed the soldiers their fort for we have profited trading our furs and hides for their knives and many-shot rifles. Like Heavy Runner, I too have signed a treaty with these Napikwan soldiers to never wage war on them. It was a treaty of peace, so I thought, a way our people could live near them without blood being spilled. But never did I trust them and today my treaty is as good as Heavy Runner's was."

Grey Bear heard the anger in the chief's words become heavier with each breath. Plenty Hawk and White Arm had murder in their eyes. Grey Bear's tired mind tried to see the Napikwan soldiers and muster the anger but then there was only Running Dog on the Marias, Running Dog and his look of horror and then letting go. That was all he had to do, hold on, but he let go. Or was it I who let go? Grey Bear wondered.

Hold on to the things you love, Grey Bear.

Cold Maker's words came to him in a flash and Grey Bear's half-closed eyes opened wide. The men all looked at him with surprise. Old Man Coyote leaned forward.

"My fellow brothers," Grey Bear said. "My band is gone save the few men who will return and the few women who have come here this day. I have seen the horrors the Napikwan have done and I agree that we must wage war and curse their name. But I have lost my only son and my heart is not right. I must go to the place of my spirit animal and build a sweat box and speak to the great he-grizzly that has given me so much medicine in battle. There is a battle now, brothers, in my heart. Only he can win it."

Grey Bear chose his words carefully.

"Brothers, if you love me as I love you, you will do this thing for me. I need a horse, a strong buffalo runner that will take me to the place of my youth, past the sacred wall in the forests to the west, to the great mountains that clouds touch. Do this thing for me, brothers, and when my heart heals I will return and join you in battle."

The men looked down and Old Man Coyote leaned back on his robe. The chief drew another breath from the pipe and exhaled, smoke catching the upward thermal of the fire.

"And it will be so, Grey Bear."

Spotted Rabbit had already laid out a robe in which Grey Bear could sleep. He welcomed this and immediately fell into a deep slumber. Next to Spotted Rabbit lay Lone Fox, watching the dying fire's shadows on the walls, seeing the many shapes of the wise and crafty fox, his spirit animal, in the flickering light.

He turned and gazed at Grey Bear, watched the matted blackness of his hair. He saw for the first time Grey Bear's missing ear, just a hole surrounded by an angry circle of redness, and the deep lines around his eyes and mouth. What horrors he had seen, Lone Fox thought. This rekindled the anger in his heart.

Lone Fox had never seen the land of Grey Bear's youth, but once when camped on a bluff with Grey Bear he heard tell of it, this land of Grey Bear's spirit animal. Many high mountains, he said, mountains that reached heights too high for the trees and the snow covered them for all seasons. He said there were many rivers, creeks, and small lakes, and in the valleys was a forest so dense that one could hardly step on the earth and must walk on fallen trunks of larch, spruce, and lodge pole pine.

The thing that most interested Lone Fox about this far-off place was the wall that guards this land on the east, a wall taller than any sandstone cliff on the Marias or any break on the Upper Missouri or any peak in the Bears Paw. It ran straight up, Grey Bear said, and when standing on the open prairies by the Sun River one's eyes could not see the end of this wall from the north or south. Grey Bear said he found a break in the looming cliff which he used to pass it.

Lone Fox stared at the top of his lodge and imagined Grey Bear as a boy, a tiny figure climbing up this break, his small legs moving higher and higher and then disappearing over it where the clouds meet. Lone Fox looked at his friend, now a broken old man moaning at the nightmares that haunted him, and wondered how he could do this thing again. Lone Fox turned his gaze to Spotted Rabbit's soft bronze skin shining in the fire's light and he drifted off to sleep.

The sun peeked over the eastern horizon, the rays seeping into the lodge's hole and onto the sleeping face of Lone Fox. He opened his eyes, blinded by the light before turning to the empty bed of Grey Bear and then to the sounds of Spotted Rabbit pouring water into an iron kettle.

"Where has Grey Bear gone?"

"He waits for you outside," she said, gesturing towards the north where the camp's wrangle horses were staked.

Lone Fox drank from a bladder of water, then stepped out of the lodge and into the biting cold morning air. Two young braves talked in hushed tones. Already they spoke of their glories in battle with the Napikwans, Lone Fox thought, and he called them over.

"Take the wrangle horses and bring in our herd," Lone Fox said. They ran in the direction of the staked horses. Grey Bear stood alone in the white prairie, his face turned away to the west. Lone Fox walked to where Grey Bear stood and together they watched the boys untie long ropes from a cluster of sagebrush. They looped the ropes around the horses' necks and tied a bowline, then mounted the two ponies and rode to the west in the direction of the windswept hills where the herd grazed.

"How many moons' journey will it be?" Lone Fox asked.

"Three." Grey Bear's voice cracked and he cleared his throat. "Three moons' hard ride west on the River of The Sun. And then I will cross the wall."

The winds picked up and Lone Fox squinted as the hard snow blew in his face.

"You will need a warm robe, some snares, and plenty of pemmican," Lone Fox said. "And Spotted Rabbit will give you an extra pair of moccasins."

"I will not forget what you do for me, brother. I am in your debt. In this world. And the next."

Lone Fox began to ask a question but the sound of many hooves on the cold earth was heard and the horses appeared on the ridge running full speed. The young braves followed shouting and whooping. When the herd reached the prairie, the horses slowed to a trot and then stopped.

A fine herd of horses, Grey Bear saw, numbering upwards of fifty head. He watched each one, inspecting them from a distance. Many fine Crow horses: piebald, bay, sorrel, chestnut, dun, and buckskin. They ran together in a fluid motion, swerving past half-buried boulders and ruts. They moved collectively, like geese flying south or schools of fish darting through water. Grey Bear focused on one of the herd's leaders, a big grulla with a dark dorsal stripe running the length of his back.

"Catch that one and bring him to me," Grey Bear called to one of the boys.

"One of the chief's finest horses," Lone Fox said. "A fast buffalo runner. He is smart and has sure feet."

The boys slowly approached the horse with ropes held behind their backs. The grulla snorted, his eyes white. They whispered and the grulla's ears moved forward, his body relaxed. One boy slipped the rope around the horse's neck and walked to Grey Bear. The grulla obediently followed.

Grey Bear brought his lips to the horse's nostrils, breathing his breath into him. He untied the rope and fashioned it into a halter around the horse's head. Lone Fox and Grey Bear walked back to Lone Fox's lodge with the grulla.

They prepared in silence. Grey Bear changed into a pair of double-layered buckskin breeches. Spotted Rabbit gave him a new pair of moccasins. They were not the watertight heyoka stitch that Yellow Leaf would have made, but they were a fine pair nonetheless. Lone Fox gave Grey Bear a buckskin pack in which to carry pemmican and snares. Grey Bear fit the pack over the blackhorn robe that served as both a coat and a blanket in which to keep warm at night.

Grey Bear placed a blanket over the grulla's high withers and back. He grabbed a handful of mane and mounted the horse. The big grulla crow hopped a little but soon was calm. Grey Bear gave the horse a kick and reined the grulla in circles, checking his feet. The horse was nimble with a controlled burst of speed, a fine mount for the journey west. He trotted the horse back to Lone Fox.

Grey Bear tried to speak but could not as he looked into his friend's eyes. Lone Fox held up a palm and Grey Bear signaled back before giving the grulla a kick.

The chief stepped out of his lodge and held his hand high. Grey Bear returned his gesture. The sound of the horse's hooves brought the people from the lodges, the children, the women, the young braves and the old. They made way for him, watching with respect.

He reached the outer edges of the camp and standing together were the women, Strong Deer, Spider Woman, Sight of Day, Calf Mother, Forest Water, and young Falling Leaf. All of them looked with wonder and fear for they had not heard of this journey. Grey Bear rode past them, staring down on their faces. Strong Deer saw something in his eyes and drew in her breath. Falling Leaf broke from the group and reached for Grey Bear's leg but he gave the grulla a kick. The horse broke into a run and kicked up snow until it reached the western edge of the windswept prairie, where they appeared as nothing more than a cloud of white.

Strong Deer put her arm around the small shoulder of Falling Leaf, and together they watched the cloud of white grow smaller until the mist dissipated. The winds flew through camp. The hair of Falling Leaf swept the lone tear from her cheek as she stared at the white nothingness.

CHAPTER TWENTY-ONE

GARLAND, TEXAS
1996

I swallowed another shot of whiskey as I thought about the poor dog. Half-dead. Laying on his side, immobile, barely moving as he labored to breathe. His left eye was covered in a milky film from the cataracts that left him almost blind, and his right eye was only marginally better.

His coat had turned to an old matted gray. His body had developed the swayback, malnourished look of all old dogs. But still he lingered, day in and day out, there in the kennel inside the workshop in the backyard.

I sat on the bed that I slept in as a child when I came to visit my grandparents. Maw Maw was fast asleep in her bedroom and I was staring with a drunken focus at the wall, thinking about the dog. Charlie.

Charlie was a wire-haired fox terrier and in his prime was a rambunctious, feisty, lovable little dog. Only Charlie was born crippled, his hind leg deformed. Dad and Maw Maw doubted he would live. There wasn't just the botched-up leg. He was a runt, one of those undersized puppies which tend to get kicked out of the feeding frenzy and were left to die. So Dad supplemented his mother's milk with formula from a baby bottle. Did that for the few weeks it took for Charlie to get some density in those fragile bones, and soon he was running around with the rest of them, albeit with a funny little gait. Dad was like that, taking over when others don't.

Dad usually sold most of the pups from his litters, always getting top dollar because of the dogs' great bloodlines. He had usually kept one or two but he knew this would probably be the last litter so there was no sense in keeping any. Customers came and went, flocking to pick out their favorites. Then somebody came in and bought the last two healthy males, and so there was only Charlie. The puppy nobody wanted.

By then Dad and Maw Maw had taken a liking to the crippled dog, so they decided to keep him. Not that there was much choice in the matter.

As a kid, I played with Charlie when I was here, which was a lot. But even later when I stopped in from college, I always said hello to Charlie, and he always came running, his crooked leg ill-timed with the other three, causing that funny bounce of his hip to compensate. He jumped up to me as best he could, often coming down not on his feet but on his side, and still bouncing back up to do it over again. Like most dogs, Charlie was full of love, but I think unlike most dogs, he was given a double helping of it, in thanks for the family who took him in.

I sat on the bed in the middle of the night, drunk, as I was most nights after Dad's funeral. Charlie. Dog wouldn't give up living as a puppy and still wouldn't at thirteen. Laying on his side, blind, every now and then getting up and staggering over to his water bowl. He didn't eat much at all. Couldn't hold it down, I guessed. But he wouldn't let go. Charlie will lay there as long as it took, hanging on to his last few moments of life.

Charlie had been out there for ten days, ten days and no telling how much longer he would endure just for the sake of breathing in and out, just to hang on to the world a little longer. To see me coming to refill his water bowl and pet him on the head. And that's why he lived, for me.

Now here I was these last ten days, going out to Charlie's bed, feeding him what little food he could eat. All soft stuff, no dry food. And water. Kept him alive out in the workshop on that shag carpet bed of his. He was not able to do anything, all day and all night, but think about living. Think about me. Just live. That's all.

Only a little whiskey left then. I rose, almost falling, hitting my knee on the edge of the rickety television stand. Everything was foggy, just off to both sides. I saw good straight ahead. Singular. I drew back the curtain, looked into the dark rain outside and at the workshop. Lightning came down, illuminating the shop and pens lined up in front, each with an entrance to the shop where the dogs can get out of the rain. Except Charlie was the only one out there.

Shop had a heater but I wondered if he was warm enough. Bring him inside for the night? Make him more comfortable maybe. But Charlie ain't gonna be comfortable ever again. He wouldn't give up. I didn't want him to suffer any more. Tired of suffering.

"Fuck this!"

I turned around quickly. Too quickly. The world was spinning. I paused, waited for my vision to catch up. I groped through the kitchen, bumped into the table, opened the back door and the cold, wet air blasted my face. I had a T-shirt and jeans on, barefoot.

The blast cleared my head and vision enough for me to make it down the stairs. The rain came down in biting pellets, hitting the top of my head, my shoulders, running down my chest. It was dark out, everything blurry, everything in shadows. Had to go on memory, on feel. My bare feet shuffled on the concrete patio, past the table where me and Dad used to fillet fish together. I saw the gate and felt for the latch.

It was dark, smelled musky. Cold despite the little propane heater in the corner. My clouded vision picked out the semblance of kennels inside, tools lined up on the opposite wall, and the big crack in the concrete floor. I used it as a guide, stepping on it, feeling the cool, uneven floor.

Through the musky odors of the old, damp shop, rotted wood and rusty tools, I smelled Charlie's old, sick dog smell. His breathing was muted, barely a light sigh as I stood by the chain link gate. I bent down and lost my balance, falling forward and crashing the top of my head into the cold metal. I fell on my side in agony, writhing on the damp concrete. The blood trickled down my face, whiskey making the pain into a comfortable, hazy throb.

I pulled myself up from the concrete and sat in front of Charlie. He didn't move, just contemplated me with his cloudy left eye.

"Hey, boy, how you doing?"

He lifted his head and then slowly brought it down again. His ear was cocked and listening.

"Me leaving you out here like this. It's my fault, Charlie. You don't know no better."

I edged up to the gate, leaned in. The damp smell of his coat wafted up from his bed. I felt his stare. My hand nudged the latch loose. Charlie's ear shifted. The gate swung out.

"C'mon old boy."

I felt around his body, picked him up and brought him out. I sat down against the metal toolbox behind me and cradled him in my lap.

"You've been a good dog, Charlie. You did real good, boy."

His body was limp against my thighs, the rough; wiry hair brushed the wet denim of my pants. The world was spinning in a sweeping series of darks and grays as the incessant rain pattered against the sheet metal roof. My desperate, drifting mind raced away, wanting something far-off and unreachable: Ivey dancing in a field of flowers, the hint of cigar smoke in an old brown Chevy, Dad chuckling and telling stories. I gave up and returned to him. A gun would wake the neighbors. A knife was too messy. This was the only way.

"I'm sorry, old boy."

I gripped the back of his head with one hand, his nose with the other, and twisted violently.

A brief whimper. A dull crack.

I looked down at his motionless body and began to cry, carefully placed him back in his bed. I stroked the old matted fur and then closed the door.

Gripping the corner of the kennel, I pulled myself up and stumbled outside to the rains.

⁊

"Calvin."

"Yeah?"

I wake up in a stupor, my head exploding from the dull ache that hit at once, subsided, then returned. There was the blurry image of Maw Maw peeking at me from the door of my room.

"It's Charlie," she said.

I forced my eyes to focus and saw the gaunt expression on her face.

"He's gone?" I asked.

"No. He's just lying there like he usually does, but he's whimpering and can't even move now. I think he's getting ready to die." Maw Maw narrowed her eyes. "Say, what happened to your head? Looks like there's blood on it."

My heart recoiled in horror. I didn't kill him. He lived. Oh Jesus, he lived.

"Um. Bumped it on the desk last night looking for something. I'll go out and check on Charlie."

Maw Maw shook her head.

"I just hate seeing the poor thing suffer. I know how much you and Dad loved him." She closed the door.

I fought against the urge to vomit and stood up, the blunt pain in my head causing me to suck in my breath. I forced myself to walk to the kennel.

I sat by his limp figure, listened to his low moans and wanting to absorb his pain. I sat until my back ached, until my legs cramped, never moving, never leaving.

Maw Maw peered in every couple of hours and asked, "Is he gone?" and I replied "Not yet."

The rains had ceased leaving the fresh fragrance of light dew on the grass. I hoped Charlie could smell the grass. I hoped he could feel the newness of the world. I hoped in his mind he was playing out there then, romping about with his awkward gait as I threw him a ball.

The wind picked up and brought the sweet freshness of life into the darkness. I looked down at my friend and saw that he was not breathing.

"Good boy."

CHAPTER TWENTY-TWO

EAST OF THE CHINESE WALL, MONTANA
FEBRUARY 1870

It was a world of white and blue. And it was in the half world of blue where Grey Bear's mind willed himself to be. His spirit was up there, floating through the light winds in the cloudless sky above the half world of white, the half world of death and ghosts. He freed himself from these things and looked with detachment at the vast prairie, the wide flatlands with the River of the Sun etching through and flowing east. He saw the lone dark figure of himself on the grulla moving west along the river to its source in the mountains.

But even in the half world of blue his spirit still looked away from the river. It was a river like the Marias, with ice reaching from its banks to its center where a thin swath of open water still flowed. The river meandered through the white flat prairie where its ice merged with the snows until it, too, disappeared where the two half worlds met. It was not the Marias, but the sight of it brought the ghosts to his mind so he still looked away.

There were no other living things in the half world of white. No sign of game, no tracks of horse or man, friend or enemy. There were only the tracks of the grulla.

Dull pain crept up the insides of Grey Bear's thighs. He was no longer in the half world of blue but back on the endless prairie. The grulla exhaled a thick stream of warm breath. The horse's eyes were steady, ears twitched, mane flowed back in the winds. Dark sweat outlined the blanket. The grulla's muscles moved in a steady rhythm.

The two half worlds of sky and earth met at the western horizon, and yet the horizon belonged to neither world. Grey Bear's dark eyes squinted, tried to see the mountains of his youth. They were too far and he gave up, focused instead on the horizon itself, a place far off, a place of nothing, belonging nowhere, a place from which he came and a place he went in this half world of white.

ॐ

The sun dipped below the horizon and everything became hazy as the blue and white merged. Grey Bear reined the grulla further away from the river. There was no cover, not even shallow coulees or low buttes, just the flatness of the wide open prairie under the darkening sky. Grey Bear pulled the reins back and released. The grulla halted and turned its head, an eye looking back at the rider.

Grey Bear dismounted, pain shooting up his legs as he landed on the hard snow. His knees started to buckle and he moved his feet to recover feeling. He let the lead rope fall to the ground. As the grulla pawed the earth and grazed on buried fescues, Grey Bear cleared a spot and lay down. He shivered, and thoughts of the cold Marias brought the doomed face of Running Dog. Grey Bear grunted and winced, pulling his arms and legs into his body. He longed for the silence. He stared into the dark sky, wanted to be back up there in his mind, away.

It was dark but there were many stars and he saw the outline of the river's edge as it snaked towards the Benton's Fort and his people.

Strong Deer.

Yellow Leaf.

He abandoned them like Kipataki and Running Dog. No, no, it was not so.

Many points of light reflected off the ice. His eyes followed the river's current to the west. A subtle movement brought his attention closer; there was something across the river.

A lone figure stood on the bank and faced him. It was a woman, her features hazy but she was dressed in white, her dark hair flowed with the winds. Yellow Leaf. She walked across the prairie, disappeared into the blackness.

He pulled his robe tighter. It was not his wife, he thought, only a trick of Cold Maker. Yes, only a trick. He watched the warm air of his breath as he exhaled, a tear sliding down his cheek.

স্ক

The grulla's soft whinny pierced the cold morning air. The horse stood just a few paces away pawing the snows and nibbling the uncovered fescues and bunch grasses.

Grey Bear rose, his legs tight. He took the horse blanket and approached the grulla as it raised its head.

"Did you get your belly full last night, my friend?" Grey Bear ran a hand down the horse's stern. With his other hand, he placed the blanket on the grulla's back and, grabbing a handful of mane, mounted the horse and reined it west.

The grulla found its gait and Grey Bear felt the steady rhythm of the horse's hooves, heard the wet swishing of hooves cutting through soft snow and finding firm earth. He reached into his pack and retrieved a handful of pemmican. He looked to the north as he chewed and noted the coming cloud cover. There was a subtle change in the winds, the air more dense.

Loneliness overcame him and he wished for his friend the hawk to appear. He thought of the spring rains to comfort him, and then of Thunder.

Grey Bear remembered the smoke-filled lodge of Old Man Coyote and the looks of murder on the faces of the men, the passing of the medicine pipe and how the warmth of the fire and the tobacco's stench turned his stomach. But the tobacco and the warmth also drew the men together. Tobacco smoked from the medicine pipe was a gift of countless winters ago to the Piegan people, a gift from Thunder.

Before the Napikwan, the Piegan most feared Thunder. The enemy Crow, Flathead, or Kootenai could be fought; the bear could be run from or tricked; sickness could be cured; but the Piegan could not escape Thunder. He shouted across the prairie, and he cried out from the tops of mountains. Thunder did not like the lone cliffs or the trees or the standing man. He toppled them all to the ground and crushed them.

Long ago, almost in the beginning, a Piegan warrior was awakened by Thunder's cries in the night. He was knocked senseless, and his lodge burned to the ground, and when he awoke he found his wife was missing.

Maybe she goes to fetch water or wood, he thought. But another moon passed and she had not returned, so this warrior was angered and sought out Thunder. On his quest, he encountered Raven.

Raven asked, "Where do you journey?"

The warrior said, "I seek the dwelling place of Thunder, for he has stolen my wife."

Raven's wings fluttered. "You dare to enter the lodge of Thunder? Know he takes without asking and destroys anything that displeases him, but know also that the lodge of Thunder is decorated with eyes, eyes of those he has taken or killed. And you wish to enter his lodge still?"

"What man can look on such things and live? But I must go," said the warrior.

"Then if you must continue," said the Raven, "take this." Raven handed the man one of his feathers. "There is only one who Thunder fears and it is I, the chief of the Ravens. He fears me because I have the vision he cannot possess, all the eyes in his lodge do not have the vision that is mine. So my medicine is the greater. Take the feather, and it will protect you."

The warrior took the feather and walked many moons to Thunder's stone lodge. He entered and his heart grew small when he saw the many eyes that hung from the rock walls. He looked with horror until a voice boomed and echoed off the high walls.

"Who dares to enter my lodge? No man enters this place and lives!"

"You have my wife. You have stolen her," said the warrior. "There on the wall hang her eyes."

Thunder rose to strike the warrior, but the man took the Raven feather from his medicine bag. Thunder shuddered and stepped back. The warrior's heart grew bigger and he approached Thunder.

"Stop," said Thunder. "Your medicine is the stronger. You shall have your wife back." And she appeared by his side.

"You know me," said Thunder. "I have a great power. I make the rains come and the grasses grow and the berries ripen." Thunder handed his medicine pipe to the man. "You and your people will pray to me every spring. You will fill and smoke this pipe, and pray that I bring you these things with the passing of each winter. Now go."

࿚

Grey Bear watched the light snows fall on the flat prairie as the grulla kept walking, and he remembered how his father would always end the story.

"And so that is how," Grey Bear's father had said, "our people got the first medicine pipe. It was long ago."

Grey Bear's thoughts returned to the meeting with Old Man Coyote. Grey Bear saw hate and venom in the other men's eyes. But then, under the quiet falling of the light snows and the flatness, Grey Bear remembered something he then did not consider. There was fear. Fear of the Napikwan. Maybe, Grey Bear thought, the Napikwan was like Thunder.

The clouds were thicker and darker, the sun just a dull haze of half-yellow peeking over the western horizon. The River of the Sun was to the north and the current flowed faster. He turned west and concentrated on the horizon which was then less distinct. The snows were falling harder. Maybe, on a clear day, he could see the mountains in the distance.

The Napikwan, Grey Bear thought, take without asking, they do not like the lone cliffs or the trees that they cut down or the standing man whom they topple and crush. They take something with them, like the eyes that decorate Thunder's lodge, only it is not eyes but something else they think gives them power and vision. They, too, covet the thing they think is real but is not.

The Raven has the greater medicine, but what is greater than the Napikwan? What do they fear?

Grey Bear thought of the vision of Yellow Leaf and his heart hurt, then of Running Dog who he will never be with again, not in the Sand Hills, not here. He was just gone and will forever be a boy, will never have his own herd of horses or a wife and children.

He was a forever boy that Grey Bear's eyes will never look upon again.

I am a father no more, Grey Bear thought, *nor a husband.*

w=His lips tightened.

He dismounted, dropped his lead rope, took the horse blanket, and kicked the snows from the earth to make his bedding. He lay down with the blanket and the blackhorn robe, closed his eyes and slept, dreamless, in neither half-world like the horizon.

⌒

There was a heaviness on his chest. Grey Bear rose, the blanket of snow scattering. The whiteness pierced his eyes. He blinked, waited for them to focus. The grulla was up the river, dragging the frozen lead rope. Grey Bear warmed his hands by rubbing them together. The sky was clearing, patches of light blue were mixed with the puffy, low-lying cloud cover. Through the sparkling whites was the outline of towering mountains in the distance, the mountains of his youth.

Grey Bear's feet sunk in the deep snows almost to his knees. He carried the horse blanket and his pack, his breath heavy with exertion.

The grulla chewed a mouthful of the frozen fescues. Grey Bear rubbed its stern and wiped a thin layer of snow from the horse's back. He laid the blanket over the horse's withers and then picked up the frozen lead rope, worked it with his hands to loosen it.

⌒

There was still only the white flatness to the three corners, but ahead was the distinct outline of the great mountains. Foothills sat below the looming peaks and he knew that in the middle was the great high wall of stone.

The grulla plowed through the heavy snows, sweat appearing around the edges of the blanket and freezing the dun-colored hair in small clumps. Grey Bear reached in his pack for pemmican and noted that there was little left. He tore a chunk in two and thought that he must set his snares once he reached the foothills.

He chewed the last bite of pemmican for a long time, savoring the juices of the dried serviceberry. He swallowed, the meat warming his body. He thought of his first journey past the wall in his youth, twenty winters ago.

The spring of his fifteenth winter, the prairie was not a half-world of white but rather of green. Fescues, bunch and switch grasses covered the prairie floor. It was a world of life, many geese and ducks and cranes on the back eddies of the river and in the sky, herds of antelope, mule deer, and wapiti. He remembered the blackhorn herd he saw in the distance one day, looking like a dark blanket on the prairie that slowly moved across its length, hundreds of the creatures feasting on the grasses.

Grey Bear remembered seeing these things through young eyes, when everything was new, young, and undiscovered. He remembered the excitement in his heart as he rode his father's best buffalo runner, a young, quick-footed buckskin mare that danced through the lush greens.

He remembered the first sighting of the wall and how his young heart grew a little afraid, how he rode its length until he found the small draw to enter the mountains.

Grey Bear's hand held the grulla's makeshift reins, trembling with cold and age, the lines running deep around his calloused fingers. He brought his right hand to his face and felt the hole where his ear used to be. The scar tissue was rough and then he felt the hard lines around his eyes and mouth. The looming mountains came closer with each step and the outline of the wall was now visible. The foothills with dense timber were then visible. But there were only outlines, still just forms of what he remembered.

"I am old now," Grey Bear said out loud. "It is good that I made this journey in the spring as a boy, and now in the winter as a man. It is as it should be. But can I make the horrible climb now that my legs are no longer young? Can my horse make the climb in the deep snows and ice?"

Grey Bear pondered these questions as he watched the sky for winged creatures and saw none. He thought of his father.

"Yes, I am afraid, like the man who sought Thunder. But I have seen sign of the great he-grizzly leading me to this place of my youth so I must go."

No, Grey Bear thought, *it was not because of the signs only, it was for Running Dog. A chance to save Running Dog.*

But Grey Bear did not say this out loud because the sound of his name brought his son's frightened face.

CHAPTER TWENTY-THREE

SEATTLE, WASHINGTON
1997

Her hand ran up my arm, her soft touch easing away the cold Seattle rains. Her head was on my chest, her dark hair spilling over me. I still smelled the humid salt through the window joined by odors of the city itself, a subtle smell of fish markets and machinery and bustle, rising up to join the wildness of mountains and bays.

"When do you go back out?" she asked.

"Three days." I was taking off for the Oregon coast. Hake season. Not as profitable as pollock.

Her warm breath against my bare chest, her face tensed in thought. I met her only that night at a bar in West Seattle. It was the first place I headed when we docked at Fisherman's Terminal after being at sea for sixty days.

"How long will the season last?"

"It's only three weeks."

It was strange being on land again. I kept getting the sensation that I was walking slightly off-level. I was tired from being at sea for so long, tired from the storms and the eighteen-hour workdays. Tired of men.

Christ, got this beautiful woman right next to me and I'm thinking about fishing. The rain was coming down outside and the storm came to mind as I stared from a third-story apartment.

❧

I clapped my gloved hands together to get the feeling back. Damn freezer hold was twenty below but the only painful things were my feet and hands. Nothing I could do about my feet, though.

More boxes came down the chute, dozens of them at fifty pounds a pop. Scott, the Inuit combie working with me, loaded them on the conveyor belt and they were heading my way.

I was a combie, too. Deckhand half-time, factory worker half-time on board the *Carla Jean*, a 280-foot factory trawler. We were a hundred miles north of Dutch Harbor, Alaska in the Bering Sea.

Ice formed on my half-grown beard. I grabbed two boxes of surimi, scrambled across the hold, stacked them, rushed back and grabbed another two boxes, and another. I worked without thinking, too cold to think, the sweat trickled down my back under my insulated coveralls, my stocking cap frozen to my head. Boxes of roe then, me dashing to the opposite side of the hold and stacking. More boxes came, relentless.

Fred, the factory foreman, stuck his head down the hatch. "Calvin! Get up on top. They just dropped and they need help with the net."

I climbed the frozen ladder out of the hold, stripped off my coveralls and slipped into my Holly Hansen bibs.

I half-jogged the length of the factory, deafening machines all around and people sorting fish, conveyors of the viscera machines, workers separating roe from the rest of the guts. At the fore of the ship they were separating the species, pulling the pollock out and letting the rest move on: the sharks, squid, jellyfish, snapper, and halibut.

Climbing the ladder to the deck and opening the hatch, the wet winds took my breath away. No ordinary storm. The stern was pitching, mountainous waves bringing the ship up and down, steel of the hull whining as it came crashing into a valley of the sea.

Couldn't see good, everything so dark, cold. A figure approached as I tried to stay on my feet. Other figures appeared in the haze, scrambling this way and that. I made out the face coming at me, the deck boss.

"Get on those nets and get them cleaned off. We just dropped," he yelled and staggered back to the chute to help the deckhands.

Fuck. Job nobody wants. Leave it to the rookie. And something else bothered me, the look in his eyes, like he had seen a ghost up here or something. The net was lying in the middle of the stern; a cable ran from it to the hydraulic pulley above. It was huge, hundred yards long when stretched out, then just a mountain of rope, ten feet tall and thirty feet long.

The deck was slick with sea water and fish parts. I gripped the nylon cords of the net and looked up. The winds were picking up, biting, cold arctic winds and the rain was driving, searing the flesh of my face.

I hoisted myself up, my fingers prying out the cords and digging in, the soles of my boots wedging awkwardly as I climbed. The winds caught the hood of my jacket, knocking it down. The salty rains hit my neck and ran down my back. I fought to ignore that, ignore my chaffed fingers as the salt burned, ignore the gray sky and the blackness below.

At the top of the mound I pulled out the mangled fish parts and threw them in the direction of the set ramp at the stern. I moved from one section of the net to the next, picking out the bones and flesh and entrails of pollock and sharks and jellyfish and creatures I had never seen.

I strained to keep my balance. The ship was heading west toward Russia and the mounting storm, going up the side of a swell, peaking, then making its descent to where the sea would swamp the ramp.

Cleaning and tossing without looking, I made myself small to retain heat. The numbness in my hands and face edged in to my bones. It was a dull ache but I was glad for it. It was something to think about besides this dark nightmare.

It came in port-side. "Rogue wave!" A mountain of black came at us. I hugged the cords as tight as I could, pressing flat on the mound.

The wave hit with a deafening boom as I buried my face in the net. The frigid water pounded my back, forcing the air out of my lungs and causing me to suck in the rancid coldness, then cough it out.

The ship lifted as the wave passed under her hull. The starboard side dove down and the net lost its grip on the slick surface. I hugged the cords, buried myself as the net crashed against the starboard railing.

The force of the slide and the weight of the net wedged its bottom half into the railing. The top half propelled over the edge and I was dangling forty feet above the crashing water. I looked down and wasn't cold anymore, not hurt. Didn't feel anything. Just let go. I heard screaming and felt my arm being squeezed. I saw the deck boss and was pulled up.

☙

We lay together, held each other, listened to the rain. The clouds thickened and the darkness settled. She yawned soft, breathed steady.

"So how did you end up in Seattle all the way from Texas?" she asked.

The ceiling fan slowly turned.

"Just had to get out of there. Lost my dad last year and had to get away from everything for a while. Didn't want to be reminded of stuff."

"Yeah. Same here, sort of," she said. "Only I didn't lose anyone. Mostly I didn't fit in back in California, like it better up here."

She kissed me on the side of my mouth.

"I'm sorry," she said. She paused. "Think you'll stay after the season?"

"I'm going to Montana in May. I worked with the Fish and Game in Colorado and one of the guys said he knows an outfitter up there who'd teach me the ropes. Think I might try it for a year."

"Then you'd come back?"

"I don't know, maybe."

Katie rested her head on my chest. Her warm hand ran along my ribs and stopped. Her eyes were shut and, with her nestled in my arms, I drifted off to sleep.

There's something over there, something dark. If I can just make it to the edge of the woods there's a clearing. Something there, moving. Is it Ben the bear? No, another bear, not Ben. He looks at me with blood on his face and I see Charlie, lying dead, eyes clouded. Don't want to, but I step closer and the bear still stares at me. Then he whispers. NO TOYS.

"Calvin!"

I searched the room, gray and unrecognizable. Katie looked at me, her face pale and eyes scared.

"You were moaning and then you screamed. What's wrong?"

"I'm sorry, Ivey."

The creases in her forehead deepened.

"Ivey? Katie, you mean? Who's Ivey?"

I got up and in the dark felt around for my clothes.

"Whoa, where are you going? It's the middle of the night! I want to talk about this."

"I can't," I said. "I've just got to go." I found my shirt. She watched me, the light in her eyes casting a glare, her nervous fingers running through her hair. I reached for the door knob. She got up from the bed.

"Am I going to see you again?" she asked.

I opened the door. "I'm sorry, Katie."

I walked down through the vacant damp streets of Seattle. The rains had moved north leaving damp concrete and empty shops and fish markets, the occasional car whooshing past throwing water on the sidewalk. I headed west, past the Pike Place Market, and crossed the street to the path overlooking Puget Sound.

A heavy mist had formed above the calm surface of the cold, dark waters. A chill ran through my body. A jolting pain hit me at once and throbbed, warning me not to move again.

Where was I? Still on the island? I searched, finding familiarity in the cabins behind me. Yes. Vashon Island. My attention returned to the waters as I lay on the beach, shirt off, shivering.

I thought about the previous night of drinking at the bar, of the music and the people laughing and the complete forgetting, the whiskey going down faster and faster, me leaving. Blackness then.

No memory.

I thought about hake season, about those last three weeks of toil and smelly fish and packing boxes.

Fish. Reminded me of apples, Dad handing me an apple when we fished. Always used minnows as bait and the apples had those little minnow scales on them when he would hand them to me. Smelled like fish. But I ate them anyway.

"Anything happened to you, I'd be in the grave next to you," Dad told me once. I rested my head on the wet sand, closed my eyes.

Me too, Dad.

CHAPTER TWENTY-FOUR

BOB MARSHALL WILDERNESS, MONTANA
FEBRUARY 1870

The grulla surged up the forested hill, the frozen pine needles brushing Grey Bear's face. He leaned down and gripped the horse's mane. They reached the ridgeline of the foothill and the firs and pines opened up. Grey Bear reined in the grulla, and he saw it at last.

The wall began its ascent slowly, the vast forest beginning its curve up, the thick timbers a pure white that formed an endless wide swath to the north where it disappeared over the horizon. Then the timbers ended and the wall shot up for a great distance; its flat ridgeline loomed high above, a massive fortress of gray stone wall that touched the heavens.

Grey Bear dismounted and led the horse to the opposite end of the ridge where he looked south and saw the looming wall disappear over the southern horizon. He left the River of the Sun where it began to wind north, but Grey Bear then realized he would have to journey further south and watch carefully for the narrow draw. The many bumps and hills below the wall were thick with snow in the bottoms, but a ridgeline ran south with the wall and he decided to follow that for easier traveling.

But not now, Grey Bear thought. I will journey south and make the climb tomorrow when I am rested.

He untied the lead rope and fashioned a hobble around the horse's forelegs to keep it from traveling far in the night. He hung the horse blanket on a low-hanging branch of a nearby fir. His store of pemmican would soon be gone. The winds picked their way through the light timbers, chilling his body. He breathed on his hands, rubbed them together before opening the pack and bringing out the snares.

The snows slick under his feet, he descended to the bottoms searching for small tracks or game trails. Halfway down the hillside he saw a frozen creek. He inspected a patch of ground until he was satisfied that no sign was there, then he moved to the next patch. Grey Bear rested a knee in the soft snow and propped a foot against the trunk of a small fir.

A well-used narrow trail of hare tracks ran through the tangled brush. Past the tracks there was more sign. Grey Bear thought of a snowshoe hare's sweet flesh roasting over a flame and his stomach growled. The sun already below the looming wall, his time was short to set the snares.

High in the timbers, mimicking him, crouched down and staring back, stood Running Dog. Grey Bear sprung up, his foot slipping on the slick snow. He fell and, flat on the ground, rubbed his eyes to peer into the timber above. Running Dog was gone. Another trick of Cold Maker.

Grey Bear threw the snares into the bottoms and screamed a piercing animal cry that echoed in the bottoms and reverberated off the wall. He roared again and scrambled up the hill, slipping on the snow and tripping on the roots. He reached the top and bellowed again. Grey Bear snatched the horse blanket and without pausing threw it over the grulla's back. He untied the hobble, threw the lead rope around the horse's head, mounted up, and reined the grulla toward the high ridgeline, Running Dog's chilled, dead face floating through his mind.

Grey Bear kicked the grulla into a gallop and they ran through the woods, branches whipping passed him. He reined the horse down the hillside and it skidded to the bottoms, ran through the flats, and then back up the opposite hill. They topped out and reached the openness of the high south ridge. He gave the grulla another hard kick in the flanks and saw the whites of the horse's eyes before lurching forward to gallop on the openness of the ridge. The wall hovered over them to the west.

And they ran, they ran kicking up snow in a flurry. Grey Bear leaned close to the withers of the sweating horse, feeling the large muscles of the animal pulse and reverberate. He screamed a thundering war cry and the horse ran faster still until the trees were nothing but a blur of whistling greens and whites.

Grey Bear reined the exhausted grulla to a trot and searched the wall.

With each step, a new section appeared from the southern horizon, each one like the last. Grey Bear stared at the imposing rock that shot straight up at the sky, like a mighty fort whose gates have been locked tight. His heart pounded, still haunted by the image of Running Dog. The northerly winds at his back gained strength and chilled his sweat-drenched back, the cold creeping up his neck. His tear-stained cheeks froze, and then in the distance the draw appeared. Appearing as a small crack running up the wall, it widened as he came closer, revealing a lush timber and a small runoff creek.

He slowed the horse to a walk. A narrow valley separated them from the mouth of the draw. Timber ran up the draw itself, began thick with the ponderosa pines and the cedars and the Douglas firs at the bottom and became less dense as the lodge pole pines climbed to the top.

The day had almost left him; the sun disappeared behind the mighty wall, light fading to a soft focus. The shadows grew long and merged in a vast darkness on the forest floor. His mind saw himself as a boy riding up the narrow passage with his heart full of hope. The image faded, though, and he saw Running Dog again, not crouched below the timbers but sitting next to him as they feasted on roasted blackhorn, his face beaming as the flames flickered in the night air.

"Father, what happens when we die?" the boy asked.

"Sometimes our eyes cannot see the things that are most real."

Grey Bear grunted, turned the grulla in a circle. He drew in his breath and, staring at the looming draw before him, the image of his father in the dream cried out.

"Kiaayo Ninaa Yaapi!" Bear Man Sees!

Grey Bear's sharp kick sent the grulla plunging off the ridge. Leaning back, he kept a tight grip on the mane as the horse's hooves slid down the snow-covered hill. In the bottoms, the horse burst through the thick timbers and jumped the narrow creek. Grey Bear reined him toward the mouth of the draw, the land rising, becoming steeper and steeper.

The timbers in the draw were thick and Grey Bear slowly weaved the tired horse through them, the steepness forcing them to climb in a switch-back fashion. The half-frozen runoff creek shot straight down to the draw's floor, water rushing beneath the ice. The air still and cold, the darkness took over, hid small branches that whipped across his arms and face.

As Grey Bear climbed the draw, the ascent was steeper still. He dismounted, allowed the horse to catch its breath. The grulla stood awkwardly on the steep ground. Grey Bear wrapped the horse blanket around his pack. He took the lead rope, began to walk up the draw.

The moon's light radiated through the light cloud cover and dense branches. Lodge pole pines shot up from the steep ground, the branches jutting from the woods and reaching for him.

Grey Bear used the sides of his feet to maintain balance. The grulla struggled to keep up, its hooves missing the mark more and more as the horse strained and lurched forward.

The cloud cover thickened, masking the moonlight. His legs strained, ankles burned. The dark outline of bumps and ridges appeared to the east, the flat horizon in the distance. The top grew ever closer but the closer he came, the steeper the ground. The grulla's missteps were more frequent.

The creek's cold waters ran swiftly, the sound deafening. His foot slipped on snows that had turned to ice and he fell on his side. He righted himself, the summit seeming to be within arms' reach. He took a step but the grulla slipped, landing on its side. The horse whinnied and struggled to get up, the ice crust breaking, flying, falling below them.

Grey Bear gasped and pulled on the lead rope to help the grulla to its feet. The horse jerked back, the whites of its eyes bright in the darkness, then he relented and attempted to rise. Hind legs shaking, it stood.

The summit lay well over forty paces away, Grey Bear almost able to touch the side of the draw. He took another step. The horse started to follow and the hard pack snow beneath its hind leg collapsed. The grulla whinnied, crashed hard and slid down the draw. The lead rope that Grey Bear jerked and dragged him down. Together they slid into the darkness.

The grulla hit a lodge pole and Grey Bear collided with the horse that kicked wildly. Grey Bear scrambled away just before it righted itself.

His hands rubbed the grulla's stern, feeling the lathered sweat, the fearful eyes of the shaking animal. He untied the lead rope, wrapped it in a loop and fastened it to his pack. His hands ran the length of the horse's dark dorsal stripe along its spine, felt the quivering haunch and tired muscles. Grey Bear gave the grulla a hard slap on the rump and watched the horse explode from the lodge poles and gallop down the draw, disappearing into the darkness.

"Goodbye, my friend," Grey Bear whispered.

Grey Bear shifted his shoulders, bringing the blackhorn-hide pack tighter against his cold body. He blew out a hard breath of air, peered up at the summit, and hiked straight up the draw. The moon shone bright, illuminating the near vertical wall of ice.

He found a quiet climbing rhythm, despite his exhaustion and the steepness of the draw. The ground flattened out as he reached the top of the wall, the western side of the rim windswept, with little snow. Even with the rocky ground flat, Grey Bear could not see well without the snows to reflect the light.

Before him lay a vast wilderness, the place of his youth, the place of his spirit animal. The many bumps and ridges and alpine mountains in all directions, the thick forests and blowdown timbers of the bottoms.

The winds were strong and his dark hair whipped against his cold cheeks. The sound of the winds blowing through the timbers and across the open summit dominated his senses; the distant rushing of the icy creek only a whisper. The smells of the old growth forest beneath him reached Grey Bear's nose. For a moment, he was again Slender Bow on the quest for his spirit animal. The feeling of youth swept through his body and he relished the silent comfort of a life wholly ahead of him.

The tight pain in his ankles and legs reminded him that he was Grey Bear with ghosts of a dead son and wife and a life passed. Stepping down into the light snows of the west-facing mountainside, he walked toward the timbers below.

Grey Bear found a narrow bench winding around the mountain and took the pack off his shoulder. With the horse blanket flat amidst a thick cluster of lodge poles, he lay down, the soft snow settling beneath his tired body. There, nestled in the snows and protected by the timbers, he slept a dreamless sleep.

࿓

His eyes opened. Soft focus, hazy white, and then the outline of tangled branches with a blackness at the center. He blinked, the image sharper, snow around him and the branches overhead. Icy morning thermals chilled his hands, his feet.

A raven glided over the bumps and finger ridges of the valley toward the western peaks in the distance. Grey Bear watched until it was a tiny speck against the dense white forest, finally disappearing over a ridge.

The sharp smells of the pines and timber flowed through his nostrils. A brief rush of joy followed by sadness. He tried to reconstruct the place where he, as a boy, built the sweat box in which he fasted for three days waiting for his spirit animal. A lone finger ridge jutting from a southern peak. An open park at its center surrounded by heavy timber. In his memory, the park was lush green with a patch of huckleberries covering its lower half, not the barren white he now saw, but it was the same place.

Grey Bear fixed the location in his mind and picked up the horse blanket, and began his descent to the bottoms.

His legs were sore from the previous night's climb. His stomach growled, but Grey Bear no longer felt the need to nourish his body. This, he knew, would make his mind clear for his meeting with the great he-grizzly. After a half day, he arrived at the base of the finger ridge, an extension of the tall mountains to the south, and climbed to the park.

In the park, an open field of white surrounded by dense timber, Grey Bear set aside his pack. The great wall shot off in a line to the east, and creeks and timber filled the wide valley to the north. High alpine peaks reached the sky to the west, and a lodge pole forest stretched from the park to the ridge and then sheer cliffs behind him to the south.

In the narrow valley ran a creek, larger than the others, still free from ice. The water tumbled over the many rapids and falls, and patches of quaking aspen grew along its edges. Through the lodge pole forest above the park, Grey Bear found a small runoff creek that fed the large creek below. Algae lined its banks, a soft cushion for his knees. He broke through the thin layer of ice and sipped the cold water.

At the uppermost base of the park, he opened the pack and his hand passed the little pemmican that sat uneaten and retrieved the flint and steel. He cleared a swath of flat earth, sat on the horse blanket, and grabbed the tool he will use to construct his sweatbox: Running Dog's knife. Grey Bear unbound the sinew cords that secured the sheath around the blade, and withdrew it, the dropping sun casting its light on the polished steel.

It is a great knife, Father. One day I will have a knife like that.

And so you will, Running Dog.

Grey Bear slipped the blade back into its rawhide folds.

అ

For the next three moons, Grey Bear toiled on the high ridge. He constructed a large fire pit with stones carried from the runoff creek, then severed thin lodge poles for his sweat lodge, binding them together with long strips of bark from the quaking aspen. Having no blackhorn hides to cover the frame, he piled on more of the thin lodge poles, leaving a small entrance. He fashioned a door with a few shorter pieces.

With the outer lodge complete, Grey Bear dug out the compact soil beneath it so that he may have room in which to sit up straight, the earth frozen, laden with stones which he removed and placed near the fire pit.

After digging a small pit in its center that he covered with small stones, he then collected bark from the cedar timber in the bottoms and carried it to his pit.

During his three moons of toil, Grey Bear grew hungry and weak. He knew he must not eat, remaining pure and clear. He drank the water from the small creek and, when the sun went down, slept in the lodge on his horse blanket in a dreamless slumber.

This will be the first moon of the sweat, Grey Bear thought the next morning, as he opened the lodge door. He sipped water from the creek, then knocked over a dead lodge pole and dragged it back to the large fire pit. When he had collected many logs, he covered his outside pit with small stones and started a fire with the flint and steel, feeding the flame with the large logs, adding as many stones as he can crowd around the burning wood.

Throughout the day Grey Bear tended this fire. He let it grow high and strong. The forceful opposing thermals on the high ridge threw the flame in all directions. Standing next to the spectacle, his eyes never moved away from the high dancing flames.

Darkness took over the wilderness, the only sight the roaring fire. Grey Bear picked up a chunk of the charred wood, smearing his face with the black ash, darkening his skin to move closer to the Shadow People. He removed his clothes save for a loin cloth and blackened the rest of his body. Carving a flat piece of timber, he scooped up the red hot rocks, placing them in the pit with some cedar bark and closing the lodge. Grey Bear sprinkled a handful of snow on the hot stones and cedar, creating a thick, sharp-smelling vapor.

The low sizzling of moisture on hot stones drowned out the winds, the lodge stifling hot with thick steam trapped and oozing out the cracks. Grey Bear shut his eyes, silent, but his mind spoke to his spirit animal, the great he-grizzly, and beckoned him to come, offer guidance, offer aid in releasing Running Dog's spirit.

Grey Bear repeated this for two moons, carrying the logs by day and sitting in the sweat lodge by night, sitting, praying, chanting. No answers. The great he-grizzly did not speak, nor the Long Ago People, nor any other spirit. Alone, he no longer heard squirrels bark nor saw fresh sign of game. Both worlds have left him and maybe, he thought, he was now in neither world, like the horizon.

As the sun disappeared to the west on the third moon, Grey Bear prepared to pray in the sweat lodge. His aching body could barely stand and the teeth in his mouth were loose. His skin had lost its color, hanging limp on his arms and legs but stretched tight over his ribs. His hollow eyes sunken in, the lines around them deep and long. But still he toiled, dragging the logs a few paces and then resting before moving them more.

He retreated to the sweat lodge, pushing away everything in his mind but the cry for help for his lost son. The night hours pass. No one listened or responded. The sun appeared in the east, shining through the door. Grey

Bear cried from despair and, exhausted, collapsed on his horse blanket, falling into a slumber.

ॐ

Grey Bear's matted eyes half-opened, still light in the day. He rolled over, hit his face on the hard ground, his swollen gums sending bolts of pain through his head. He rose to his hands and knees, his joints stiff and aching. Sweat covering his blackened body, he crawled to the makeshift door and with the hardest push he can muster, it landed flat. He screamed.

"Grey Bear," the grizzly whispered in a deep, guttural voice.

The great he-grizzly's massive paws sunk into the earth, his great dish face taking up the sky. His forepaws came to rest on the door, his brown face and cold black nose close enough to touch.

"Grey Bear." The grizzly's breath foul, smelling of death. "You have come here for me, but I have been with you all your life. Always in the shadows. Always I watch over you."

The grizzly shifted his huge frame, the hump on his back twitching. His black eyes bore into Grey Bear's.

"I have seen you," said Grey Bear. "Sometimes, you're a flicker in my outside vision. I see you in dreams."

He was bigger than Grey Bear remembered from his youth, twice the size of any bear he had ever seen, with dark, silver-tipped fur, the bear's claws larger than his knife.

"I have heard your cries," said the grizzly. "But I knew that you had seen me, seen my signs. I knew you would follow me."

The grizzly's great shoulders shifted and he moved his head even closer, his dark eyes narrowing.

"You can never see Running Dog again. I cannot help you with this. I brought you here to die a good death and I will guide you to the Sand Hills to be with your wife and other children and your people. I will guide you there, like I have guided you in life."

"I have failed Running Dog," Grey Bear said. "Failed my son, disgraced him in front of the women."

Grey Bear rose to his feet and the great he-grizzly reared up, towering over him.

"I will die here, as you say. But my spirit will never rest and will never go to the Sand Hills until he is with me."

The grizzly came down on his forepaws, the ground reverberating.

"If that is your wish, it is so," said the bear. "I will be with you always here in this land of your youth."

Grey Bear returned to his sweat lodge. When he came out, the bear was gone, leaving only the cold winds and the broken door and the great tracks.

Heavy dark clouds moved in from the north and the winds died down. A stillness on the ridge, the air moist. From the western rim of the park Grey Bear gazed down on the fast-moving creek, its cold waters crashing through blowdown timbers. He glanced at the great wall to the east and imagined the vast plains beyond, thought of the Marias in the spring and Yellow Leaf running barefoot through the tall cattails, smiling, laughing.

❧

He heard the steady sound of his son breathing and knew that Running Dog dreamed. Grey Bear wondered what his dreams were, and guessed them to be of future glories in battle and of horses and a lodge his son can call his own. Maybe he dreamed of his own vision quest, his own spirit animal. Or maybe he just of Yellow Leaf and the food and comfort she offered.

These were the dreams Grey Bear wished for him, anyway.

❧

Grey Bear removed the knife from its sheath, held the blade up to the setting sun. The blade of high temper, the wapiti antler smooth in his hand. He turned the knife around and, with his last strength, plunged it deep into his chest. He dropped to the ground, his lifeless eyes facing north to the blackness of the approaching clouds.

CHAPTER TWENTY-FIVE

BOB MARSHALL WILDERNESS, MONTANA

SEPTEMBER 1997

Two weeks ago, I arrived in lower camp with empty sawbucks, having dropped a load of twenty bales of hay. Tired, I hurried to unsaddle the lathered horses and mules. Rick, the cook, helped, and then we walked back to the kitchen tent. Rick lit a cigarette, sat across from me. A small, wiry man in his late forties, he had worked for Cecil for years. Staring blankly down at my boots, I really wanted to go sleep. He peered at me with bloodshot brown eyes through a screen of cigarette smoke.

"You heard him out there yet?" he asked in his gruff voice.

"Who?"

Rick started to chuckle, then coughed, cleared his throat. "Nope, guess you ain't. The Blackfoot. Blackfoot warrior up there."

My eyes were heavy with fatigue.

"C'mon Rick, I'm not in the mood for your damn ghost stories. I'm going to bed."

I poured some cold coffee from the stove, swallowed it down. Rick put on his weathered hat, the mouth underneath his gray handlebar mustache set firm.

"You'll hear him. He's out there and he's real."

He turned, shuffled out of the tent, whistled up his black lab and got in his truck, the fading taillights of the old Ford disappearing into the timber.

"Yeah, Rick. Go to the bar and tell your drunk friends about it."

I took one of the Coleman lanterns from the kitchen to my tent, set it on my little homemade cedar nightstand, lay down in my cot, and put the day out of my mind.

Three nights later, I was coming in from bale deliveries, tired and sore riding the ten miles back. About halfway to camp I heard the chanting. I blinked into the nothingness, shaking my head, trying to push this thing away. But it was real, he was real.

Silence for a moment—then horse hooves came down in cadence, steel on rock and dirt. The gentle creak of cold leather as the empty sawbucks shifted on sweaty withers. The tightness of the lead rope in my hand, the dull pain. Black.

The chants came from high on the ridge to the east, flowing down the mountain face. It was human but not human, deep but hollow. Like a shadow.

I stifled my breathing, sat still, ears focused. The chants stopped.

I was afraid at first, but then there was only a sadness.

࿇

Twenty slow paces, then a pause, walking on the sides of my feet by placing my heel down deliberately and rolling my foot forward. I fought the urge to wipe the sporadic rain drops from my face. I examined the forest floor, looking for elk and deer tracks, the trees for rubs, bare marks where the elk and deer have rubbed the summer velvet off their antlers. I scanned the forest ahead of me, to the south below and to the north above, looking for moving legs or a patch of hair, listened for a branch breaking below or the crunch of frozen dirt above, for a grunt from a traveling bull or a delicate mew from a cow elk, for a squirrel bark in response to a presence.

My cold nose worked in synergy with the other senses, smelling the sweet bear grasses and far off patches of ripened huckleberries. I smelled the subtle, pungent odor of the swampy bottoms, a decayed smell of old dead wood and stagnant still water laden with moss and algae. I smelled death, a cumulative smell of a lost struggle with the victor the unforgiving winter and the lion and the wolf and the bear. A smell of starvation and violence.

These I detected under the cover of the dominating pine, a sharp, pleasing scent that was the father to these sons of death and rebirth.

We hiked briskly for a few hundred yards. The bench began to widen so I found a spot overlooking the valley floor. The tips of the pines obscured our vision directly beneath us, but still afforded a decent view of the river bottom and the timbered mountainside a quarter-mile away. I unslung my rifle, leaned it against a thick blowdown cedar that afforded a comfortable backrest. Al took off his pack, sat beside me.

There was a low-lying cloud cover, but the rains had ceased. Winds with their midday thermals shifted direction every few minutes, bringing the penetrating cold that seeped through my damp thermal underwear, chilling my back, torso, and feet.

My day had begun at 3:30 a.m. when I wrangled and saddled the horses, and with all that's happened since, my sore body relished the rest.

Al and I perused the river bottom, the open parks, the barely visible timberline.

My forehead creased in thought. "Is it everything you thought it would be?" I asked Al.

He bit into a candy bar. "And more. Beautiful. Absolutely beautiful."

I studied Al out of the corner of my eye. He pulled his stocking cap back on his head, revealing wisps of thinning white hair matted with clumps of sweat. Two day growth of white beard stubble, he had a kind face, weathered, the age lines creasing his forehead and crow's feet visible even with no expression from his bright blue inquisitive eyes. Al kept his focus on the distant peaks as he smiled.

He drew in his breath. "You know Justin, my boy? You met him in camp."

I nodded.

"He's probably your age, maybe a little older. I was a contract engineer for the government while he was growing up. Always on the road, flying to South America or California or India. Always gone. All those baseball games I missed. He loved his baseball, you know. But I only saw him play a handful of times and I remember how his face just beamed when he looked at the stands and saw me."

I glanced sideways at Al, my hollow heart pained and pushing away a memory.

He stared at me for a moment and he continued, his voice softening.

"I retired from the government three years ago and bought some apartments. Justin and I manage them now. Get to see him every day and we do something like this every year."

Al twisted the cap from his water bottle, took a swig, a droplet of the water dripping from his mouth.

"He's married now, got married last year to a real good girl. I guess I failed him growing up. I just want to make up for lost time while there *is* still time, you know?"

I drew in a deep breath of the pines and sharp cedar.

"Yeah, I do. I know," I said. "Aaron was really looking forward to taking Justin out, says he's a real good guy." I grasped for words. "He's sure lucky to have a father like you, despite everything."

Al cocked his head, white tufts of his hair changing directions with the wind. He studied me, his eyes narrowing. The old Stetson I wore resting on the grasses beside me, my brown hair rustling about in sweaty clumps. My green eyes pained by the sun, straining to meet his gaze.

"What about you, Calvin? Your father here in Montana?"

I gazed into the valley below and struggled for an answer.

"No. He passed away last December. He was my grandfather, actually. Called him Dad, though. My real father left when I was little."

I raised my eyes to the horizon of jagged peaks.

"He's dead, too."

Al's head bowed. "Oh. Well, I'm sorry."

I glanced at him.

"It's okay. I'm fine. I'm going to grab a short nap. Animals are bedded down now. We should too. Wake me in an hour or so. If you can't sleep, you can watch those open parks across the valley. A bear might wander by."

"Calvin."

Crouching above me, staring, a little puzzled.

"Yep, I'm up."

"You were moaning in your sleep."

I rubbed my eyes, refocused.

"You were mumbling about somebody named Ben. Who's Ben?" Al said.

"Ben? Just a friend of mine."

Al grunted, reached for his rifle. I glanced at my watch, 1:30.

"You ready to work those bottoms, Al?"

"I'm following you, boss."

I gathered my gear and we began the sheer descent to the bottom.

The grade gradually became less sharp and the geography more forgiving. But then there were the blowdowns, hundreds and hundreds of dead timber. The ever-present lodge poles littered the forest floor with sporadic cedar and a sprinkling of downed Douglas firs in the wooden maze of decay. The standing, live trees provided a darkened canopy, casting shadows and creating spectral rays of light from the peeking sun revealing the solid blanket grasses and the knee-high alpine timothy and the thick green mountain brome shooting out the wooden matrix.

Beneath the canopy, the wind negligible, my wind powder shot up, swirling, dissipating. I peered into the darkened gloom. It smelled of slow decay brought about by the waters of the river and runoff creeks and insects and time. The occasional branch broke caused by some far-off animal, and the creaking of old-growth forest against gravity and the light winds produced the grinding of the live trees against the leaning dead, and the leaning dead against the fallen dead.

His face pale, beads of sweat fell from Al's brow.

"Let's make our way to the river," I said. "Believe it or not, elk will move through this like it's nothing. They'll use this thick timber, too, for cover and for food."

I pointed to the deep greens of the fescue grasses and Al nodded.

"I'm going to be looking for sign as we move through," I said. "If you would, keep your eyes peeled for movement."

Al adjusted his rifle sling. "Yeah, you bet."

We moved slowly, stepping over the fallen timber, sometimes ducking under a massive cedar or leap-frogging a series of down lodge poles. With the timber smooth and moist, more than once we lost our footing while stepping on a log, our feet crashing through the crevices into the grasses and wedging into the soft earth.

After 200 yards, I found a lone bull track, heading south towards the river. A fresh track, less than an hour old.

Raising the brim of my Stetson, the perspiration seeped down my unshaven face. I deliberately took one step at a time, following the tracks but taking a side path to avoid disrupting their pattern. We followed the bull out of the blowdowns and into the brush and marshes that clung to the waters. He was heading straight for the river.

Around us the world changed. Out of the darkened gloom of the decayed and the dead and into the greens that spring from the life-giving creeks and the river. The smell of the fresh elk sedge seeped up my nostrils, mixing with the Baltic brushes in their tight clusters of bright greens and contrasting dark flower beds.

I peered in through the tangled masses of brown leaves and pine cones. The wind lightly swirled around us; we had no way of knowing if the bull had picked up our scent, negating our efforts. Al, with sweaty concentration, surveyed his surroundings.

Gritting my teeth, I contorted my body to slide past the myriad branches, mindful of the sound but comforted by the river's flow masking our fumbling efforts. I hoped against hope but the truth reared itself at the river's edge.

"The son of a bitch crossed the river," I said.

Flowing swift and deep, the river ran ten yards wide.

Al remained silent, waited for me to make a decision. I tried to fix the details of the opposite shore where I suspected our bull continued his walk, then searched downriver for a better place to cross. I spotted a fallen cedar about fifty yards downstream which had landed on an exposed boulder where the river was wider and calmer. I didn't like it, but I also knew we couldn't give up. Still early in the ten-day hunt, Al was still fresh. But then, Al might not want to do this. After all, crossing the river was dangerous, and the prospect of hunting while completely soaked for the rest of the day was a problem, too. Damn.

"What do you think, Al?"

His eyes never left the other side of the river. "He's close, isn't he?"

I hesitated, then said, "If he hasn't winded us. He was still just plodding along when he crossed."

Al's eyes met mine. "Let's see if we can get him."

We made our way downstream, precariously balancing on the few inches of river bank the crowded alders afforded us, often gripping the tangled branches for support. I eyed the down cedar and swift current, wondering if it was shallow enough to keep our packs and rifles dry. In front of me, Al grunted as he crouched under branches and stepped over half-buried rocks. Eyes narrowed in pain, he gave me a smile.

The embankment underneath him collapsed.

Al cried out as he dropped, he and the clump of muddy earth hitting the current with a crash. He held his rifle high, his head disappearing beneath the freezing water, then emerging again. His rifle above the current, he began to frantically paddle toward me.

The ground beneath me began to weaken. I dropped to my stomach, lay my rifle down, and started to crawl. The current took Al downstream, but he fought his way to the edge. I wormed my way down the bank. He made it to the steep embankment, his free hand gripping an exposed root.

"I'm coming, Al." My forearms dug into the wet earth, my feet finding the exposed rocks and roots. A clump of mud underneath me collapsed and I scrambled out of the way, grunting. I reached Al. My fingers gripped the shifting mud and I hung my arms over the drop-off. Al looked up at me, pale, wet.

I took his rifle, set it down. "Give me your free hand," I said.

He latched on with a cold, wet grip, and clutched my forearm with the other hand. I pulled with my all the strength, straining, gasping for air. He slowly emerged from the water. Al's face locked in a grimace, his feet kicking, he searched for anything to propel him. The soft earth underneath me shifted so I maneuvered him back onto solid ground. The tendons in my arms burned, muscles strained to exhaustion.

As I stepped away from the bank I let go of Al and he weakly stood, staggering to the safety of the thick grasses and he lay down on his back, his chest moving up and down. I lingered closer to the shore for a moment, my hands behind my head, caught my breath, and then sat down next to him.

"Al?"

"Yeah?" His voice weak, hands trembling in the cold light winds.

"I'm going to go get the rifles and look around for a place to build a fire. You've got to warm up. Got to get those clothes dry."

~

The cold and wet penetrated my skin and held a death grip on my bones. We saw nothing on our hunt back to the horses; the winds picked up and the temperature dropped and we lost light. We fumbled our way back to the horses shivering in our still damp clothes.

Al stood, waiting patiently for me to untie his horse and put its headstall on. I knew he was hurting and tired and just as miserably cold and wet as I was, yet he said nothing. I led his horse away from the tree to a place where Al could mount up. I took his rifle, slid it into its scabbard, and tightened the horse's cinch. Al put his left foot in the stirrup and hoisted himself up, easing back in his saddle, groaning. My guide horse, Toby, stood half asleep at his tree. The cold steel of the little flashlight in my mouth made my teeth ache. The ice plastered to my wool pants forced me to strain to mount up. I took the lead and Al followed me up the trail for the two-hour ride back to camp.

Hurt, tired. But there, then, was the nothingness and the silence. Only the steady clomp of horse hooves on rock and dirt. I saw nothing. Pure black. The wind vanished, clouds gathered in masses and obscured the light of the stars. The sound of the hooves faded from my consciousness; I was above it, beyond it. My legs were the only tie now to the forest; I sensed Toby's mood through our contact and the small reverberations in his body. I thought about the Indian, wondered if he was out there.

Toby's coarse mane brushed my hand. I looked with unseeing eyes into the nothingness. The gentle inhaling and exhaling of the horses and the beat of their hooves fade. I listened. I smelled.

A tremor reverberated down Toby's shoulder, his ears on alert, nostrils flared. The stagnant icy air subtly changed to a foreboding gloom, thicker, heavier. My lungs filled with the darkness, my thoughts raced, tried to ascertain the source of this unseen threat. A mountain lion perhaps in the large expanse of boulders above us, perched on its nightly vigil. Or a roaming grizzly, with its massive blackened nose dictating its movements, sniffing the unfeeling winds, smelling us, seeing us.

I tensed. Toby shifted his neck, listening, alert.

My moist left hand squeezed the leather reins and my right hand at my side slowly clenched and unclenched, staying warm and pliable. The air became lighter and I felt Toby's tension soften. His ears retreated to a neutral position.

❧

Water splashed beneath me, and the tent lights flickered through the tree branches. Muted voices through the forest, a horse's whinny.

"Looks like we made it, eh?" Al whispered.

I rode Toby into camp. Taking my right leg out of the stirrup, I worked my pained joints back and forth to shake the ice off my pants. My knees almost buckled when my feet hit the ground. I gripped the fender of the saddle until my strength returned.

"Good hunt today," I said. "We almost had him."

"Yeah. We'll get him tomorrow." His pained face managed a wink and he staggered off to his tent.

The tack stowed, I glanced at camp, lit up and inviting. Seven wall tents in all, not counting the tack tent, set up in the old-style way with lodge pole rails and cross beams. Three tents for the hunters were lined up and beside them was the kitchen tent, twice the size of the others. Behind it, out of view, was the cook's tent where Rick sleeps.

Across the clearing was Cecil's tent and the guide tent where Aaron and I bunked. In the center of it all was a fire pit, flames shooting up, smoke dissipating in the cold night air.

The smell of the sweet meats cooking and the sound of Rick's gravelly voice reminded me of my hunger. I turned the horses out to the corral. They both bounded to the hay troughs lined along the makeshift lodge pole fence, joining the others, twenty head in all. With new competition for food came the inevitable kicking and biting, reminders of the herd pecking order.

Things settled down soon, however, to only muffled sounds of grinding hay and swishing tails of contentment.

CHAPTER TWENTY-SIX

BOB MARSHALL WILDERNESS, MONTANA

1870-1997

The moon's light seeped through the low cloud cover, blanketed the dark greens and grayish-whites with a yellow hue. The thermals of the peaks and high ridges swirled, the cold winds no longer sure of their course. The life of the sun was no longer, then was the time of the moon, which gave off false light like the false darkness of the shadow.

The nocturnal hunters began their nightly rounds, the lions perched on high boulders above game trails, waiting for a passing deer or elk. Wolves roamed through the open parks and dense ponderosa forests, their noses scanning the erratic winds for blood. Black bears emerged from their winter slumber and plodded down the southerly slopes of the bottoms seeking winter-killed animals, feasting on the fresh shoots of alpine timothy and mountain brome.

The great grizzlies, too, emerged and roamed the lower forests, noses to the ground in search of elk calves that cowered in the tall grasses. Their ears worked in synergy with their noses, twitching in anticipation of a newborn elk's high-pitched call. The grizzlies, like their smaller brothers, feasted on emerging grasses and pine nuts and exposed roots.

Grey Bear, perched atop a high ridge, was a shadow, his sun then the moon. He stared at it, the yellow-grays passing through him and reflecting off the boulder beneath his feet. He heard with shadow ears the faint rushing creeks as they journeyed to the main river that ran up the interior of the forest. He heard the roaming animals, both predator and prey. The winds continued to swirl, but they blew through his shadow and he did not feel their biting cold. Darkness and cold were now his friend.

He walked up the ridgeline to its crest at the base of the barren alpine peak. The moon's light reflected on the snow-covered rock, not the blinding whiteness of the living but a hazy image of a dull gray. He stopped at the west-facing slope where it dropped to the forested bottoms. He stared at the night, no longer a nothingness but a world of hazy life, a world of far-off sounds and sights.

Grey Bear began the ancient chants his father had taught him when he was a boy, chants of the dead who cry for the spirits in the Shadow Lands and the Long Ago People and the Above Ones and Below Ones.

"Akayimm Inn! Akayssi Ksahko!

Amsskaa Pipikaniikoaiksi Omahkai'stoo

Omahkai'stoo

Akayimm Inn! Akayssi Ksahko!"

His voice carried down the cliff, the echo running under the sounds of the living. He was quiet, listening for sounds from below, but all was silent. They have heard my voice, Grey Bear thought. Through the tangled alders and the thick branches of cedar and ponderosa, he watched the deer and elk and bear below.

They stood still, ears poised, sniffing the winds. High on the east-facing slope across the valley was a lone nanny mountain goat and she, too, stood still with fright as she studied him. The winds blew stronger, their thermals shooting up the cliff, the bare lodge pole pines groaning. Grey Bear brought his hands to his ears and found that his ear was torn away still, as it was in life. The surge of loss returned, his heart darkening.

"Ahi Imita! Running Dog!"

Nothing but the winds and motionless animals as they watched him, afraid.

⌘

Many winters passed, many moons of darkness. Springs came with greens peeking through the melting snowpack, the young game growing stronger, and the roaring waters gaining strength from melting runoffs. Then the summers of cool nights and lightning storms and rains followed, bringing lush greens of blowdown jungle bottoms and lodge poles up to the timberline of the high country where pockets of snow remained on alpine peaks. In the fall came the bugles of the bull elk. High-pitched, they were an escalating series of notes that started with a low grunt, moved higher in tone, and dropped suddenly back down. They echoed off the canyon walls and peaks. Then the winters came again with heavy snows and high winds that blew through the shadow of Grey Bear as he watched it all from the high ridge.

One summer he saw what he thought was a sign. A strange thing in the sky, a large bird, larger than he had ever seen in life, of silver with unmoving wings, flew through the dark sky as he watched in awe. He remembered this thing, its thunder, as it rushed past and disappeared over the easterly peak.

Grey Bear contemplated this for many moons, thinking it was a giant bird sent by Napi. It was a sign. The great bird flew east back to his home on the Marias, but he could never return there, not as a shadow. He must remain here because it was the will of the great he-grizzly and the fate of all of those who live a dishonorable life to haunt the place of their death.

He prayed many nights and chanted many old songs seeking wisdom and meditated in his sweat lodge, but the great he-grizzly never came, and Grey Bear did not see nor hear nor feel sign from any other thing. Whatever this was or meant, it had nothing to do with him or Running Dog.

He thought about that long ago night as he walked to the high ridge for his nightly prayer. He began his chants with prayers to Napi and the Long Ago People for guidance, for a way to release Running Dog from Cold Maker's prison. He prayed that Yellow Leaf and his other children were faring well in the Sand Hills and that one day Running Dog may join them.

This was the time of the wapiti's bugle, the lead bulls rounding up their cows in the bottoms. The satellite bulls challenged the herd bull that often rounded up his cows, disappearing over some far-off ridge. But sometimes, the herd bull became angry and sought out the challenging bull, Grey Bear witnessing the two great wapiti lock horns and the victor claiming the cows.

Grey Bear finished his chants and anticipated the bulls' familiar piercing wails. None came.

Then, through the dense alders along the creek, a Napikwan on horseback appeared riding north through the narrow valley. Alone, he led six horses, all strung together with light rope. Each horse carried packs covered by canvas cloth tied with a heavy hemp rope.

Grey Bear stood on the high ridge and watched this interloper to his country, the first human he saw since becoming a shadow. A sliver of anger ran through him at the whiteness of the interloper's face but this was quashed by the yearning to hear another voice, a human voice. The rider wore a large brimmed hat that hid his face, but he glanced upward and Grey Bear saw that this was an older man. The interloper rode under Grey Bear's diligent gaze and past him, disappearing around the mountain.

For many winters after, Grey Bear saw more and more of the Napikwans with their horses. He always ceased chanting when they appeared or when he sensed the animals' silence. He thought that, like the animals of the forest, the Napikwan might also hear his voice and bring more whites who would find his sweat lodge. With each passing winter he let them cross through, silently, his lost soul becoming less angry and his heart becoming more accepting.

These Napikwans wore no uniform but leather dusters and shotgun-style chaps. They always appeared in the fall and returned with the outline of elk quarters strapped to pack horses. These were not the soldier-killers he knew as a living man, these were like the cowboys he had seen as a boy in the summer who wandered into the Piegan camp to trade their beef for blackhorn robes.

One night, a few winters since he first saw the Napikwans, Grey Bear sensed them coming and did not cease his chanting. Rather, he stood at edge and let his cries ring through the blackness.

"Akayimm Inn!

Akayssi Ksahko!

Amsskaa Pipikaniikoaiksi Omahkai'stoo

Omahkai'stoo

Akayimm Inn!

Akayssi Ksahko!"

Grey Bear fell silent, waited, watched. The animals, already alert, were now immobile, listening. The Napikwan's horses, too, were jumpy, their eyes white with fear and their ears pointed in his direction. The Napikwan rode as before, making no movement of surprise. He did not look up.

☙

One hundred and twenty-seven winters passed and the shadow of Grey Bear still chanted, still prayed, his shadow heart still hollow. The coming of fall brought several Napikwan hunters from winters past, but then a new one: dressed in a leather coat and chaps like the others, but the hat brim black and new, his face clean, eyes bright.

Grey Bear watched this young Napikwan with many horses carrying empty panniers. The winds blew the light rain sideways, the waters flowing through the still shadow of Grey Bear. The young man's eyes shifted from the trail to the flowing creek and then up at the ridge. Grey Bear's shadow eyes met his.

He is a fallen-in man, Grey Bear thought.

Grey Bear looked to the cliffs, taking in this new despair. He saw the young Napikwan's heart and knew that he was lost, not because of a long-ago war, but because of his father. And then Grey Bear thought of Running Dog's eyes on the river as he let go of his hand. Running Dog's eyes spoke of letting go, of accepting his fate. The young Napikwan had looked up at the ridge with those same eyes. Grey Bear's heart twisted and he stood, crying out:

"Hold on, my son!"

The young Napikwan's eyes shot back up the ridge. Grey Bear ran down the ridgeline and into the timbers, to the open park where the ancient lodge still stood.

☙

For six moons more Grey Bear returned to his vigil on the ridge. He no longer began his chants alone; he waited for the young Napikwan and rather than singing the old songs he chanted the same verse in cadence.

Grey Bear Sees

Grey Bear Hears

No thought in the chants and prayers. He looked into the young Napikwan's heart and listened to his stories, stories of his father, of his grandfather. The scenes flashed before Grey Bear like lightning, blinding flashes of light in a world of darkness.

The face of a Napikwan, eyes bloodshot, the smell of whiskey, he walked closer, something in his hand, a toy for a child, lifting his arm, threw, the sharp pain running up Grey Bear's back.

"No toys," the Napikwan said.

A young woman lay down, sobbing, blood on her face, her eye purple and swollen shut.

Choking, cannot breath, no air. A white arm wrapped around Grey Bear's neck. Desperate, helpless, a tear dripped from his face, and then the arm released Grey Bear and he was on the ground, looking up, trying to breath, staring at the face of a Napikwan.

The Napikwan again, crouched in a corner, his face hidden, whispering words of some long ago war. Grey Bear across from him, behind a table, doubled over, making himself small. The pistol in the Napikwan's hand, coming up to the Napikwan's head and then the deafening boom, red on the white walls. The half-face with a single vacant eye and no more words.

A Napikwan girl, about the age of Falling Leaf, her long flaxen hair caked with blood, her crumpled, naked body lying lifeless on a wooden floor.

A man in a coffin. Not the younger Napikwan but an old man, and suddenly his heart felt hollow, empty, and a surge of pain coursed through him, dull and lasting.

Grey Bear blinked, his shadow eyes focusing on the lone rider. For the first time that night, he thought of Running Dog. His son immersed in a dark hole of ice, his hand holding on to his father. Grey Bear looked at his shadow hand, its form, the blackness and winds and rains rushing through it. He then saw his hand as it was in life and the hand of his young son holding on and then at once letting go. Grey Bear drew in a breath of blackness, gazing at the young Napikwan disappearing into the timber.

Grey Bear's sharp cry echoed through the valley. The young Napikwan glanced back and their eyes met for an instant. Then he disappeared into the thick alders and pines.

A flash again, but this one less clear. A flash not in the past but of a future, it seemed to Grey Bear. The scene vague, hazy.

It was winter, past the time of the wapiti that sang. Only whiteness, deep snows all around. It was familiar. Grey Bear concentrated.

The outline of the ancient sweat lodge, buried under a heavy blanket of fresh snow. The young Napikwan, his hat off, brown hair covered with ice, looked at the narrow valley. A sea of white surrounded him.

The young man reaching inside his leather coat, the black pistol in his hand, the thumb cocking the hammer, the barrel rising to his head.

The light flashed, was gone, and Grey Bear screamed.

CHAPTER TWENTY-SEVEN

BOB MARSHALL WILDERNESS, MONTANA

SEPTEMBER 1997

C'mon in Calvin, Aaron."

Cecil's eyes were tired, bloodshot, deep lines reaching out from them. His broad shoulders hunched over a fold-out table, the front of his green wool shirt stained with sweat from the day's exertion. His powerful old hand clutched a cup of steaming coffee, and I inhaled its earthy smell.

Aaron sat down next to his hunter, Al's son, Dan. Flickering shadows covered the large tent canvas and the smells of fried pork chops permeated the warm air emitting from the wood stove. Rick's back turned to us, his arms moved quickly, turning the chops over in the large cast iron pan and frying up a batch of sliced potatoes. He shifted his stance, half stumbled.

So he's been drinking today. Rick glanced back at me, grunted, bloodshot blue eyes staring out from the matrix of age lines and a beard of white, the sweat-stained brown brim of his old cowboy hat casting a shadow over his face. He turned back to his cooking. Two Coleman lanterns hung from the tent's ridge, the mantles burning bright, their hollow noise sounding like a giant man exhaling slowly. Rick's old black lab slept next to the stove, curled up with his head buried between his paws.

The heat from the stove stifling, I removed my long-sleeved wool shirt and hat and hung them on the makeshift rack next to the tent's entrance. Al sat next to Dan drinking coffee. I gave Al a friendly pat on the shoulder and sat next to him.

Al winked before turning back to Cecil's hunter, a short, boisterous, heavy-set man named Stan telling everyone of his day's adventures. Stan was a top-level executive with Ford in Detroit. His bushy eyebrows moved spastically when he spoke, and his rosy cheeks appeared almost unnatural, like they were painted on.

"I told Cecil that the elk is moving toward the open grass to feed, and I would hike around the pond and get the wind in my face and ambush him there," said Stan, gesturing wildly with his hands.

"So I do that. I get around the pond and start to move real slow, kinda creeping up on him." Stan craned his neck, moved his head side to side like a rooster.

Cecil watched Stan with a tired half-smile. Aaron shot him a quick, knowing look. Poor Cecil, the look said. Having to put up with this bastard all day long.

"I'm close, right? So I get down on my hands and knees and start crawling toward the edge of the park and what did you say the elk did, Cec?"

"The elk turned and—"

"Yeah, the elk turned and looked my way real quick and trotted in the other direction. The damn thing ran right by Cecil on the other side of the goddamn pond!" Stan laughed and Cecil almost winced. He took a sip of coffee, his shadow wavering behind him.

"I told you about that jacket you're wearing," Cecil said. "I've got one extra in my tent I'll let you wear tomorrow. Fleece. It'll be quiet and won't make all that racket when you rub against those branches."

"Aw, bullshit," Stan said. His plump belly quivered with a chuckle. "Wind just shifted a little, that's all. Hell, tomorrow we'll just—"

"Chops are done, dive in if you wanna eat," Rick said as he dropped the steaming pile of pork chops on the table. He turned around to get the bowl of potatoes still on the stove, but stumbled and moved sideways to catch himself.

"Somebody's been hitting the sauce this afternoon." Stan chuckled. Everybody looked at Cecil, whose eyes stayed focused on his mug of coffee.

"He cooks better when he's been drinking," Aaron said with a smile.

Rick approached the table holding the plate of potatoes and onions, his body swaying.

"Look at these spuds. Turned out beautiful. I make the best goddamn spuds you'll ever eat." Rick set the potatoes down on the table between

Al and Dan, both of whom leaned away in fear that Rick would spill it.

The food passing around the large picnic table, I chewed slowly, shifted my weight in the chair, the tightness in my legs from the cold sending slivers of pain up my back. My feet were warming up, but the coldness lingered in my bones.

The men ate, the chewing reminding me of the horses. It was the way of men and horses, the contentedness of company and food after a hard day's toil that made communication unneeded. I focused on the canvas wall, tried to make sense of the shadows as the flicker of the Coleman lanterns made them dance in the half-lights. Shapes flashed before me, ghostly images taking form and dissipating.

"Good grub, cookie," Stan said.

"Yes, Rick, great job with supper tonight," Cecil said.

Rick took an apple pie from the cast iron oven. The pie's fresh steam wafted up from its crust, filling the tent with its sweetness.

"Best goddamn spuds you'll ever eat," Rick said, and then cleared his throat. "Put your bones on a separate plate there when you're done with 'em."

I rose from the table with my mug.

"Coffee, Calvin?" Rick gripped the coffee pot and brought the spout to my mug. Rick's hand, callused and wrinkled, trembled as he poured. His mouth set, concentrating.

"Anyone need another cup before dessert?" I asked.

Cecil and Al waved off the offer, but Dan, Aaron, and Stan nodded.

"Go ahead and set the pot down, Rick. I'll get it."

Rick grunted and I poured the rounds. The pie was passed around and everyone relished the slight bittersweet taste of apples and delicate crust.

"Where to tomorrow, boss?" Al asked, pushing the last few flakes of pie crust around his plate. Cecil, his mug to his lips, cast a glance at me.

"Well, the elk we ran into today winded us, so let's back off a bit. Tomorrow morning we'll head high, I'm thinking—"

"I tell you what you ought to do, you ought to go where Cec and I were today," Stan said. Flakes of pie crust littered his T-shirt. "We seen plenty of sign, and they're still there, I'm telling you. They're still in there."

"No," I said, trying to keep my annoyance to myself. "I'm thinking the burn above Pony. They'll be up high, and there's plenty of good feed."

"It's a good place," Cecil said. "A guy oughta do fine up in there."

Al nodded and I continued.

"We can ride up in the morning and—"

"You're not going to give that dog those small bones, are you?" Stan asked Rick as he picked up the pork chop remains. "He'll choke."

Rick glared at Stan, then tossed a bone to the dog, who woke, gnawed on it.

"He'll eat it or he'll fucking die," Rick said.

Stan laughed nervously, and the rest of the crew chuckled at him.

"Well, fellas, early day tomorrow," Aaron said as he stood up. He turned to Dan. "I'll see you bright and early and we'll go get 'em, huh?"

A flicker of excitement shone in the young man's eyes. I glanced at his camouflage pants and long-sleeve shirt, his feet in new hunting boots. He'll remember this for the rest of his life.

"You bet," he said.

"I'm gone myself," I said. "Al, we'll talk in the morning. Get some good rest. Night, Cecil."

"Good night, Calvin."

Aaron and I walked to our tent. The black sky had clouded over and the rains were falling, the frigid water pelting our hats and shirts; we splashed in the pools of water littering the slushy mud. A rumble of thunder in the distance, and then a brief flash of lightning illuminated the camp. Once inside our tent, we closed the flap and tied the cotton strings together.

I put three big half-logs in our cast iron stove, resting them on the bright orange embers which popped and sprayed orange sparks. I pushed in the spring handle of the door and locked it in place, and then closed the damper.

"What's this?" Aaron asked. I turned around. Aaron held up a sort of leather pouch.

"It was on your bed. Is it yours?" he said.

"Nope."

The pouch the size of Aaron's hand, he loosened the whitish cord that pursed its opening. With two fingers he probed its contents and brought it close to the lantern on his makeshift nightstand.

"What is it?" I asked.

"Grass. Just a few blades of grass." Aaron tossed the pouch over to me as I sat on my bunk. The pouch a soft leather. Not cowhide, for sure. Deer or elk. The whitish cord and the binding material was sinew.

"Pretty neat little pouch. Maybe something Al picked up in Missoula somewhere and wanted me to have. Why there's grass in it I have no idea."

Aaron unlaced his boots.

"Dunno. I don't see how Al could've left it for you, though. He was in the kitchen tent the whole time we were. Before that, only you and I were here."

I sighed, placed it next to the lodge pole stump that served as my nightstand. "We'll figure it out in the morning. I'm too tired to think."

We lay down and twisted the knobs on our lanterns, cutting off the fuel. The hollow sound waned, the blinding glow dimmed, the shadows on the tent's walls expanding, meshing. I lay on the bunk relishing the comfort and watched the brightness of the mantle dim until there was nothing but the outline of reddish hue until it, too, died down to nothing.

My eyes grew heavy with the warmth of the stove. The angry reds of the embers shone through the small crack in the damper. They popped and fizzled, contrasting with the rain pelting the canvas in a series of small thumps. The thunder grew more frequent, louder, moving closer.

I stared at the ridge of the tent, thinking of the ride back, and my frightened horse. What did Toby see? Or feel? And then I thought of the pouch, but dismissed it. It's nothing. Just a gift from Al or one of the hunters. I inhaled deeply, and a sadness came over me. Not the incessant underlying sadness, but something more profound, something here now. Direct and absolute, confronting me.

Just let it go.

CHAPTER TWENTY-EIGHT

BOB MARSHALL WILDERNESS, MONTANA

SEPTEMBER 1997

The shadow fire's dark flames shot high in the open park, tiny black sparks surging, fluttering to the ground. The rains pelted harder, shooting through the fire, the flame's roar unaffected.

Grey Bear's shadow face painted with black coal, he danced around the shadow fire, his feet shuffling through the wet earth, his arms extended as he circled the black flames. He cried in cadence in song:

Ooyah Oh Bear Man Sees

Ooyah Oh Bear Man Hears

The winds raged, the rain drove sideways through the spirit of Grey Bear and through the dark flames. He danced, looked to the black sky, determined, no longer in the land of white or blue but in the horizon. Lightning creased down to the valley soundlessly and then the dull rumbling of the Thunder rolled past him, through him, and the darkness returned. He cried chants that ignited from his soul.

Ooyah Oh Ooyah Oh

He stopped, the last cry dying. But he felt it. The earth's tremor in cadence with great paws that moved through the forest.

Through the thick lodge pole pines the great dish face appeared, the massive hump in his shoulders swaying with each step.

Grey Bear stood motionless in the torrid rains, the great he-grizzly on the other side of the dark flames.

The bear's thick fur matted wet, bristled on the wide hump of its shoulders. The beast sat back on its haunches, stared into Grey Bear's eyes impassive, reading him.

"I hear your cries," the great he-grizzly said, its low guttural voice booming through the rain. "And, I see the Napikwan boy as you see him. I see his heart."

"Yes, you see his heart," Grey Bear said. "You see that the boy will soon no longer be among the living. He will take his own life as his father has done, as I have done."

The great he-grizzly's dark eyes rested on Grey Bear, silent.

"My father, now in the Sand Hills, was a great man. A wise and kind father. A man of medicines and a healer. He healed the sick and grieving and made them strong, whole. He took his brothers and sisters in and made many hollow hearts full again."

Grey Bear peered upward, searching.

"I have not been as great a father to my son, Running Dog. The strength and courage I showed I gained only from you. But I failed him, and could not save him."

The black flames billowed skyward.

"Running Dog led our people to safety across the great open in the dead of winter, just a boy. Just a boy, but I followed him along with the women. I thought of many things, thought many times of my father and the old stories he told me, of the fallen-in man of long ago, who was cast into a pit and left for dead but saved by wolves and made into the half-wolf who provided meat for them in thanks."

The bear nodded.

"I have watched the Napikwan boy for many moons, thought of the treacherous things his people have done to my family. The hate in my heart is deep and is a forever hate, but there is a thing which is stronger between a father and son."

Grey Bear took another step forward.

"You gave me respect among all Piegan. You gave me honor in battle and helped me in times of loss. Like my father, you too can give power and make a man whole. You have been with me in life and death. You are part of me now, a greater me."

The grizzly lifted his forepaw out of the snow and rested it down again. He lowered his head, deep voice rumbling.

"Yes. I am that."

Grey Bear's hands trembled. "I want to give you to him. To the Napik-wan boy. I want you to save him from his hollow heart."

The bear remained still. His dark eyes black pools, swirling, considering. The storm raging, the night winds drove the sideways rain hard into the earth.

The great he-grizzly rose, the muscles in his shoulders shifting to and fro.

"For me to leave you," the bear said, "you have to die the twice-death. You must become one with a member of the living world. If this person or thing dies while you are with it, you will die the twice-death. I can then leave you to guide another."

The great he-grizzly gave Grey Bear a menacing stare.

"But I must warn you. After the twice-death, you will wander eternally in a world of void. It will be a white nothingness that is unending. You will have no one, nothing. You will belong nowhere. Forever."

Grey Bear opened his mouth to speak but the great he-grizzly's voice boomed.

"There's more. I have great medicine with many creatures of the forest: the bear, the lion, the wolf. If the Napikwan takes his own life, his spirit will go to the Napikwan Sand Hills and to his Great Father. But if I kill him, I can take his spirit and offer it to Cold Maker in exchange for Running Dog."

The bear's eyes softened.

"Grey Bear, you will never be in the Sand Hills with your wife or family. But I can bring Running Dog to you. You will have him here, with you, forever."

Grey Bear turned his back to the bear, walked a few steps away, dropped to his knees. He focused on the muddy earth, angry drops of rain falling before him. His shadow hands caressed the ground, the downpour passing through his arms. The earth trembled as the bear lumbered toward him. Grey Bear turned his head.

"You have more power than that," Grey Bear said. "Just this once I think I am the better part of us."

CHAPTER TWENTY-NINE

BOB MARSHALL WILDERNESS, MONTANA

SEPTEMBER 1997

The thunder bellowed through the tent walls, a deafening, murderous boom. I lurched out of my dreamless slumber, sat up in my bunk. Aaron's brown eyes stared in fear at me over the edge of his sleeping bag.

A low, guttural groan. A deep voice, barely audible. Then nothing but hard rain against canvas.

Three explosive reports and then a long, primal roar, loud, deep. And Rick's distinctive voice. "Better get out here, I'm out of ammo!"

I jumped from my bunk, forcing my feet into my boots. Aaron swung out of his sleeping bag, grabbing his single-action. I untied the tent flap.

A bolt of lightning illuminated the camp. Fifty paces away and walking toward Rick was a massive grizzly. The bear's lips curled up in a snarl, the cool black eyes staying trained on Rick. Wide paws sunk in the mud under the great weight.

I stood transfixed, the rain pelting my head, streaming down my cheeks. In my peripheral vision I saw Aaron, the black iron of his revolver, the hammer cocking. The hunters peeked through the flaps of their tents, faces pale and wet, staring silent at the great beast as it edged closer.

The grizzly saw me and lumbered in my direction. His eyes never wavered from mine, his brown dish face never turning. An easterly thermal blew the rain sideways. Lightning flashed, closer. The bear only thirty paces away, his mighty head low, the hump of his shoulders moving in a slow, steady rhythm. His eyes two shadows of recessed pain.

Aaron trained the big revolver's barrel on him. His breath steamed, the barrel's muzzle quivered. He inhaled, pointed it up into the air, squeezed the trigger. The shock of the blast caused me to twitch, heart sinking. The great bear stopped ahead of us, a colossal hazy figure in the open. He stood for a moment, his bulk almost imperceptibly swaying in the winds.

The growl began low, barely audible. The great bear shifted his weight, powerful hind legs lowering, the silvertip hairs on his humped shoulders standing on end. His lips parted, teeth visible. The growl grew louder, deeper, coursing through the rain and the dark, through the men. The black eyes stayed on me, focused. The bear stepped forward, his forepaw sinking into the thin mud, long claws boring into the wet soil.

Frozen in place, my legs immovable as stone, heart squeezed in fear. No thoughts. Nothing but me and the bear, our eyes locked.

Lightning flashed close to camp and revealed the wide swath of blood behind the grizzly. The thunder broke the trance and the bear roared. The grizzly took two quick steps forward, eyes focused, teeth flashing. Aaron trained the revolver at the great beast and fanned the hammer. The sharp reports of the .357 came in a rapid succession, the orange sparks of the gunpowder blinding. One of the slugs severed the great bear's spine and its hind legs to dropped flat to the muddy earth, useless, ten paces away.

The grizzly's massive jaw opened wide, the bellow came from deep within. His forelegs held up his torso, the brown silver tips of his fur matted red and caked with mud. The roar deafening, the air sick with the smell of burning flesh and blood. The bear's eyes, locked on mine, flashed white with anger.

The grizzly reached with front paws and crawled, the claws digging deep into the mud and pulling his dead lower half. A paw slapped down into the mud inches from my boots, the brown dish face coming closer, its breath smelling of death and decay, black eyes burning hotter.

A blast from a shotgun rang out, smoke swirling away, Cecil's pale face lifting from the shotgun's stock.

The buckshot hit the grizzly in the shoulder, breaking bones. The bear collapsed in front of me. With deep rumbling moans, it attempted to look up, but then his head dropped down on his foreleg, his breath labored, erratic.

The hunters crept toward it. Cecil, his shotgun trained on the bear's head, eased closer. Rick appeared from the recesses of the kitchen tent, his empty pistol in hand, shirtless, rain spilling down the creases in his old cowboy hat.

Rick cast a sideways glance at the hunters. *"Stay back*—he's still alive."

The great bear turned over on its back and wailed. The sound started low and faint, escalating and deepening like the swing of an ancient oak door. His death wail.

I stood silent, still. The rain continued to fall, but the wind died down to nothing more than a smooth wisp. The powerful sound flowed through me where the winds could not, a deep haunting ache that inhabited me, became me.

The bear's great paws outstretched, his black eyes gazed at me and as his wail died, his eyes mellowed, lost focus. The grizzly drew in a whining breath, moaned one last time, releasing a flowing pillar of hot steam that dissipated to black.

I stared down at his great form, now silent, still. Blood flowed from him in thick clumps, worked its way through the tangled, matted fur and dripped to the wet earth that cradled the body. The rains ceased, the dry winds swirled and carried the scent of death, a feral smell of burned flesh and fur and gunpowder.

Aaron watched me, the subtle creases around his eyes deepening, his lips parted to speak but then closed. I knew his thoughts questioned me, asked things I knew but for some reason could not tell him.

The hunters whispered, approached the giant, still form. Stan, gaunt and pale, confused and searching as he shuffled forward, the laces of his boots trailing. Al, his white hair tousled, his bloodshot eyes cast toward me in concern, his son at his side. Rick removed the spent shells from the cylinder of his revolver, slid it into the holster.

"He's dead, right?" Al's son whispered.

Cecil glanced at Dan, his face softening. "Yes. He's dead."

Stan cleared his throat but said nothing.

Hands trembling, Rick remained focused on the bear. "Aaron, Calvin, let's move him over by the tack tent. I'll ride out tomorrow morning at first light and report it to fish and game."

"I'll help," Al's son said.

We took the dead grizzly by his limp paws and strained to drag him through the bloody slosh. I gripped him by a forepaw and my fingers ran across his long, sharp claws. My boots slipped in the sloppy wet earth. His massive frame moved across the open slowly, a foot at a time, the bear's body stretched out, human-like, his big dish face hanging loosely, his unseeing eyes vacant and downcast.

The other hunters and Cecil walked with us, respect for the bear in their eyes, awe. We pulled it to the side of the tent and I gently lay his paw on the ground, the weight of his frame shifting and then lying still. We stood for a moment, all of us, hovered over the great beast. Cecil glanced at the shotgun still in his grip and I saw that he had forgotten what he was holding so tightly.

"Let's get some rest," he said. "Long day tomorrow."

"I'll see you in the morning," Al said to me.

The hunters all turned, trudged back to their tents.

Aaron, Cecil, Rick, and I walked away from the bear, our feet sinking into the mud. I breathed in the dry air, no hint of rain. The night clouds receded and stars appeared, a hint of moonlight creasing through a break in the fading cover. The bear's scent lingered in the air, subtle and constant.

Boots and socks removed, Aaron sat on the edge of his bunk looking across the tent, not at me but past me at the damp canvas wall and the changing shadows.

"Hey, you all right?" I asked.

His lips tightened. "You didn't take your rifle when you heard the shots. You went without it. With nothing."

I glanced at the rifle, loaded, leaning against the corner post of the tent, as if seeing it for the first time.

"After Cecil shot the bear," Aaron said. "You stood there with that monster wailing, right up on you."

The Coleman lantern running low on fuel and the light dimming, the hollow sound grew faint. The shadows still danced, the lights moving across Aaron's face.

"That look on your face," he said. "It was, peaceful."

He slipped his feet into the sleeping bag, put his hands behind his head, stared at the ridge of the tent, eyes half-open. I lay down in my bunk, tired muscles letting go.

"Yeah. Don't know why, but I felt something. Better now. I can't explain it, but you know how I wake up sometimes in the middle of the night?"

"Yep."

"Well, I don't think I'll do that anymore."

CHAPTER THIRTY

BOB MARSHALL WILDERNESS, MONTANA
SEPTEMBER 1997

The next morning Al and I took a hard ride up a steep bluff under the cover of darkness. After I tied up the horses, we hiked to the bluff's edge overlooking a grassy park surrounded by thick clusters of ponderosa pine. Heavily laden with alpine timothy freshly sprouted from the burned timber and earth, a fire caused by lightning, I thought the park would be a good place to sit and watch for feeding elk at daybreak. As we reached the edge of the rocky bluff, Al was out of breath, his face strained and half-hidden under his wool cap.

The darkness fading, it gradually gave way to the coming sun, a barely discernible orange hue over the eastern peaks. The open park just a hazy image, it revealed itself subtly in the minuscule light.

Al, then breathing normally, whispered, "So what do you think, boss?"

"This is good spot for an ambush. Sit here and watch this park and I'll move over there." I gestured toward the west side of the bluff. "I'll watch the timbered bench leading up to the open, in case any bulls hold back from feeding at light and are in the area. If there are, you might get a shot."

Al made his way up to edge. He moved slowly, carefully, legs sore, and I imagined him wincing with every step. He stopped, awkwardly removed his pack, and sat down with his rifle resting on his lap.

I found a spot on a flat, moss-covered rock and sat down. The cool dampness sent chills up my back. Wearing my pack, I leaned back on it, put my hands in my pockets to keep them warm as the thermals from the valley stung my face and chest.

My legs ached as I watched the growing light in the valley.

A twig snapped behind me.

I turned, my heart recoiling in horror. There, in the dark recesses of the timber, a great grizzly sat on its haunches, bigger than the one in camp, watching me.

I couldn't breathe. Sweat beaded on my forehead.

I glanced at my rifle. Can I reach it before he charges? Can I chamber a round? Just grab it. Wait. Move slow. I looked back up.

He was gone.

As if he were never there.

I scanned every nook and cranny of the thick woods looking for him. A patch of fur. Dark eyes.

The morning light came revealing every spot, uncovering every possible place to hide. I rose, rifle in hand, and hiked over to where I saw him.

No tracks.

I scoured the surrounding area, searched the wet earth, the moss.

No sign.

Perplexed, I sat down on the wooded bench. I could see Al, the back of his head just above the maze of down timber and rock. He had removed his cap, and his matted white hair swayed with the upward thermals. I imagined his eyes searching the edges of the open park, his hand on the rifle that rested in his lap, his finger tapping the trigger guard. What did the Indians call elk? Yes, wapiti. The gray ghosts.

I leaned back on my pack, brought up my binoculars to study a game trail winding through the thick timber. I started at the closest point and worked back, looking for a patch of fur, the movement of legs.

Was the bear real?

The sun peeked over the alpine mountains, making the vertical walls of granite gleam at their tips. The sky a magnificent blue and orange, sunlight spread thin across the forested valley to the west, illuminating the lush greens. The arc of the valley focused light into a wide swath and my eyes followed its path up to the valley's source where the timber grew sparse, gave way to wide patches of ice on peaks not far from the Chinese Wall, a great mass of vertical stone that made up the eastern border of the Bob Marshall.

No, the bear was not real. I only thought I saw him. With what happened last night, I was thinking of bears and so this morning I mistook a shadow or a boulder for a bear. That's all.

The sun now halfway over the eastern rim and shooting rays of light through the dark timber's canopy, I felt its heat. And something else. Some inner warmth.

I was protected.

I unbuckled my pack and swung it around, unzipped the main compartment and took a quick swig of cold water from my canteen. At the bottom of my pack, a patch of tanned leather revealed itself from underneath a folded map.

The deerskin pouch.

I held it in my hand, felt its soft texture, my thumb running across something hard and sharp inside. I pulled the object out, held it in front of me.

An arrowhead.

Somewhere deep down, my heart told me not to question where it came from. I gazed at the eastern horizon and its jagged peaks, the sun shining just above them; the sharp smell of the pine awakened my senses, awakened me from the darkness. The sun on my face, radiating smooth and constant. I smelled the subtle, pungent odor of the swampy bottoms in the blowdown jungle, a decayed smell of old dead wood and stagnant water laden with moss and algae. I smelled death, a cumulative smell of a lost struggle, the victor the unforgiving winter, and the lion and the wolf and the bear. A smell of starvation and violence.

These smells I detected under the cover of pine, a sharp, pleasing scent, the father to these sons of death.

And rebirth.

About the author

Mike Hancock is a former wilderness guide and commercial fisherman, having spent seven years working in the mountains of Montana, Idaho, Wyoming, and New Mexico. He holds a B.A. in English Literature and a MFA in Writing from Southern New Hampshire University. Today, Mike teaches online American Culture and Spoken English to university students at Huaihua University in the Hunan Province, China. He lives on the island of Leyte in the Southern Philippines.

In a world of swords, be a pen

For more information on this and other exciting
new authors, please see ArtisanalPublishing.com
www.ArtisanalPublishing.com • reachout@ArtisanalPublishing.com

Made in the USA
Monee, IL
30 September 2020

43679294R00139